ABOUT TILLY BEAMIS

ABOUT TILLY BEAMIS

SUMNER LOCKE ELLIOTT

A GROLIER COMPANY

FRANKLIN WATTS
NEW YORK TORONTO 1984

Library of Congress Cataloging in Publication Data

Elliott, Sumner Locke.
About Tilly Beamis.

I. Title.
PR9619.3.E44A64   1984   823   83-26008
ISBN 0-531-09834-6

FOR
WHITFIELD

ABOUT TILLY BEAMIS

1978

"Why didn't you run after her?"

"Then?"

"Then and there, Rose. Why didn't you get up and follow her out of the restaurant and catch hold of her and simply confront her and ask, 'Are you Tilly?'"

"Honestly, Edward. Supposing she had just said, 'No, you have mistaken me for someone else'? It was, as I've *explained* to you, only a second's glance."

"But she stopped and looked at you."

"Not stopped, hesitated. There was a moment's hesitation when she looked at me and then they went on out, she swept on out with the boy behind her."

"Because she *knew* you."

"Or maybe thought she *might* have known me. But you know how often that happens, how often one thinks, 'Do I know this person?' It was no more than that and it wasn't till after they'd gone that the thought struck me. It takes a second or two to take in the inconceivable."

"But that's when you should have got up and run after them, they might have still been putting on coats, waiting for the doorman to get them a taxi. I absolutely cannot understand you, Rose."

"For one thing, you know those big heavy tables at the Quadrille, even if you're just going to the girls' room, you have to wait for the waiter to pull the table out so you can sidle out trying not to bump your behind on the next table. It's one of the things I don't like about the Quadrille, the tables against the walls are so close they almost overlap, and it was the height of the dinner hour. By the time I could have caught the waiter's eye they'd have been in a cab and half way down Park Avenue."

"It didn't, I suppose, occur to you to call the maitre d' and simply ask could he tell you who that woman was that just went out with a young man, as you've just described her to me, red dress and gold chains and so on."

"No. I was—transfixed. It took me perhaps five minutes to even *consider* the thought, it was like falling and then thinking, 'Oh, I have fallen down,' and then I said to Woody, 'I must interrupt you. I think that woman who just went out with that boy was Tilly Beamis.' Of course Woody never *knew* Tilly and he's imperturbable anyway. If you told him, if you said, 'Look, there's Jesus Christ,' all Woody would say would be, 'Oh, come *back* has he?' "

"And on top of everything, to be flippant about it, Rose."

"I wasn't meaning to be flippant, Edward, but I'm sorry. I mean I'm sorry I told you now. I've been wondering all day if I should tell you or let dogs sleep on."

And, Averell thought, looking at her husband and sister-in-law and at the two profiles so sculptured alike they could have been two Roman coins; even at a moment of contingent catastrophe (she saw the woman in red with gold chains sweeping out and there was something too haphazard about the incident for it *not* to have been Tilly Beamis, Averell condoned the haphazard) they were still in cahoots, Edward and Rose. From the moment Rose had said, "Something weird happened to me last night," she and Edward expressed identical dismay.

Because she could think of nothing else to do for the moment or to establish some foothold in their exclusivity, Averell got up and turned on a lamp in the darkening apartment.

"Of course," Rose said, "it may just have been a spooky flick of the subconscious, the goose walking over one's grave."

"But you *said* Tilly."

"Because certainly if it *had* been Tilly she's greatly changed."

"How?"

"Well, how does *anyone* change in all those years, people change out of all recognition, Edward. Our own mother might hardly recognize *us* now."

"How changed?"

"Tilly, do you mean? If it was. Larger I'd think."

"Fatter do you mean?"

"No, larger I thought, though it may have been the dress which was, I think, layers of chiffon over something, and there was a *difference*, I don't know how to explain. Different, an air, as if—I don't know—not like she was—*bold*."

"But you had this psychic hunch."

"I suppose you could call it that, a recognition at the moment she glanced at me. But on the other hand—"

"What other hand?"

Rose sighed, arching her fine eyebrows, assumed a coolness.

"Well, it's been said, hasn't it, that every person on the globe has an exact double."

"If you're backtracking, Rose, you're only being exacerbating. Don't open cans and then pretend to close them."

Edward stood up and looked down at his sister with that insinuation of tall dignity that only small men can assume at such lengths.

"And I'm not convinced of your indecision about telling me, I'm only surprised you didn't call me the moment you got home. But if you had any mild intention of upsetting me with this—this bizarre story, I can only tell you that you most certainly have upset me very much. Very much indeed."

And now in spite of doctors' warnings, he will have a drink, Averell thought, watching him go into the bar and switch on the green glass lamp. She looked at Rose's impassive long face on long neck, Modiglianilike, under the strong dark hair and wondered if Rose, like her, expected to hear the creak, the crack of doom in the quiet room and then, hearing the clash of ice, if Rose was considering what furies she had let loose with her story begun so trivially ("You may just laugh at me but something weird happened last night, I think I saw Tilly") and whether Rose had either the compunction or even the sense to know that Edward would pursue this thing, whatever it was, coincidence, specter, to the bitter end, however damaging it could be to him, to herself, to them all.

She got up and looked out at the early evening

where, downtown and across the park, lights speckled the pervasive twilight blue and traffic moved silently.

And is Tilly somewhere out there? Is Tilly there tonight, breathing, doing her hair, getting dressed to go out somewhere, looking at her older self in the mirror (how old would she be now? forty-six, forty-eight?), unconscious of us, talking to someone on the phone about something inconsequential? There were no hobgoblins, werewolves, demons, boggarts, banshees out there in the calm night to affright the guilty heart. But supposing Tilly Beamis were out there somewhere at this moment putting cream on her face?

Averell turned away from the window, switched on another lamp and, as Rose turned an unquestioning face to her, she managed from some deep reservoir of her strength to summon up a feeble laugh.

"Speaking of Jesus," Averell said, clasping her long fingers, "your joke about Jesus. I wonder if it has ever occurred to anyone that Lazarus coming back might have turned out to be a nuisance in the long run."

Monsieur le Maitre at Quadrille, button-mouthed with disapprobation, turned the pages of the leather-bound reservation book, eyebrows in sky-high dudgeon. His fingernails were impeccable. Well, they had so many people, monsieur, so many reservations, and it was generally not the policy, et cetera. Great sighs emerged from him.

"In red, with a young man," Edward persisted. Edward was not one to be put off by ersatz style, no matter how Gallic. Edward leaned forward to read the names listed in purple ink. Perhaps, Edward suggested, the woman might be a regular.

"*Reg*ular," Monsieur le Maitre's back stiffened. "We have regular every night, we have mostly all regular. Vendredi, Vendredi," the polished fingernail went down the page. Jensen, Castlemain, Keene, Schultz, Grayson, Van Zandt, Dreffle. The finger stopped and went back to Van Zandt.

"Er—Madame Van Zandt, *she* comes with a young man. Per'aps, per'aps not."

"Friday evening?"

"Yes, yes, Friday night."

"Do you have an address? You bill her?"

"Monsieur, we are not permitted—you are from the CIA?"

The reservation book slapped shut.

Nine of the eleven Van Zandts in the telephone book denied ever hearing of the Quadrille restaurant. Was this an advertising survey? they asked in some annoyance. Edward discounted one on West One Hundred and Tenth Street, and the Van Zandt H. on Beekman Place was answered electronically declaring herself out and asking that a message be left on hearing the beep. The electric voice sounded slightly British but with nasal overtones of American and something else. The voice of Mrs. or Miss Van Zandt titillated Edward.

"Have you thought she might not be listed?" Averell asked, clinging to a straw. The mouthpiece of the telephone was sweating with Edward's persistence. "What will you do, go through the electoral rolls?" She put a useless hand on his arm. "Will you please not go on with it."

She closed her eyes.

"What name?" the doorman at Beekman Place, lifting the house phone.

"Patterson."

"A Mister Patterson to see you, Mrs. Van Zandt."

After a pause (for astonishment? momentary amnesia?) a voice barked something, chark chark chark.

"Very good, madam."

The doorman hung up. "She says she doesn't know any Mister Patterson, sir, and that you have the wrong person."

The doorman had the gray boredom of all doormen.

"Tell her, would you call up again and tell her it's in connection with the note I wrote her."

Sighing, the doorman dialed again, waited, and delivered the message. This time an uncertainty seemed to be manifest at the other end as though she might be considering momentous options. Edward clung to his umbrella and even more to his resolve. A minute, it seemed, went by, world turning, comets colliding in space.

"Very good," the doorman said, summing Edward up in a glance lest descriptions be asked later. "Seventeen C."

Two women on the elevator assured each other that the rain was needed. The one with the standard black poodle got off at the ninth, the one with the child in a yellow plastic raincoat at the twelfth. Each time the elevator doors took an eternity to close.

And now, Edward thought, stepping into the long green-carpeted hall wallpapered in excessive banana plant, let it not be her, let all return to normal, let her have been true to me unto death, O Lord, allow me to say to her, "Do pardon me, I've made a mistake."
He rang the bell.

1976

She overtipped the bellboy.

For after all, there were four bags as well as her zippered hanger carryall; not yet certain how long she would stay, she had arrived like Sheba. She was holding her makeup case with a precaution that intimated it contained her emerald and sapphire crown.

As if to acknowledge the tip, the bellboy bent and switched on the television; an orange face ballooned against a cruel blue background. An unfamiliar voice said, "And this afternoon at Randwick the starting prices will be————."

"I don't need it on," she said.

The bellboy snipped it off, the orange face collapsed. The bellboy opened windows, a gust of saltish air lifted beige marquisette curtains. "You get a nice view of the Opera House," he said.

"Ah yes." She caught a glimpse across buildings of mother-of-pearl and beyond, blue water.

As if in obeisance the bellboy turned a switch and pink lights swam before mirrors in a marble-floored alcove lighting up closets, dressing table, sink, and washstand.

"Very nice," she said with finality, and he went out, closing the thick walnut door softly, leaving her to her fate.

The room was instantly hushed, insulated except for the muted sounds of traffic and the distant hoot of perhaps a ferryboat.

Now, what would Tilly have done?

Tilly would have sat on the bed probably, to judge if it were too hard, too soft? Tilly would have smiled at the bellboy, very likely asked his name, even where he came from, had he been in Sydney long? Was he from the country or just an outlying suburb, whatever town or suburb, Tilly would have known or pretended to know. Tilly would have been chummy. It was one of her precipitous mistakes, entrapping her with people so that later she would be made to suffer fools gladly. People she could barely place, if at all, would pounce on her in lobbies or elevators saying, oh we had such a nice chat, didn't we, at the soandso, in the whatsis, going over on the ferry, on the bus, the train, remember? Are you walking this way too, I don't believe you've met my hubby, I didn't quite catch your name, dear. "But *I* am Tanya," she said aloud to the amethyst mirror, taking a comb from her makeup box and running it through her crisp shortcut blondish-gray hair, as if to assure herself before she took another step in a strange country, in Tilly's country, of her own immaculate self.

Because the feeling of danger was everpresent and something to which she was not accustomed, outrageous, possibly jet-lag but nevertheless must be contained, vanquished. This outrageous feeling in the heart, ever since she had walked out of Sydney airport following the old man with the humped back wheeling her baggage (luggage here?) into the extraordinary sharpness of the sunlight and the clarity of Australian morning, the vibrant air tipped with the pepperyness of eucalyptus and the violent, really violent, feeling of recognition.

"Your first visit?" the cab driver asked her into his rear mirror.

"Yes," she had said, uncertainly, ridiculous because it was her first visit, for *her*.

"I'll take a bet you're from New York," he said. A. Grubb, his license read.

"They always sit in the back seat," he said.

"Oh?"

So she had committed a faux pas in this most democratic of countries, a commonwealth, the commonweal, you sat in the front with the driver, matey-like, chummy. Tilly would have instantly scrambled in with the driver, before they had got out of the environs of Mascot she would have been hearing about his wife's rotten mastoid and the ingratitude of kids today. This bloody government.

She gazed silently at the drab suburbs of brick cottages crouching behind starved gardens, hydrangea. At corner pubs with doors open revealing, even this early in the morning, crepuscular interiors where men sat in shirtsleeves drinking, she supposed, with her skin creeping at the idea, beer. Decaying rows of Victorian terraces with iron lacework balconies, dusty fields where, on this Saturday morning, boys were playing soccer, blue and red jersey figures.

"Hyde Park," A. Grubb later announced. "That's the War Memorial over there." She saw a hulk of pinkish marble, art deco-ish.

"For the First World War. My dad was in it and I was in the Second, New Guinea, Lae, all that. The way things look, we'll have another one one of these days and what's your President Ford going to do to stop it and that U.N., that's a farce if you arsk me."

At the Wentworth, paying out the unfamiliar bills (notes?) while the liveried doorman was whistling for the bellboys, she said, rather too artfully, "The reason New Yorkers don't ride in front is it is not permitted for reasons of safety unless there are four passengers. Don't take it to heart."

She could not recall how she had come by this information, she herself had never spent more than days at a time in New York, but these spooky flip-flaps were not uncommon to her.

While she was unpacking, lining up her Gucci shoes, her boots (she was prodigal with footwear, often changing shoes two or three times a day), the door buzzer rang and it was the bellboy with the obligatory fruit, cellophane-enclosed pears, oranges, a pineapple. Compliments of the management. It had the slightly secondhand look of all hotel fruit baskets. The card read "Mrs. H. Van Zant," misspelled. Besides which, they never gave one a fruit knife.

"Just put it anywhere," she said, "oh, over there out of the way."

She changed out of her flight-crushed pants suit into a safe navy-blue dress, not knowing what was or was not de rigueur for lunch at posh hotels in the Antipodes. Unlocking her attaché case she took out Tilly's worn dog-eared address book and placed it by the bedside telephone. Time for that later, when she was more in possession of *herself* (for she had had, for the first time in years, a sense of slipping out of character, of being outside of herself looking in). But a good night's sleep would fix that, she would order dinner in her room, she would resume herself.

In the elevator (lift?) two Australian matrons, looking too carefully prepared, combed, sprayed, corsaged (it defeated their intended chic), were conversing in thin disdainful voices.

"And look, they're utter rooks at that restaurong."

"Go *on*." Gow orn.

"I said to Warren, 'You ort to complain. Look, the escaaargoes were *dry*.' "

Squashed into a corner table in the bar, she felt incongruous in the noisy camaraderie of the little groups pressed close together, drinking, judging by forests of tall dark-brown bottles, beer, the extrovert Australian laughter and debunking voices ("You're just a ratbag, Peg," a male voice shrilled nearby), the muscular young men wearing shorts and knee socks casually sitting in half embrace with the girls, some of whom were still sporting miniskirts, long out of style at home. She felt acutely alien (she was brought a Bloody Mary and a cocktail napkin with a what bird? Kookaburra? How had she guessed that? on it). Not alien from being American (the lobby had swarmed with them; "We're with the Milwaukee group," a woman had said loudly to a streaked-hair dame wearing shrieking heliotrope pants), but because in the midst of these heart and soul careless free-and-easy young people (it was, she had been warned, a nation of young people now, the only nation left with a future if they could handle it), she was so deeply rooted in her inbred detachment that rejecting their instinctive naturalness, their jollity, fell on her like a rain of tacks. She became conscious that the man sitting at the next table (but so cheek by jowl they could have clinked glasses, had she smoked she could have used his ashtray) was casting sidelong looks at her, not so much by turning his large well-proportioned body (he was immaculately dressed, he gave off an expensive aroma of spice) as by osmosis; his sidelong interest in her was transmitted like his after-shave lotion. He was tapping on the brass tabletop with his half open pack of Parliaments; he cleared his throat.

"That's an unusual stone you're wearing."
The well-educated affluent Australian accent, the businessman's accent tempered in the fires of good Scotch and fine brandies, had the self-assurance of one who knows the names of barbers in hotels from Bangkok to Beverly Hills.

"It's a white emerald," she said, but drew one hand over the other like a snail drawing into its shell.

"Go on."
Well, the last time he was in London he'd been up and down Bond Street looking for just such a gem for his wife. He was pushing away the silverfoil from his Parliaments and holding out the pack to her. No? Good for her. There was a roguishness in the way he congratulated her on not smoking. He was often in the States, he informed her, when in New York he put up at the Mayfair Regent on Park Avenue. He was with Ampol, he said, indicating *noblesse oblige*, and when she didn't respond he added reverentially, petroleum. Statistics flowed from him. Recent off-shore drilling in the Bass Strait

had now precluded the importation of forty-six million dollars worth of foreign petroleum. He was relentless. At any moment he would produce snapshots. She looked around for the waiter.

"Look here, won't you let me buy you a drink?"

"No thank you."

The bored lonely businessmen away from home, chumming up with anyone they could entrap, even a forty-six-year-old widow like herself.

She ate a single mutton chop in the deserted grill. After lunch she went out, walking rapidly, not knowing nor caring where she was going but needing to absorb, to orient herself with this new-to-her old place, Tilly's place. On this abstract Saturday afternoon the city seemed deserted, brooding in the sunlight and shadows of empty business buildings, banks and travel agencies, their windows blazoned with inducements to Spain and Italy, the Algarve. "This Year make it Copenhagen." They seemed unreal, remote as the stars from Hunter Street, Sydney with its ponderous stone and granite funereal buildings that mixed unhappily with the frivolity of glass skyscrapers. She paused in a quiet intersection and read on a small obelisk that this had been the site of the first church built by the settlers; she saw, fleetingly, the vanished bushland and, on this very spot, black men with pendulous bellies wearing loincloths and with their faces painted in mysterious white streaks, holding spears. Their continent was gone now, they were pushed up north, scattered into dust bowls and mulga, into reservations or worse (who had told her this? had she read it?), herded into suppurating slums where they became drunks and degenerates. Such information was not included in the glossy brochures handed to you by smiling QANTAS stewards in immaculately-pressed scarlet jackets.

She turned onto Castlereagh Street and walked briskly as if she had some errand and as though she had a familiarity with it (the thought was somehow threatening) and with dim names on glass over shut doors; Chalmers Building, Garrick Chambers, to King Street and down back George Street, eventually to find herself in the hiatus of Martin Place, where, in a pedestrian mall alongside the great Victorian arcaded General Post Office, plastic green grass had been spread and fiberglass chairs placed here and there among tubs of sooty pansies and salvia in a forlorn attempt to achieve the pastoral. She sat down in one of the hard chairs, and at that moment the GPO clock (dismantled and taken down during the war, she had read in John Gunther's book, for the bizarre reason that it might direct Japanese bombers to the very heart of Sydney) struck three. As the giant leaden strokes boomed over her head and reverberated in the silent mall, she felt them shatter under her feet, dissolving around her as though she herself were being struck right through to the heart with astonishment and terror, as if tearing herself out of an ugly dream, she had awakened to find it a reality.

Boom. Boom. Boom.

She put her hands over her ears but there was no refuting the testimony of living sound assaulting her with the thought, the incredible suggestion. She had heard these bells before. This clock had struck over her before.

Now silence and in it, birds cheeping in a harmless square where a few people drifted aimlessly or sat staring. She got up and walked weakly along the colonnaded side of the Post Office. But all this nostalgia was nonsense, a flash of metaphysical inference when she was tired, too suddenly in a new time zone, jetlagged, in the alien smell of Sydney's air, warm, and salt sea air. She leaned against a granite arch, breathed in deeply. Nonsense, she wasn't going to be hoodwinked by such hobgoblins, not her, not Tanya, she was not about to be daunted by memories which were, after all in the true sense of the word, not hers.

"April 15, 1950. I'm *here.*"
Tilly's country-school handwriting in a fat exercise book, written in pre-ballpoint pen days with obviously a scratchy nib dipped into a bottle of Penfold's blue ink which had now turned a glittery bronze. Tea stains made little islands among the words.

Tanya lay on the bed and turned the pages with indifference to them, only hunting, darting like a goldfish in and out of slimy weeds for a crumb, a name, an impression or opinion, and remembering that Tilly's opinions were, for the most part, as valueless as gold in Ophir, for they were all golden.

"After changing into the night train in Tamworth where there was a counter place open so was able to get a pot of tea and a scone before getting on the big train which was sitting in the platform with no lights on but a nice porter told me this was the Sydney train all right and not to worry, they'd be putting the lights on soon as they put the engine on, you're early he said and I told him I'd come in from Bogong on the local at five o'clock which was the only connection, so we had a good chat about the local trains, some of which only run once a week so for instance if you lived out Merimba way and wanted to get anywhere except on a Tuesday you're out of luck. The porter's name was Kev. He had terrifically red hair and he expects to be made station master next year. He showed me snaps of his two kids and when the lights finally came on in the Sydney train he helped me into a nice clean second-class no-smoking box car with one other lady in it about 50 or so, a Mrs. Day from Tamworth who was going to Sydney because her older son who works there is an engineer and had had an accident, how bad she doesn't know until she gets there, poor woman. She had a thermos of tea with her and shared it with me and I made her have one of my hardboiled eggs and a tomato sandwich because I was too excited to eat and I told her all about how my brother Barry had bought up the rest of the family's shares in our dairy property after our dad died and so I'd got my share and was going to Sydney to stay with my second cousins until I found my feet as it were and it was peculiar because as I was telling Mrs. Day I had the absolutely certain feeling I'd never go back, that something very final was happening to me and it had to do with that very private feeling I've never let on to anybody that I didn't belong to my family, as if I was a changeling. Like that late afternoon walking along Bandicoot Road in the sunset when I had the REVELATION and saw through the bark in the trees where the sap was running and into the red earth and into myself as if they were all the one thing and maybe that was what God was.

"By the time it got to be daylight I gave up trying to sleep and watched the suburbs hurtling by and later factories and slums and then there we were in the great big Central Station where my cousin Loli was waiting. I knew her right off because I'd been told she was half Chinese (all my cousins are by a different father). She is about the most beautiful girl I've ever seen with her almond eyes and petal skin and no wonder she is a model. She was in a watermelon pink suit and alligator shoes and God knows what I must have looked like in my crushed white muslin and my new straw hat (Sydney girls don't wear hats anymore). I said she was a jewel to get up so early to meet my train and she said (she speaks in a breathy bored way as if she can't bear to live another two minutes), 'I was up anyway. I was at a party.' She seemed a bit aghast when I hugged her, I guess Sydney people are more aloof than country cousins and I realize that I am a cliché but better to be a full sized one than a pretense. *I can't help being myself.*"

Here the journal was startlingly interrupted in violent ink by an interpolation in capital letters, "OH NO?"

"———the tram hurtled through the great empty

city, this being a Saturday, down to Circular Quay. I am going to be stunned by it all until I get the oats out of my hair, there seems to be no end to it. On the Lane Cove River ferry we sat outside so that Loli could smoke and I just leaned on the rail and let the wind blow through my hair. High up along the harbor slopes are big houses in gardens and some with their own little coves and jetties. If I'd had a megaphone I'd have called out across the water, 'Cooee, I'm Tilly Beamis from Bogong and I'm here at last. I have arrived!' "

Tanya switched on the bed light in the darkening hotel room. She got up and went to the little refrigerator, took ice and fixed herself a moderately strong Scotch and water. Taking up the journal again, she turned pages, skipping. How Tilly ran on. But then at this age she had had no real knowledge of herself, there were yet no boundaries.

"————I *love* them all. My cousins, the Gardenses. Panthia, their mother, has jet black hair pulled back into a comb, penciled eyebrows, and purple lipstick. She smokes endlessly even through meals and she is huge and can only move like a great brontosaurus since her accident. Jumping onto a ferry that was leaving, she fell between the ferry and the wharf where she was partially crushed. They have been suing the ferry company for years, and haven't succeeded in getting a penny out of them. But they ignore trouble. Bother doesn't exist for them. They live in sunlight day and night and are totally individual. Panthia has been writing a play about Joan of Arc for seven years and says if and when it is ever finished it will be better

than Mr. Shaw's. When she was a girl she hob-
nobbed with writers and poets and knew Norman
Lindsay and Banjo Patterson and had the three
children by different lovers, which is why they are
all so different. Dorothy who was got by rape is
tall and graceful and teaches ballet because her
height (five foot ten and a half) militated against
her dancing. Loli whose father was Chinese and is
herself lovely as Ming is sought after by hosts of
goodlooking boys who come for her in the evenings in sporty cars. Geoff is a tender brigand with
his ink black hair and dark eyes, tremendous body
in swimming togs, deadly, deadly serious (I have
yet to see him smile) about himself and his composing of Aborigine themes set to odd instru-
ments such as the didjeridu. There is a kind of
timelessness to living here. We sit on the front
veranda in the evening having sherry and looking
at the lights on the river. Sometimes if the wind is
in the right direction we can hear the choir prac-
ticing at St. Ignatius across the bay. No hurry. Wait.
Don't run, don't press. Everything will happen,
Panthia says, if you give it time. So we live in a
timeless country ruled over by a mythical queen,
Panthia, where no one has ever heard about strain
or necessity, like being in a tapestry of castles and
unicorns, like being inside music, like their lovely
name, Gardens, like happiness. Last night at dinner around the big scrubbed plain deal table where
we sit on benches under the glassed-in roof, Panthia suddenly said, 'Oh look, the moon is in my
wine,' and held up her glass. And it was.''
Here the handwriting became epileptic, metamor-
phosed into defiant stalagmite printing as though

someone had seized Tilly's pen and written, "I THINK THEY WILL COME TO NOTHING. . . ."

The telephone call had been myopic, opaque, like people phoning each other across the plains of Saturn (the number had long ago been changed but she found a Gardens, D., Hunters Hill in the Sydney directory), and after at least eight rings, a harsh gravel voice that sounded like a man's said, "Hello." After she had introduced herself in her American voice the man (Geoff?) asked abruptly, "What's it about?" But it could have been a woman's voice grown harsh with a long life of anger and nicotine. "What," it demanded, "do you want?"

"I knew Tilly Beamis."

"Who?"

"Tilly Beamis. I knew her in America."

Silence. Either affronted or forgetful?

"Oh yes?"

Not interested perhaps, aroused from heavy sleep, not wanting to stir up the mud from around Tilly at the bottom of the river.

"To whom am I speaking?" Tanya asked.

"This is Dorothy. Say your name again?"

Eventually, grudgingly, after consultation with someone in the background, a date for afternoon tea was arranged.

But Tanya would have to go out to Hunters Hill, Dorothy was crippled with arthritis, hadn't been "into town" for over two years. Was a wreck, she said.

The halting tone implied Mrs. Van Zandt was an

intrusion, the whole idea was a nuisance, tea included.

"*Any* day," Tanya said affirmatively. She wrote down directions. Get off the boat at Valentia Street, walk up the hill, third house on the right and so on. But with her peculiar perception, or as if she had dreamed of it many times, she knew the house before she even reached the gate and read on the peeling board over the front entrance the name 'Valhalla' as the house portentously proclaimed itself, rearing itself up as if in reproach to the newer residences and brick apartment buildings with their television antennae, which had surely not been there in Tilly's day. Once white, the big clapboard house with its gabled windows and generous verandas was now a dirty tea color; a decrepitude hung over it behind the wisteria vines clinging to the balconies; an attenuation, such as occurs to people in very old age, appeared to have shrunken the once bold outlines, and, withered, it leaned on the natural rock wall behind it in the perennial shadow of the giant Moreton Bay Fig tree, whose roots might be sucking the last life out of it. If Tilly had conjured up unicorns and peacocks in the garden and slopes that ran down toward the Lane Cove River, now there were only dusty manuka bush and wild ti-tree, rose bush gone to thorn and, as she opened the wooden gate, half off its hinges, as though to synonymize the exact statement of this moment in time, an aged dog wobbled toward her, dripping saliva.

A voice behind the wisteria vine said, "Be careful, there's a broken step there, watch out now."

And as Tanya stepped onto the veranda, a little

wiry woman with blackberry eyes, wearing an apron over a starched white uniform, seemed to pop like a Jack-in-the-box out of a sagging rattan chair.

"I'm the part-time nurse, I'm Mrs. Lovell," she said perkily and the beady eyes took in every nuance of Tanya's appearance, dismissed it as being over emphatic, too Yankee for her tastes (she sniffed continuously), her buttoned-up mouth imperfectly lipsticked in tangerine declared a cynicism, a flair for finding fault in perfection, in anticipating the worst and pride in vindication.

"Found the way then, did you?" Mrs. Lovell said heartily, and dragged a dirty cane chair over the dusty unswept boards. "Sit down then and get your breath, that's a bit of a climb, isn't it? She'll be down in a tick," and as Tanya sat down, "I've got the kettle going so we'll all be right as rain in no time. This your first trip to this part of the world?"

"Yes, as a matter of fact."

"Go on! Must seem a bit strange to you, I bet."

"No." Tanya put her capacious handbag beside the chair. "No, not really. The world is becoming interchangeable."

"Yairs, I suppose. Oh well, what can you do about it? I'll go and tell her you're here." Mrs. Lovell clumped to a door and called up into gloom, "The lady's here, Dorothy."

Mrs. Lovell sat down again and beamed at Tanya malevolently.

"I said when she said you rung up, 'Oh, that'll be nice, dear, that'll make a nice bit of a change for you,' I said. She can't hardly see a thing, did you know? She can't see the telly even. But she'll be right once she has the cataract operation. And she's well taken care of with the invalid pension and she has Meals on Wheels the days I'm not here. Come on, dear," Mrs. Lovell cooed, hearing the canes blundering inside, and darted forward to assist the figure looming out of the dimness of the house.

Grown huge perhaps with inactivity, the knotted hands like pigs trotters gripping the canes, the former ballet teacher was guided to the sagging grubby cretonne-covered armchair like a liner being berthed.

"I can't find my hairbrush," Dorothy said petulantly, "did you move it?"

"We'll find it, it'll turn up, dear."

"But I haven't even combed my hair because the comb was *in* it."

"That's all right, dear, Mrs. Vanzan won't mind, will you love?"

Dorothy Gardens was assisted to the chair, where she groaned and lay back against buttocks of pillows.

She held out one of the knots of hands and Tanya touched bones gently; the milky eyes searched for her.

"Nice of you to come all this way, Mrs———"

"Tanya."

"I meant to comb my hair for you, I must look a sight, don't I?" King Lear, the white hair ballooned from the great jowled face, she must have been pretty, the mole on the chin now sprouting bristles, a young woman turning men's heads to see her cross a street. Dash, she may have had a certain dash, the movements of the head were quick and graceful. "Queenie," Dorothy glared around sightlessly, "Where's Queenie, Nell? You didn't let her out again, did you?"

"Oh now, dear, she's around somewhere, she likes to lay in the sun when there's a bit of the autumn nip in the air." Mrs. Lovell spun over to the edge of the veranda and piped, "Queen, Queen, Queen," and the ancient dog appeared, slobbering up the wooden steps and moved jerkily, like a wind-up toy almost run down, to Dorothy, where it offered a running nose to her seeking hand, licked the knob of hand and then collapsed on its side, letting out a stertorous fart. "She's eighteen, blind as a bat," Nell Lovell said cheerily. "But we're all that fond of her, aren't we, dear? Are you comfy, dear? I'll leave you to talk to Mrs. Vanzan while I go and get the tea. My word, you don't often have a visitor from America, do you, love? This is a bit of a red letter day for you, isn't it, dear?" Dorothy lay back on her pillows and glared toward Tanya, said in a sepulchral undertone:

"Three days a week I have to put up with her. It's the joviality that kills me, oh Christ, the joviality." Dorothy heaved with a dark inner laughter and out of a large tapestry bag hanging on her arm, she took a pack of Marlboros and a box of wooden matches and waved them in Tanya's general direction.

"Light a fag for me, would you. Have one yourself."

"I don't."

"One of my only pleasures. I was a dancer you

know and all my *career* I had to abstain but now I'm a crippled wreck I smoke like Etna."

Tanya lit a cigarette and handed it to Dorothy.

"Ta," Dorothy inhaled greedily. "You out here on business or just pleasure?"

"Neither. In one sense I'm out here looking for Tilly."

The milky eyes were searching for Tanya in the eternal white night in which Dorothy lived. "How's that?"

"I'm trying to fit her into some perspective. I thought perhaps something could be clarified by visiting her native country."

To explore, she had said boldly to the consular clerk in Los Angeles, asked the reason for her trip. That was it, wasn't it? You'll need more than six months, the clerk said, it's vast.

"How are you finding it?" Dorothy asked.

"So far I am not finding it as she made it out to be."

"No, well you wouldn't, I daresay. Everyone sees a place differently and anyway the *changes*. She wouldn't recognize it now. I was thinking after you phoned, how old would Tilly be now? My God, forty-*six*. Can you believe it? You were close, were you?"

Tanya looked down at the dappled water, boats.

"As close as two people could be and be total opposites."

"Sad, wasn't it?"

"Yes."

"Quick I hope."

"Oh, quick I imagine."

"Poor little soul. We'd never of known, only that friend of hers Jean Magnus wrote us."

"Oh, yes."

"Of course, I was never that close to her as my sister was. Lo was closer to Tilly, they were nearer the same age, and besides at that time I had my career, I was running the Branowski ballet, she may have told you I was an *arteest*. We were the pioneers, we toured, we were invited by the governor general to dance in Canberra and I've often thought, no harm mind you, I'd like to have said to Tilly, well put *that* in your pipe and smoke it, after she said flat out I'd be a failure. Not that I hold it against her, you couldn't hold anything against her, she was too sweet."

Too sweet indeed.

Tea was wheeled out. On the traymobile were set out dry little scones and a slab of teacake. "Milk and sugar?" Mrs. Lovell poured.

"Just black."

"Oh, you like it black, do you? Rightyo."

Dorothy was handed her mug. A pause descended. Cicadas chirred in the guava trees.

"Sometimes late of an evening she'd come and perch on my bed before I went to sleep and talk and talk, pour out her heart to me about all the things she wanted to do and be and sometimes, do you know, I got the peculiar feeling something quite different was going on inside her, that whatever she was saying wasn't *it* at all, it was the direct opposite. Did she ever give you that impression?" Tanya stirred her black tea carefully.

"She never lied to *me*," Tanya said.

"Oh lied, I didn't mean lied. Just that there was often more to her than met the eye."

"There was more," Tanya said.

In the silence a bird laughed.

"Kookaburra," Mrs. Lovell said cooingly. "Where are you, love? Come out and let's see you, darling."

"But as I say," Dorothy continued, "it was my younger sister Lo who'd be able to tell you more than I could about Tilly. They were close. Lo can tell you, *if* she gets back while you're still here. It's her day with the Prudential; she services the typewriters for them and sometimes she doesn't get home till after seven."

"Your brother Geoff———" Tanya began.

"Oh, did she remember him?"

"Yes."

"He's got a garage business in Goulburn, he's doing all right. He and Gwen and their brood, *they're* all right from what we hear when she bothers to drop a line, which isn't often except for the odd Christmas card. Oh, he escaped, he took off, shot through and *we* were left with mother."

Dorothy laughed and the unseen kookaburra taking the cue from her laughed in the tree; the calm air rippled with their mirthless glee. A gate squeaked, slammed.

"Speaking of angels———"

Tired steps, a defeated walk, the lugubrious green of chartreuse crepe-de-chine, Oriental face under salt-and-pepper hair. The beautiful Loli becalmed, beached, the years lapping over her. She came up the steps lugging her heavy case of tools, then straightened up seeing Tanya sitting there in the cane chair, put down her tool case and took a quick step backward, then sideways as if she had trodden on sharp broken glass. Blinking, she put a hand up as though to ward off a terrible glare in her eyes.

"Tilly?"

Then Loli took a little step forward peering into Tanya's face.

"Is it Tilly?"

"Don't be mad," Dorothy said, "Are you batty, Lo?"

"The likeness has been often remarked on," Tanya said coolly, putting down her cup. "We were often mistaken for one another."

Loli came forward, still staring, absorbing every molecule of Tanya's uplifted face in the sunlight.

"How do you do," Tanya, emphatically herself, said in her bold American way.

"You must be mad, love," Dorothy put in.

"I knew it *couldn't* be," Loli said, sitting down, laughed at her foolishness, and then said irritably, "Well, of course I knew it couldn't be, Dot, but just for a second, it might have been the light in my eyes or something, I thought I *was* mad, seeing things. Well anyway, it's been so many years—we could pass in the street and not know each other."

Mrs. Lovell said she would bring another cup and that Lo looked worn out.

Loli sank now into a faded deck chair and said, "I've got to take off my shoes if you don't mind." For a woman with beautiful legs it was shameful that her shoes were ugly and cracked. She massaged her feet.

"It's a cow of a job, up and down stairs and that darned toolcase weighs a ton."

Lethargy, exhaustion, framed Loli the one-time model, her Oriental face was drawn inward like a slowly deflating balloon. She reached down and tickled the old dog who, roused a moment, nudged a dry nose toward her and then fell back.

"How long you been in Aussie?"

"About a week."

"They treat you all right at the Wentworth? *I've* never been in it."

"Not bad."

The veranda boards creaked under Mrs. Lovell's feet, their dry rot. The Gardens sisters grumbled between themselves, the cake was dry, had Lo forgotten to get the bread? had there been anything in the post? had the laundry found the missing cardigan? was there any news of soandso? Soandso was worse, it had spread, she had been taken to Saint Vincent's Hospital. Oh, well. How was your day? *My* day, you must be kidding.

Tilly was right, they had come to nothing. The dancer, the dream-girl model, the exuberant composer-son now attending brake linings in Goulburn, the stilled voice of their crusading mother exhorting them on, on, to brilliance and success to justify her failure, placing invisible garlands around their necks like halters, calling on cherubim to light their way to glory, they had fallen into desuetude and silence where once Tilly had written in her diary that often her voice could not be heard over the din of egos.

Like chimney sweepers come to dust, like Tilly. Fish darting through a cage of bones.

But she would like to see Tilly's old room, Tanya said. Only a box room now, they said. Yet Tilly had done a painting on the wall and they'd never kalsomined over it, but you'll have to excuse the mess. She followed Loli upstairs; the house smelled of old linoleum and stale cinnamon, tenebrous oil paintings in battered frames hung on the stair wall, assaulted taste with dim stags in glens, horsemen reared up on the edge of impossible abysses. Loli led the way toward the front of the house past glimpses of unmade beds and the pale glimmer of wardrobe mirrors and opened a door onto a stuffy little front room overlooking the tangled garden, piled with boxes, cartons, a rickety baby carriage (pram?), an oldfashioned wire meat safe. She had had a nice view though, Tilly had, you could look right out at the river then, before the vines grew over the window.

On the wall facing the window by the iron bed-stead, on which were piled rotting mildewed Australian Womens Weeklies and hat-boxes and chipped china plates, was Tilly's painting, obscured here and there by patches of damp and seepage. It was pale blue, painted directly onto the white plaster in what seemed watercolor. It showed, in what was probably meant to be an Impressionist style, the house as seen from the river slopes standing among blue trees between which a hammock was stretched and, among azure bushes tinted here and there with mauve, two figures stood, ghostlike girls, one slightly behind the other, slightly taller. Whether by design or the invasion of damp, the figure standing behind had enlarged in splotches so that it merged in and out of the foreground figure, overlapping like the penumbra on an imperfect television picture.

"Who are they?"

"She never said or we never asked, I forget."

Loli brushed away a thin cobweb.

"How was she when you last saw her?"

"Last saw her?"

"How was she? Happy? Unhappy?"

Tanya paused. Happy, unhappy were too definitive for the depths and tides in Tilly. "She was herself," Tanya said without sense of evasion.

Loli cleared a little island in the debris on the mattress and sat in it. Her mooning olive-shaped eyes were longing for clarification, famished for secrets. She had imagined, obviously, that Tanya's asking to see the room had been a ploy to impart secrets too awful to be said in front of the older sister. Tanya stood at the window toying with the acorn at the end of the cord on the shade (blind?).

"She was engaged, wasn't she?"

"Yes."

"You know the bloke?"

"On and off."

"She was a bad picker," Loli said, and as if Tanya might not have heard or understood, she reiterated it: "She was a bad picker."

"I was aware of that."

But Tanya might not have spoken. Loli was suddenly on fire from years of smoldering. Oh, the pity of it, was the theme, the waste. When she was capable of such generous love. Not everyone is given such a talent for loving as Tilly was, a genuine talent, and to let it be wasted on such a no-hoper as she did. "I had boyfriends," Loli raged, "but Tilly had *love.*" It was dumbfoundingly easy to see that Loli was rampaging on about herself. "And all the time, Geoff, my brother was dying of love for her. She could have had him by snapping her finger."

That had been true, no doubt. But there had been pitch-dark chasms between them, Tanya knew. Unbridgeable by snapping fingers. And to think that Tilly had written in the journal that Lo was the "one with brains"; so many of Tilly's unicorns turned out to be goats.

"I wondered if America had changed her at all."

"Oh, it would have taken more than America."

"Is your husband living?" Loli switched Tilly off like a bedlamp.

"No. He died rather young. Ours was a short marriage."

"But sweet."

"No. Perfect. Not sweet."

Loli sighed deeply. She may have once believed in perfect marriages. She stood up. "Well?" she said, cheated out of any revelations that might have been savored gluttonously.

She opened the door and Tanya said quickly, "What's happened to him?"

"Him?"

"Jack Quist."

"Oh you know about that, do you?"

"Naturally. Is he around? Can I get in touch with him?"

"How much did she tell you about him?"

"Everything."

"Oh. Well then you know." Loli was defeated, bilked out of revelations.

Loli tittered.

"Well, you can never tell about people. I'd have expected he'd have conked out on the booze. Well, this'll make you laugh, it would have made *her* laugh, God knows. He went into the Church. Can you believe it. He's the Reverend John Quist of the Saint Whatever Church of England in some little place out west near Lithgow, Bullagulla, preaching the gospel and giving communion, and butter wouldn't melt. And knowing all the time what he did to her. Talk about hypocrisy."

"Atonement?"

"Oh don't make me laugh, dear. I don't think he ever had a regretful bone in his body, otherwise he'd have got in touch with her at one point or another. But she never had so much as a line from him from the time when he shot through to New Zealand. I can remember her saying to me, 'It wouldn't be so bad if I could only have heard from him once.' Oh well, she got over it. We all get over things in the end. She was too trusting, that was her trouble."

"Not *too* trusting."

"NO? You don't think so? Well, I do. He was a bastard, out and out."

"She didn't think so."

Loli laughed again, it was full of snidery.

"I ran into him in Pitt Street a few years ago and when I saw him in that get-up with the white collar turned around I couldn't believe it. I said, 'What are you doing in that costume? Are you in some television show?' He'd been an actor, you know. Oh no, he said, he'd been ordained. It'd been his secret desire all his life, he said straight-faced, to work for Christ. It was all I could do not to laugh in his face when he said Christ in that pious way, the times he used to blaspheme easy as breathing, Christ this, Christ that, Christ the weather.''

"Did he ask about Tilly?''

"Not a word. Oh she was just a little incident in his life by then, forgotten, put out of mind now he was sanctified. I suppose I should have said, 'Why didn't you ever write to Tilly, you bas-tard?' '' But it was all in the past by then. She'd long ago gone to America with Jean Magnus, she'd made another life for herself, what would've been the use?''

"Bulla what?''

"Bullagulla,'' Loli spelled it as Tanya wrote it with a gold pencil in her little leather notebook. "Why would you want to see him?''

Tanya said, "I'm on a voyage of exploration, he is part of the coastline.''

"I see,'' Loli said though clearly she did not. Thought Tanya was a dark horse, an enigma. Tanya knew Loli would say to Dorothy, "Well, she's a dark horse all right, a cold fish, I wonder what Tilly saw in *her?''*

"How soon is there a ferry?'' she asked going downstairs.

The spark left after the fire had gone out was not here, the vestige of Tilly she had hoped to resur-rect was not in this decaying house. She pulled on her gloves as Loli sat down in the deck chair to sip her tea gone cold while Dorothy stared blindly affronted, sucking at her cigarette. Nobody had noticed that the old dog had died. There was a little pool of bloody sludge alongside its mouth and the gray flanks no longer rose and fell, the body looked deflated, flat as a doormat. "I think your dog is dead," she said. Loli with quick alarmed steps went over and knelt, Dorothy made swimming movements from her chair, moving her arms blindly toward the floor. Loli, kneeling, her ear to the furry chest, gave out a squawk, "Queenie, Queenie."

"Is she?"

"I think maybe she is, I can't hear any heartbeat."

"Run and ring the vet, Lo, run."

As Loli ran cannoning into Mrs. Lovell.

"What's up, love?"

"Get the vet," Dorothy screamed, and began to moan and rock in her chair.

"I'm sorry," Tanya said to the commotion. "Goodbye," she said to the hysteria beginning, at such overstatement, since the dog was eighteen, hadn't they said? She walked away.

Tilly would have stayed to console, wouldn't she? Get them tea or drinks, help put tissue paper over the lifeless form until whoever came to dispose of it. Wouldn't she? Cry.

But then that was Tilly. She was Tanya.

At Bullagulla railroad (railway?) station, which was nothing but a corrugated iron shed and red dirt, there was no sign of any conveyance except a utility truck, onto which a man in shirtsleeves was loading oranges in wooden crates that had come off the train. Taxi? He took in the myth of Rodeo Drive inexplicably brought here by the same little two-carriage puffpuff train, the local trunk line from Lithgow, took in the tasseled loafers, the Gucci overnight bag, the Irish tweed slacks, the London Fog raincoat over her arm; she might have been some griffon come to life and flown off a distant cathedral all the way to this dusty scrub. Give you a lift to town if you like. Hotel? There was only the pub and they'd stopped putting up guests years ago. You might try Mrs. Berry, who uster let out a room if it wasn't for more than a night or two. Not many people stop by here anymore, not since the tin mine closed fifteen years ago. They bumped along rutted dirt roads, by split-rail fences and telegraph poles that marched up and down across hill and dale of this vacuous desolation.

"Town" was a paved main street on which stone and old red brick two-storied buildings clung together in despair, where little dark shop windows announced Millinery, Ham & Beef, Fred's Barber Shop ("Ladies Beauty Salon") under the shade of tin-roofed canopies. Spindly dogs dodged the utility truck. A two-storied verandaed stone-painted-white edifice simply bore the inscription, HOTEL, where outside the pub door sporting tarnished mirror signs of KB LAGER, RESCH'S ALE, men in T-shirts lounged, beer mugs in hand and wearing greasy fedoras. She was let off outside a yellow brick bungalow where at every window the shades had been drawn down as if to discourage conviviality. Sparse cosmos offered meager consolation over a tin fence once painted a Mediterranean blue. Mrs. Berry was dubious.

"Well, if it's only for a night or two. It's my daughter's room. She's away in Lithgow seeing the dentist for a couple of days. I expect her back the day after tomorrow."

"I expect only to stay the night," Tanya said.

After an uneatable stew at the ABC Cafe, where she was regarded with the deep curiosity of the few patrons, she asked the waitress where she could find the rectory.

"Rectry?"

The girl tasted the word, frowning. She was the color of lead under the fluorescent light.

"Where Mr. Quist lives."

"Oh, the parsonage you mean."

She was told to go up to the end of the street and turn left on Butter Street, then left again after passing the church. Not far. Nothing was far in Bullagulla, with dusk it seemed to shrink, as though the encroaching bush were threatening to devour it and it might not be here tomorrow. A dusty wind had sprung up, stirring little eddies of sand and leaves around her feet. Cows mooed in the distance, and adding to the sense of solitude were the faint artificial voices of television through the lighted windows of the scattering of houses where the miracle of modern technology had brought the reruns of old American sitcoms to the wilderness. What had brought the carefree, careless Jack to this unlikely dot on the map, too small even to be on the one she had bought in Sydney. She paused outside the small wooden church and read in white plastic letters under dirty glass, "St. Thomas Church of England. Rector: Rev. John Quist. All Welcome. Sunday service 11 a.m. Vespers Wed. at

7 p.m." The sermon for the previous Sunday was entitled "God and Cucumbers"; the analogy, so purposely perplexing, suggested he had not lost his talent for titillation. Or as Tilly once said, "playing tennis without a ball."
The rectory was a small stucco house to the back of the church, dim light showed through blue and red leadlight glass.
And now? And now?
After she had rung the doorbell twice (and what if he were visiting in some other parish, suppose she had come all this distance and he had succeeded in evading her?) a light was switched on over the porch, and the door was opened by a tall blond boy wearing blue jeans and a T-shirt reading WOMBATS. He was about eighteen, she would have guessed, and she knew instantly by the remembrance of the snapshots that he was, in the planes of the face and the skeptical mouth, the reproduction of Jack Quist.

"Hello," he said pleasantly, the on-tap-twenty-four-hours-a-day pleasantry of the vicar's son. Our Door is Always Open.

"I'd like to speak to Mr. Quist."

"He's not in right now, can I help? I'm Eric, his son."

"Will he be back shortly, do you know?"

"Hard to say, he's over visiting a parishioner who's sick."
He wasn't looking at her as though she were some strange object. He smiled, and as she put her hand up to the hair blowing in her eyes, he said, "Look, won't you step inside, there's quite a breeze."
"Brerees," he said in his Australian accent and

closed the front door after she had stepped into the linoleumed hall. Something was being cooked in the kitchen.

He led the way into a small parlor where the furniture was of such diversity as to suggest donation. Fumed oak argued with blond pine. "I'm Mrs. Van Zandt," she said. "I'm a friend of someone who used to know your father."

He smiled again, a pleasant smile. "Yes? You're American, are you?"

"Yes."

"New York?" He appeared to light up at the thought of New York.

"California."

"Still you're quite a bit off the beaten path then, aren't you?"

"I'm in Sydney for a few weeks, so it's not *that* far off. Just a long dirty train ride."

"I'm sure he'll be flattered. Get you a cup of tea?"

"No thank you."

So this was the son Tilly might have had, had things turned out differently, this tall lanky fair boy with his long legs twisted around each other as he sat looking at her clear-eyed, a trifle rattled, disconcerted by this bolt from the blue turning up out of the evening, out of the wind as it were, in desolate Bullagulla. What would Tilly have done? Tilly would by now have embraced him, told him he was nice looking, asked if he had finished school, had a job here, plans for the future? Tilly would have liked a cup of tea, gone with him into the kitchen, sat on a stool while the kettle boiled, venturing, intruding as she always did, into the heart until later she might dismiss him as dull or vacuous. Just as she so often did, down into blind alleys. Her over-generous estimation of people too often resulted in disappointment.

"New York," Eric said, "is where I'd like to go, but I guess the movies are the nearest I'll ever get to it. Excuse me while I turn down something in the oven."

No, his Mum was dead, some years ago, he said in reply to her question. There were only him and Pa, he looked after Pa now. Not much else to do in *this* place where there were only dairy farms and one iron mongering factory. Nice of her, he implied, to show the slightest interest in him. He squirmed in his chair with the spark of excitement she seemed to have lit in his inertia, as if the mere fact of her remoteness in place and time and her cool acceptance of the situation, her sitting with her hands calmly folded on their sitting-room lounge were like a Roman Candle exploding, fizzing in golden rain in the dull little room with its mezzotints of biblical scenes, its gray-green wool table cloth with a fringe of disgusting-looking bobbles. He played with the bobbles, casting her sidelong looks from under his dull gold hair, urgent looks as though to beseech her not to yawn or glance at her watch, not for a minute at least. Well, he'd wanted to go to the Uni., University of Sydney. He was "keen on art" (said quickly, furtively as though it might cast aspersions on his masculinity, had perhaps been disparaged in this country where the male held sway and where circumstances had arranged themselves in such demeaning fashion that he must learn to compose casseroles), but Pa wasn't keen on the idea. And anyway, Pa was a no-hoper when it came to cooking and housework, and the parish was so poor there was no way to pay anyone to come in so————.

He shrugged.

He was stranded on this darkling plain.

And he was keen on art.

Had she been to the Sydney Art Gallery, he asked. No. Well, it was worth a visit to the Australian wing to see the work of Sidney Nolan, William Dobell, Russell Drysdale. He was especially taken with Drysdale with his scope and rhythm and use of burned colors. He had spent a week in Sydney last year on a holiday and gone to the art gallery every day (he was working up to something, she could tell) except for one at a football game (he was on the local soccer team, he indicated his T-shirt), and once to the beach. Look, he said springing up, as a matter of fact he "mucked about" a bit with painting himself, would she care to see one or two?

She recognized the main street of Bullagulla, the hotel on the corner, and the little tin-roofed shops under a sinister lemon sky whose light threw the buildings into sharp relief and created an effect of shadows in which figures moved threateningly. Another was of a house standing in a barren field beside a water tank and what seemed to be the figure of a little girl leaning on a post in the foreground. The sense of forlornness was exemplified by the dot of blue which might have been the girl's pinafore set against the dryness of the burnt umber fields. There was one of a rotting shed under skeletal gum trees, another of a stark little wooden post office standing against a piercing electric-blue sky, the railway station with a ghost train. In all of them the ominous light portended doom as though he had caught the apocalyptic flash before the bomb that would annihilate the planet.

She knew nothing of art, she told him, she couldn't know if they were technically good or terrible. But they were *arresting*, she said, looking into his pleased, excited eyes.

"Would you like one?"

"Well, thank you Eric, but if you're sincere about wanting to be a painter one of the first things you must learn is not to give your work away."

"Once they're finished, there's nothing to do with them. Nobody here's interested."

"But one day if supposing you became famous they would be very valuable."

"Famous," he said with such deadly skepticism, the word stuck in his throat like a fishbone.

"But I might like to *buy* one."

He looked astounded, his lower lip drooping.

"The small one of the railroad station. How much do you want for it?"

"Oh I wouldn't know. Anything you like, you say."

"Twenty-five dollars?"

"Oh that's more than enough, I'd've said twenty, it's the smallest."

She took out her purse. He didn't seem to know how to take the money, she had to prod the bill into his flaccid hand where he left it.

She rolled up the small canvas and put it into the

big handbag. "Well I like it," she said. "When I get back home I'll have it framed."

"It's the first thing I ever sold," he said, stunned, still not looking at the money.

A car was heard to stop abruptly.

"That'll be Pa."

He was hurriedly collecting his canvasses and stuffing them into a cabinet as though they might have revealed some stratum of himself he didn't want to be found exhibiting.

A door opened.

"Eric."

"Someone to see you, Pa."

A face, well known from obsolete photographs, appeared around the door, broke into a smile. There was no scintilla of recognition or surprise. Bland.

"Well now, whom do we have here?"

Well, he'd been on the stage once and now he was consolidated into the role of country parson, agreeable, unctuous, ever ready with the right note of enthusiasm, condolence or chiding. The handsome face had weathered into deep grooves around the full mouth, the dark bushy hair was sprinkled with dusty gray, but Tilly would easily have picked him out of a crowd even in the distance of years; the distance of the heart to the first beloved is said never to diminish, the wound never to heal completely, the anguish never to be altogether assuaged. Thus, summing him up, taking him in in the harsh glare of the white ceiling light, mightn't Tilly have felt or heard the heartstrings tinkle like thin glass pendules?

She noticed there was a faint rime of dandruff on his black jacket collar.

Eric was stumbling, shambling, saying, "from America."

She accepted Jack Quist's long hand.

Giving him her searchlight look. "I knew Tilly Beamis," she said. "She was my greatest friend."

"Tilly."

The eyes narrowed as if he were trying to pick out the speck of a person on the far horizon in a dimming light. But if there had been a crack in the ecclesiastic armor, a tic, a spasm, it was deflected by Eric asking did he want his casserole now.

"Just leave it in the oven, old son. Had yours, have you? Well cut along then and watch your telly. Isn't this 'The Waltons' night?" Eric looked reluctantly toward Tanya but Mr. Quist had invoked the atmosphere of the confessional from which outsiders must withdraw. Eric shambled out and Jack Quist sat down opposite Tanya in a flowing manner of a concert pianist, hands thrusting away invisible coattails.

"And what brings you so far afield, Mrs.——"

"Van Zandt. I'm researching Tilly's life."

"For a book?"

"No, for myself."

The fact that he made no reference to the likeness was, she thought, significant.

"Can I get you a spot of sherry, Mrs. Van Zandt?"

Cool as God and a cucumber. He opened a pickle pine cabinet and took out a bottle of pale sherry and two glasses. She took hers being careful not to touch his fingers, there was something physically repellent about his having been Tilly's lover. As though she could see through the black clothes to a hairy chest.

"Good health," he clinked glasses with her. Drank, paused, then,

"I knew Tilly through her cousins the Gardenses. Oh, those Sundays at the Gardenses. They invited the cream of artistic Sydney."

Artistic. The plebeian little word seemed to sum him up and the sum of him was less than he imagined. She recognized his type of conceit; he was the kind of man who would memorize the name of one good French wine to throw around, two or three lines from *Paradise Lost* to convince people he knew Milton.

"———they were all talented, especially the son, Geoff, who composed some Aboriginal thing, chorale, jolly original it was and their mother Panthia, a poet, wrote a play about Joan of Arc which I was to be in, I acted in those days. For some reason or other it was never done and I had to be content, alas, with being in 'Dingo and Daise,' which was a very popular radio series then. Ah, but the Sundays at the Gardenses or *Dimanches aux jardins* as the more erudite of us would say."

He was veering, tacking. And what else, Tilly might have asked, would you expect? He was a practiced evader. He was evading Tanya's stare (pouring himself another sherry), evading Tilly.

"———round about the time I was involved with Loli Gardens. My goodness, what a beauty she was, half Chinese———"

"I've met the Gardenses," Tanya said, "it was through Loli that I got your address."

"Really? Well, she was ravishing then. Well, she ditched me, she cut me off finally in seven words, she said, 'Why do you wear such terrible ties?' "

He laughed, a drop of sherry ran down his chin and he wiped it away with the back of his hand.

"So after I was ordained we met in the street and I said, 'Loli, as you can see, I've given up ties.' "

That he might have been different, less translucent when he was young, less preposterous, Tanya doubted. People don't alter that much. Of course he had been handsome, but couldn't even Tilly have gathered he was incapable of depth of feeling? All she had ever said was, "Well, he could be bliss for five minutes." And she had kissed the dead flowers. Dead pansies that she had pressed in a copy of *For the Term of His Natural Life*, gone the brown color of moths, and Tanya had snatched them and flung them into the fire and said, "Don't be such a fool, you can't kiss the dead back to life," and Tilly had said, "Well, they were all he ever gave me."

Now in the brief pause that had at last opened up (he was staring into the sherry glass), she leaned forward, her arm on her knee, chin on hand.

"Did you ever love Tilly?"

This time he filled the sherry glass to the brim, a little overflowed, and he wiped it off and licked his finger. She saw that his hand trembled. He stared down at the glass for a long time and when he looked up she saw that his face had lengthened, narrowed, and he had the mournful look of a saint in a triptych.

He said, "Well, there are degrees of love, wouldn't you agree?"

"Did you ever love her at all?"

"Why, may I ask, do you wish to know?"

"Because *she* wanted to know and you cheated her out of knowing."

"Not so."

"It *is* so. And because she loved you with all her heart and being."

"Is that what she said?"

"No. It wasn't possible for her to put it into words, she couldn't expose it even to herself. That would have been worse for her than the pain itself. But now, after all these years, *I* want to know. Simply yes or no."

He half emptied his glass.

"How do you know it hasn't been painful for me, too?"

"I would hope it has."

"Have you come all this way from America to assure yourself of that?"

"Partly."

"Then you may rest assured. You may rest assured." He gave her a crooked smile, emptied his glass, repoured.

"Dear Tilly," he said, "Sweet Tilly. The fawn in the woods as it were. Can I get you another sherry?"

No, she said. She hadn't come here to be hedged by fawns in woods. Nor for that matter to watch the Reverend John Quist get stoned, something, she felt quite sure, that was not altogether occasional. Eric's worried face confirmed this. Didn't he want his casserole now? Eric's worried face in the doorway. You ought to have something to eat, Eric said.

No, no, cut along old son.

As soon as Eric had cut, the reverend quickly bent and took out a new bottle of sherry from the cabinet. He sat down and crossed his long legs, lit a cigarette, a little unsteadily.

"You come like a thief in the night, may I say."

"Because I knew perfectly well if I'd written first or telephoned you'd have palmed me off with excuses, Reverend." She underlined the word and he smiled. There was beautiful irony in the smile, showing his perfect teeth.

"Very good of you to bother to come all this way, I'm immensely flattered."

"And," she said with impatience, "I have a very early train to catch in the morning to make my connection."

"What you don't know————" he said, emptying the first bottle and placing it carefully on the floor. "What you *don't* know, dear Mrs. Vansart, is that I warned her that I was a no-hoper larrikin, which in Australian translates into ne'er-do-well or just plain bastard. I made it perfectly clear from the start that the pursuit down the primrose path with me would only be the worse for both of us which, as you no doubt know, it was. But I couldn't reason with her outrageous innocence and impetuosity. She had no sense of her own emotional potential. She was captivating in the worst sense. Any man could have told you that. But she had ambi-

tion beyond her own good sense. She wanted *me.*
It would have been better maybe if she'd never left
wherever it was she came from and married some
stock-in-trade cowhand and had a barnful of——
—"

He pulled up short before the word that would
have swept him beyond tactlessness into bathos.
He passed a hand across his forehead as if he were
brushing away a night moth.

She said at once, "Yes. And what *about* the
child?"

"Naturally, I didn't know about the child until
later."

"Naturally."

"I give you my word of honor. I was in New
Zealand. On tour."

"She never believed you were on tour. It
seemed too convenient."

"My dear woman." He feigned outrage. "You
don't invent excuses to go to New Zealand. You
obviously haven't suffered through an Auckland
Sunday, especially in those days. Oh, I was on tour
all right. She could have got in touch with me, she
never did. I had no word from her, ever."

"She said, if I remember correctly, she would
have preferred to cut off her hand."

"Well then, it was her own sin of pride, shall
we say. Of course I would have replied at once,
tout de suite. Certainly I'd have sent her money. I'd
have scraped up what I could to cover——" That
brought her to her feet.

"Money?" she spat, hot with anger. "Money
wasn't what she needed. What she needed desperately, despairingly, was word from *you.*" He got

up and closed the door to the hallway. Eric need not hear recriminations, justifications, presumption. Presumption was all it was, on her part, he indicated, sitting and pouring sherry unsteadily but with a twist of the wrist that suggested contempt.

"As you were not there at the time, you can only surmise that."

"No."

"How can you be so em——emphatic? You're very quick to pass judgment long-distance, as it were."

"I haven't come to pass judgment, Reverend. That's *been* passed on you and you ought to know it by now."

A gust of gritty wind startled the plastic Venetian blinds. He rose and closed the window, stood feet apart looking at her with half-closed eyes as if he were trying to place her in perspective, as if, had she been Tilly come back to life, it might have warmed him into some kind of emotion, as if something odd had begun to obtrude both alarming and wistful.

"What satisfaction can you get, what possible good can come from raking over coals now merely to put me on them?"

But she had never thought about satisfaction, she said, there was no thought of vendetta or reprisal, she said, more calmly now (because just observing him trying to regain a certain balance both physically and morally, trying to assume his theologian advantages, however hazily, a pathetic boozy parson in this duck's neck of a town out back of nowhere, just seeing the nowhere and nothing of him was justification enough. Even Tilly would have known that. Even dumb Tilly who had kissed the dead flowers but later kissed him off at the edge of the cliff. Judas, she said).

"Just to see that you have an iota of conscience would be enough. I'd settle for that, for her."

He smiled a greenish smile.

"Do I need to show you a letter on my chest? I believe you're an intuitive enough woman to know you got what you came for. What else can I say? Mea culpa? You talk about betrayal and conscience as if they were things to be bartered at the supermarket and you have the audac——audac—ity to classify and pass judgment on a rigmarole of second-hand information from which you form a pontifical accusation of me. I must remind you of your own conscience when it comes to such accusation from fifteen thousand miles away and twenty odd dead years as dead as Tilly. Why not let her rest in peace?"

"Because she liked to tidy up. After all this time she would like to know why."

He turned and stared into the empty grate where a dusty paper fan emphasized the coldness of no fires.

After a long time he said, as if his head had cleared, "There wasn't any job in New Zealand. I just picked up and went because——. I was like someone with a bad sunburn moving into the shade. I could no longer stand the glare of her, the intensity, honesty of her, that's all. That's all it was, pure and simply. So how does one explain that to a girl in a few words on notepaper or on the phone from an airport? An explanation that can be put into as few words as a telegram, good-bye. Talk about sins of omission. My God, they are sometimes forced on us."

He sat down heavily into the leather sofa and stared at his dusty shoes.

So often the truth was as simple; so simple as to be devastating (she saw Tilly's upturned face burning Jack Quist's face with its intense trust), and the simplicity of his reason, unembroidered with self-righteousness touched her suddenly with its plausibility as if, seeing him momentarily stripped naked, she was obliged to accord him a measure of dignity, even decency.

She picked up her handbag.

She said, "Then perhaps you did right."

She was seeing something else in him, a dreary morality and that what he had failed in being was the rake, the roué he had enjoyed proposing himself to be and that the masquerade of the surplice had been the final metamorphosis of that failure, the dressing up in the robes of a private innocence he had tried to repudiate. It had been this innocence that Tilly had blunderingly uncovered, seeing through his cock-a-horse affectations that he was virtuous. No wonder he had fled from her.

"Good-bye, Reverend," she said, this time without mockery, and opened the door into the hall where Eric was standing, looking helpless. He opened the front door onto the blustery night. His wan face hypothesized that this would be one of those nights of getting Pa undressed and into bed.

"Goodnight then, Mrs. Van Zandt," he said dutifully, the young churchwarden screwing on a grin. "Can you find your way home?"

It would have been a moment of genuine poignancy for Tilly, the child grown up into lanky manliness, polite, hopeless, futureless.

"Oh yes," Tanya said, and impulsively (for her) put a hand on his thin arm. "I hope you get out of here one day."

Jean Magnus, after recovering, had Tanya sit where she could "see the view."

But you had to admit———, Jean Magnus said in her deafening voice (the voice of the deaf) that she had had quite a start when she had opened the door and there was . . .

Mrs. Magnus had tottered, tilted on her high golden heels as if she were on the deck of a ship rolling in heavy seas, she had put out a hand to steady herself. Then reason returning she had said loud enough for all the tenants on her floor to hear, "Jesus Christ, for a second I thought it was Tilly back from the grave."

With her usual patience, Tanya had explained that the likeness had often been remarked on.

The apartment (flat?) was also deafening with color, from the expanse of hot rust wall-to-wall carpeting to the violent guacamole walls that were crowded with abominable paintings so thickly daubed that they resembled petrified chili. Outside, the harbor blazed in quicksilver against the overpowering sky; flotillas of sailing boats keeled around little Fort Denison (Jean pointed it out as Pinchgut, said the poor convicts had called it that after the dreadful food they were given). Jean also pointed out that the day was so "aysure" you could see clear out to the Watson's Bay lighthouse. Wasn't that near the Gap? ("There's always the Gap," Tilly wrote in a despairing moment.)

Jean Magnus also blazed. In shocking pink trousers and shirt. She was hung around with so many heavy gold chains it was a wonder she could keep erect, and her small dimpled hands were weighted down with tremendous topazes and aquamarines. On her right wrist was strapped a man's platinum wristwatch.

Her hair had been expensively twisted into clots of gold and white streaks and she wore a lot of blue eyeshadow and false eyelashes.

"Well aren't you sweet," she shrieked, "to call me up and come and see me, aren't you a doll?"

What must she be now? Seventy, seventy-five? Deaf as a post, she had no control over decibels. Her voice was a curious amalgam of Australian and New Yorkese. "Wouldja care for cawfee, honey?" The former Miss Australia, the former Jean Botts, a nice Melbourne lass, pretty as a little budgerigah, good sport (nice Joe to Americans), spotted by Mackinaw "Mindy" Magnus, a Hollywood talent scout, later to be president of Schonfeld Arts Management, signed up, sailed away on the old *Sonoma*. Never made a foot of film. Married Mindy instead. Widowed at thirty-five. In her late sixties came "home" still a perfect size ten. Now pouring herself a squat Bourbon at four in the afternoon, why not? "I've never gotten caught by that Australian afternoon tea thing, even though at heart I'm Aussie to the core.

"But now I've got you in a better light, Tanya." Jean pronounced it with the short "a." "I can see the difference, especially about the eyes. Tilly's eyes were a seaweed green, weren't they? But it's more in the manner. In the manner you're as different as chalk from cheese."

"Yes. We were antitheses."

"What?"

"Poles apart."

Jean swept a silver frame off a table sporting a dozen or so.

"This is us in Yosemite."

In a fading color enlargement Jean and Tilly stood humbled by El Capitan in slacks and sweaters. There was a shadow of a smile on Tilly's face, it looked rueful, forced, in contrast to Jean's orthodontic grin. The manner in which Jean was gripping Tilly's elbow gave an impression she might be a jolly policewoman taking the girl into custody.

"My little pet, my baby," Jean shrieked. "The year she arrived in America with me. That'd have been before you knew her." Jean returned the photograph to its place among the others.

"She was my *baby*. Right to the end. No matter what she did, I forgave her. Care for some Turkish Delight?"

She held out a wooden box of trembling pink jellies.

"No thank you."

"I like a Turkish Delight with my drink."

Jean sat down on striped pink and avocado satin and engorged a piece of quivering pink, licked her fingers.

"Gratitude," she said through jelly, "is not what

I want, you can take your gratitude and shove it. But she was like my own child, do you see? I took her to the States, you know. See, by that time I had citizenship because Mindy, my husband, had said to me, 'It's better you should be an American citizen just in case anything happened to me.' And so you see I could sponsor her, which I did, and it was through a pal of mine she got her first job in perfumes at Bonwit Teller and we were happy in my big old place over on Central Park West, all white it was and she had her own room and could just come and go as she liked, we were like sisters." Mrs. Magnus' baby hand groped in the wooden box and brought another jelly to her mouth. "Except, she was secretive, kinda. Most of the time she wouldn't say where she was going, where she'd been, she kept her friends apart from each other in boxes. That's probably why you and me never met. And then too sometimes she would get this funny look, not like herself, long drawn out look as if she was listening to somebody talking very softly to her when there was no one else in the room except me. It used to give me the creeps. Also I think she usta talk to herself. I once stopped outside her closed door, I wasn't eavesdropping, just curious, I thought maybe Irma, my maid, was in there with her. She and Irma were great pals, always whispering and giggling together. In a funny way she was closer to Irma than she was to me, it riled me just a weeny bit, and so I knocked and sang out to her, 'Is Irma in there with you?' and the talking stopped dead for a few seconds and then Tilly said 'No, go away.' Look, I wasn't so much stunned by the rudeness as by her voice, it was a hard horrible way she said it in such a strange cold voice. 'Excuse *me*,' I said. Later on when she came in to get me my five o'clock bourbon and ginger, I said joking, 'Talking to yourself's the first sign of madness,' just joking, and she just went on putting ice in my highball, but she had that indrawn look on her again, sort of sad, and she put the drink down and came over and put her arms around me and she said, 'Oh, poor Jean, poor Jean, you'd never understand.' I couldn't get over it. But as I say I loved her like my own and I forgave her right along to the end, even if it did all come apart and she left me. What of it? Everyone leaves you in the long run, it's part of life, I guess, and no one likes you for giving them too much, they resent it, I found that out too late. Did you know this rich guy she was going to marry?''

"Somewhat," Tanya said.

"We were never introduced, but I wrote him a note after it was in the paper they'd found her luggage on the bus, and I received a very nice courteous note back from him. What was she doing way out in Pennsylvania anyway?''

That could not be entirely elucidated, the room was too bright for any further clarification, she and Mrs. Magnus would be blinded, and anyway there was no total truth to Tilly, one could just as well fictionalize. But as it happened, for no reason, Tanya told the truth.

"She was coming to meet me."

"Oh really? You were living there then?"

"I was nearby in a little place called Temple."

"Terrible."

"Yes."

"Ghastly."

Tanya stood up.

Tilly wasn't here. There wasn't shade enough in this overt atmosphere for her to have protected herself from the unflattering truths about Jean Magnus, that she was a vulgar, generous, possessive collector.

"Oh, must you go so soon?"

"Afraid so."

"Oh, have a spot before you go, a little vodka or something." Tanya was walking toward the hall with Jean protesting in loud squawks about hoping they could have had a little dinner together.

"Oh, wait just a *sec.*"

Jean disappeared. Drawers were heard to open and shut. She came back brandishing a little glitter.

"I want to give you a little Australian something to take back with you, Tanya."

Incredibly, it was a little rhinestone boomerang. Jean fastened it onto Tanya's blouse.

"Oh, you were adorable to come visit me," she screamed.

In Macleay Street, Tanya unpinned the boomerang and tossed it into the first trash bin she passed.

On the last afternoon, gusty with April wind, she took the bus out to the farthest reaches of Sydney harbor where cliffs divided and the Pacific rolled in.

"Up that way," the bus driver said, pointing and giving her a sharp look, perhaps for asking for the Gap. But surely she didn't look suicidal (she gave him her calm stern look getting off) in her tailored gabardine pants, her Gucci loafers, swinging her capacious bag.

She walked up a path to where a protecting fence had been put around a curving shelf of rock. Two hundred feet or so below, the ink blue ocean boiled and heaved over the jagged rocks. The Gap. Desperation Point. Where they had flung themselves over in hundreds during the Depression, it was said.

Only a mention of it in the journal: "Oh well, there's always the Gap," Tilly wrote and appended three exclamation marks.

Inconceivable.

But had it been a turning point? Had she, in a moment of despairing aberration, come here one twilight, come probably in those days in the old tram, got off and walked up the path and stood at this fence? Looked down at the sizzling white water curling and uncurling over the fearsome seaweeded rocks, felt the sticky spray in her face, taken off her shoes, put a note under a stone, climbed the fence to stand on the edge?

Not Tilly, inconceivable.

But could she have come to this brink to dare herself not to deny her strength? Could she have felt then in that moment, at the moment of wind and falling, sky and sea over and under, at the uttermost moment of truth that there was something, some reason to step back, to continue?

Was it me? Tanya asked the air, the sea.

Yes, it was me.

1951

It had rained during the night.

When Tilly opened her window, hearing the toot of the seven o'clock ferry below on the river, there was instantly the strong aromatic smell of wet eucalyptus and musty lantana bush. It was the early morning smell of the bush, of Bogong, of her childhood, and it made her think of damp red earth and corrugated iron water tanks and the wood stove in the kitchen on damp mornings and of her mother laying out tin spoons on the breakfast table for their porridge, which they ate hot winter and summer, sprinkled with brown sugar to be followed by (for her brothers) two fried eggs and a pork chop or a porterhouse steak smothered in fried potatoes and mopped up by chunks of mealy bread, because nobody but a jackass would have started a day's farm work on less. And nobody talked at breakfast, it had to be got through fast and so out to the cattle feed. And Mum stood through it as she did through all meals, just having a peck at something in the kitchen and saying nothing, occasionally moving her false teeth around in her mouth because they hurt her, had never fit right from the day they had driven her all the way over to Tamworth when she was eighteen to have all her teeth out, which her mother had assured her was to save her any future dental problems, them living so far out. Only after the boys had tramped out did Mum sit down and have a mug of hot tea and rest her poor feet while Tilly got out the dishpan to wash the dishes in greasy lukewarm tank water. This was the beginning of the day (in winter by lamplight) every day of the year except Sundays, when they slept in until nine and got later into their best, the boys shaving, to drive the thirty miles to church.

Here at Valhalla (and what a name for it, the bloated old house lunged over the bay like a hippopotamus) the Gardens family treated breakfast as an irrelevance since everybody got up at different times. Someone left a pot of tea gone stone cold and long steeped into bitter dark red tannin, and whoever came down next plugged in the electric kettle and watered it down to tastelessness. Someone might open a tin of pineapple juice, but the day you fancied a piece of toast the bread crock would be empty. Often they left notes for one another: "Mum, the line you were trying to think of is from Winter's Tale, 'daffodils that come before the swallow dares and take the winds of March with beauty.' G." "Tilly. Could you sew a button on my pink linen dress before you go? I've left it on the sofa. Lo." Leaning out of her windowsill beyond morning glories and breathing in the sharp air, which had in it a smack of spring, Tilly saw that the dining room chairs had been left out all night in the rain. They had been moved out last evening because there had been a full moon and so Dorothy had wanted to dance free movement on the lawn. The younger folk had stretched out on the dry warm grass or on steps and perched on the rockery, but Panthia's older friends, the wrecks and mildewed poets, had required chairs. The yellow paper lanterns which had last night glimmered with their little candles in the lower branches of the Moreton Bay Fig hung like huge wichetty grubs. Sodden pillows lay round about.

Because nobody here assumed authority. Because nobody here interposed in anybody else's way of life. Unlike life on the farm where everyone had an assigned task and did it at the assigned hour, nobody did anything here until it was decided that the situation had gone on too long, the refrigerator reeked with the six-day-old fish, four people had almost broken a leg falling down the back step where the light bulb had expired a month before. The stopped-up lavatory was because of the used tea leaves they constantly put down it, but being unstopped they paid no heed to the plumber and went on pouring the tea leaves down it to save them the short walk to the rubbish bin.

There was no consultation among them; they exercised their rights and privileges as people living independently in a family unit, and, taking everything for granted, were freed from responsibility and strain. ("They have never heard of strain," Tilly wrote in her journal. She often wrote about them in the late evenings, it subdued her need for screaming at their sometimes selfish eccentricity and impracticality.)

Like the time they had decided on a goose for Christmas. Elaborate purchasing of esoteric condiments had occurred, someone had found the recipe for a luxurious gravy to be prepared with mouthwatering spices, potatoes were to be roasted outside on coals, pumpkin whipped with walnuts and raisins. But when it came time for Geoff (who was by far the best and often the only cook) to start roasting the goose, there was none. "I thought you————" "I thought *you*," they said to each other.

Yet, in spite of the inconveniences (there was no closet in her room, every dress she had was hung on a big nail on the back of the door) and the invasions into her free time with their requests, Tilly still felt the thrill of enthrallment to them. If she were away for only a night she would telephone just to ask how was everyone. Were they missing her? Strange, she had never felt as closely knitted to her own family, rather, she felt a changeling. But the Beamises were a close-mouthed unresponsive lot. Work and sleep were all they knew. They sat at meals and chewed their food silently like the ruminants in the sheds outside, got up from the table, went their separate ways. She could not remember her father making a personal observation about anything apart from the price of fodder, possible drought, how much one could get for a good heifer calf. At his funeral, she tried her hardest to respect him with a tear or two but her honesty was too much for it. Once Mum had surprised her. Mum had laid down the torn sheet she was patching and said, as if in answer to the question, "Well, I woulda liked to see Paris. That's why you was named Matilde. Dad fancied June, but I had my way. I'd read this story about Paris where the girl was named Matilde. So you got Matilde for me and Anna for Dad's sister. Well, I got to see Sydney on our honeymoon and we went out on I think they call it the Manly ferry and it was all right, I didn't mind it. But I woulda liked to see Paris."

Poor old Mum. Tilly would have liked to give her

a bit of a hug but the Beamises weren't given to hugging. Mum would probably have thought Tilly had lost her marbles. Even at the train station, leaving forever, she had had to do the hugging. Mum would have simply handed her the shoebox of sandwiches and said, "Well, ta-ta Til, take care of yourself." That was how Mum was.

But Mum had recognized some need of burgeoning in Tilly, said, "When you get your fourth of the property perhaps you might like to go off to your cousins in Sydney, my cousin Panthia Gardens and her bunch. They're artistic, I've heard. If you'd like I'd drop her a note." So now, the contrariety, she felt she had come home to her own family after a stay in the outback with these dairy people. She learned in no time where everything was, the Delft bowl for roses, the goblets for the wine, where they kept the mincer, the heavy silverware wrapped in flannel but gone black. Here in this old house heavy with wisteria attitudes were expressed, disagreements aired, and people conversed, communed, disputed, admired and abused each other. But there was constant give and take, not sterility; the Gardenses commented on each other without impingement. There were guidelines, as she had found out to her disconcertion, that even violent confrontation was statutory. She had nervously intervened in a hotfisted confrontation between Panthia and Dorothy in a dogfight (Panthia's black painted fingernails gripping her canes, her huge menacing back with her fat black pigtail like a colossal Indian squaw ready to do battle, Dorothy backed against the piano trembling, ashen-faced with wrath) and Tilly had rushed in where angels would have feared, to separate and calm, widening her thin arms between them in an outmoded stage gesture and in the affronted silence, Panthia had clicked a lighter to her "Capstan" cigarette and said cuttingly, "Tilly, you must learn not to intermediate in the quarrels in this house." Half an hour later she had come upon the two of them laughing over something in the *Bulletin*.

Now she combed her short crisp hair, peering at her little heart-shaped boyish face in the mirror, where you had to dodge the tarnish to find yourself. On the stairs lay a pair of emerald-green satin shoes that Loli had dropped (quite often it was Loli herself to be found on the stairs where she had dropped). Tilly picked them up and cast them away in the downstairs closet like someone throwing fish back in the river.

In the big flagged kitchen, the glasses and dishes from Sunday's *Baquamier* free-for-all were stacked high (and more would be found eventually under ferns and bushes). She put water on to boil and got out the instant, heard a step and knew it was Geoff before the arms were around her and he had her pinned from behind in his grip of iron (he was six four with the strength of an anaconda, it was presumptuous to stir), and so they stood together in silence, looking, she was sure, rather foolish, feeling his breath disturb her hair while the pot was taking forever to boil. Unable to move, clamped to him, she merely sighed and said, "The dining room chairs got left out all night in the rain."

"Oh well," Geoff said, she could feel the reverberations of his deep voice through his chest, "no matter. When you think of it, chairs last longer than people."

It must fulfill something in him, this embracing, a compensation or apologia for his day-long silences. He let go of her and sat at the kitchen table folded in thought, the long dark stare.

"Till," he said.

"What?"

"Till."

As she sat, he drew a long fingernail down the inside of her arm and smiled to her face as if they had deep entrancing secrets, which they did not. The only deep secret between anyone and Geoffrey Gardens was himself. When she was newly arrived, he had taken her out to French's Forest "for the view" in his third-hand old Packard, a relic from the thirties, battered as a broken-down Hong Kong taxi, and on a secluded back road a tire blew out, and while he was lying on his back in the dust and she was handing him this, that, the jack, the spanner he had reached up and drawn her down beside him and held her mutely beseeching something of her which in her shock and inexperience she could not read or define by the gesture, something so strong that she felt her heart beating in response to his urgency and with the rush of this brand new cognizance of herself, put a hand inside his shirt where it was poking out at the waist and touched his hot skin over the navel until he had rolled away and stood up, tucking in his shirt and saying waggishly, "Now Till," as if she had led him on.

Always the gorilla embraces and then nothing. She wondered whether he might be, might be queer or impotent.

Some nights after a day of silence broken only by "Butter please" or "Did I get a letter today?" he would make the house shake with music all the way down to the ferry wharf with his Aboriginal nocturnes on the piano with their antipodal rhythms and atonal chords that sounded like the jargon of the blacks themselves in corroboree thousands of years ago in some hot night cave, pointing the bone. By day he sold sheet music in Albert's Music Store, who advertised, "There's no song we can't find for you."

Now as suddenly as he had appeared, Geoff vanished, gone while she was hunting for a clean teaspoon.

The front gate slammed, the full stop.

They were like that, cut you off in midsentence with a thought of their own more important or impudent. It was like their half hopes, halfway completed plays and sonatas, half accomplished love affairs, like Dorothy's eight-year engagement to the Russian dancer Mischa Branowski, who everyone knew was queer as a coot and as much a fixture of Hyde Park evenings as the Archibald Fountain. It was like Lo changing lovers like coats in a fashion parade, it was like Panthia's everlasting play which went forever on like Penelope's weaving.

But they're my family, Tilly said to herself, going out the gate and turning to see the early sun blazoning the windows on the house containing them. I love them.

Then as if she had caught her leg in a sharp nettle, she gasped, and as if it came from the lantana bush another voice said raspingly, "But dilettantes at everything, even life. They'll come to nothing."

"Yes, can I help you?"
She must say it sixty times a day. It occurred to her there might be something symbolic about going through life asking strangers could she help them. Certainly characteristic. She was ideally suited for it by nature. She wore a crisp pale blue linen suit with IA (for Interstate Airlines) embossed on the shoulder in darker blue. She enjoyed the big cheerful office with its powder-blue carpeting and bright posters of the Barrier Reef, Mount Kosciusko, and Ayers Rock. It was her habit to stop every morning and buy one red carnation or rosebud to put in the bud vase on her desk next to her name plate, M. Beamis.
She had a vicarious sense of travel, of floating in blue air, while looking up schedules and a sense of gratification when she obtained a last-minute booking for someone on desperate business. "Eureka," Tilly would cry, "we can get you space on the ten o'clock flight after all." "Good news," she crooned into the phone, "good news, Mrs. Hastings, there's been a cancellation on the eight-fifty to Hobart, but you do know, don't you, there's a half hour stopover in Melbourne."
She was chided by Mr. Toogood for being too chatty. The airline, Mr. Toogood reminded her, only required she check the flight availability and make out the ticket, she need not enquire

after relatives or look at snapshots of grand-
children.

Some of her steady clientele brought her small gifts,
barley sugar in jars, or a box of handkerchiefs. But
her ebullience occasionally landed her in jeop-
ardy. Mr. Mooney, fifty if a day, who travelled in
and out of Brisbane twice a month for Penfolds
Wines, suddenly short of breath, wheezing, leaned
across her desk and said, in hoarse undertones,
"Miss Beamis, wouldn't you, won't you have dinner with me at my club one night?" Mr. Mooney
had the look of the tomcat regarding the flounder
left unattended on the kitchen table. Tilly smiled
and said, "Now Mr. Mooney, I'm here to make
reservations, not dates."

She supposed herself as liberated as any girl her
age in postwar atomic-age Sydney; she had never
attached any significance to virginity (it sounded,
she thought, like something one carried in one's
handbag like a vanity case. What are you looking
for? My virginity, I was sure I put it in my bag),
which she had yielded up at eighteen literally in
the hay, behind the big stack in the number five
paddock to a husky youth named Keith Hardcas-
tle, and when it was over they'd dusted themselves off and gone their separate ways forever.

But the heart was a different matter. When it came
to her heart she was as strictured as a crusader's
wife, chastity-belted in a locked tower awaiting the
return of her husband. Of him. Him.

The only one.

But when she thought about "him" it was never
somehow in the context of marriage, nor of love
affair, it lay in a limitless region between the sol-

emn and the frivolous. But it would be, when it happened, undeniable, it would be like the perfect chord struck, the exact color, synonymous with morning, light, ocean, dew, night, serenity, and words that delight the heart. It would be like awakening after a troubled dream to find yourself in a safe familiar room. Ah yes, you *knew*.

Him, unoutlined, just there.

She was already profoundly ready for him, her lamp trimmed, in the window.

She was sharply aware of sham.

Like the boy and girl kissing in the dark outside on the ferry. She heard the boy say, "Care for a cig, dearest?" The tone was so prefabricated it made you wince. He might have said "muttonfat" for all the honesty that came with that deplorable "dearest," flat as cow dollop, phony as a tin sixpence.

Standing beside the couple, waiting for the little wooden gangplank to be dropped, Tilly saw that the girl had the waxy glow of being overkissed, was transported by bogus passion. She had the stupidity that produces the catastrophic marriage.

Clack. The gangplank fell.

"Watch out, he doesn't love you," Tilly said to the girl and went lightly up the gangplank.

Not like her at all (she saw through the back of her head their thunderstruck faces, of all the cheek, they said, the nerve, the girl must be balmy), not a scrap like her.

Her religion, although made ornamental by Methodist hymns, was her gift of love, her talent for people. She cast the sunlight of her interest on them and warmed, they opened petals up to her, and then caught in their misconception of her she had to struggle, to wound in order to shake herself free of them. She basked in her popularity and at the same time was contemptuous of it. She was wise enough to know there were perils to this chameleon existence, that this obsession of being everything to everybody might someday annihilate her real self, that she might vanish entirely. But what was her real self? Whatever it was it alarmed her, it was both relentless and alluring.

She had been eight years old when she had had her Revelation. It was early evening, the time when the antipodean sun, turning toward winter, drenched the bush in an umber light so clear that every leaf stood out on gum trees and every gnarl on wooden fences was as defined and articulate as the craters of the moon seen through a giant telescope. Not a breath of air disturbed the trees along Bandicoot Road, and the silence was intense and archaic, as though the huge country had just been born out of the molten heart of the planet, not twenty million years ago. Then, as she stood there on the red earth country track (no cow mooed, no bird uttered a cry), she suddenly felt thrillingly— entirety. One with everything, with leaf and bark and ants moving, the underground springs, the air she breathed silently, the planet itself whirling in space and it was as though she could see *into* the trees and into the earth under her feet where the sap ran up from the roots. For a few exalted seconds she *saw* entirety and that time and space and the air and cows and the rusted tin can of IXL raspberry jam by the prickly Banksia bush and herself in her faded cotton pinafore were all the same thing and had been since the beginning of time and would be until the last star went out forever. So this is the thing they call God, the child thought, wondered if she could die this moment would she be frozen into the understanding forever like a fossil in an Aboriginal cave. But then a cow mourned for hay in the nearby field, wind stirred leaves and dust, crows fretted, and as though an invisible hand had stirred the divine pool the vision was disarranged back into the fractured world of animal, vegetable, mineral.

"Well," her Mum said, scraping a black pot, "you look as if you just seen the ghost of the jolly swagman."

Couldn't say to Mum, I seen God out by the Cameron's place and He's a tin can.

"You look a bit liverish," Mum said. "Teaspoon of castor oil for you, my girl."

"Tilly, meet Jack Quist."

She was coming in the gate holding a watermelon as though it were a big green baby and the sun was in her eyes so that she could only see gauzily windblown brown curly hair and a lot of smiling teeth. Geoff's pal, Jack.

Who was "keen on himself," according to Loli, thought himself irresistible. Loli was at pains to take him down a peg or two. But then, she was at pains to demote most men. Her repudiations were often bizarre, she had broken her engagement to a highly eligible son of a prestigious family because he wore shoes with crepe rubber soles; the squishing of them made her feel sick, she said, her almond eyes clouded with disapprobation.

"My cousin, Tilly Beamis," Geoff said.

"Well, hello, Tilly Beamis," Jack Quist said. He had a darkly resonant voice with, surprisingly, because she had heard he was a successful radio actor, a strong Australian accent, an outback accent as strong as tea brewed in a billy can.

"Sorry, I can't shake hands," she said, nursing the watermelon to her breast.

"Let me unburden you of that," Geoff said, reaching for the melon.

"No I'll manage," she said.

Strangely ill at ease suddenly with the fact that the actor's concentrated stare was too precipitate. The way Jack Quist leaned against the brick wall was too consciously casual, the pipe held by a grin, too euphemistic, it might never be filled. She wasn't prepared yet to deal with its insincerity.

She carried the watermelon inside, letting the screen door slam.

The Gardenses were having one of their literary Sunday blowouts, this one constructed around old Cristabel Pinkney who under the *nom de plume* of Henry Wolf Wister had written a famous historical novel in the nineteen twenties, the more famous in literary circles for the fact that, verging on starvation, she had sold it outright for one hundred pounds (then a small fortune) only to have it go into twenty-one printings for which she received not sixpence. Nor had she been able to follow her *Tasman* with another success and she had declined into being a legend. The legend, looking like a cadaverous vulture under an ancient mossy tricorne hat of bile green, sat on the veranda next to the recumbent Panthia and surrounded by lesser poets, faded women novelists, and editors of obscure quarterlies. Panthia served them tinned salmon and mayonnaise on wilted lettuce and Pilsener served in jam jars to save breakage and referred to them in absentia as the Porolds. Porold Gwynneth, Porold Ken. She was succored by their lifelong struggles against borderline poverty and lack of recognition and, herself uncomplimented, unencouraged, fed on their mortification with barely-concealed gluttony. They came to her Sundays, Tilly concluded, because they had nothing else to do, poor things.

As she crossed through them, cradling her watermelon and giving them quick smiles, someone was heard to say, "Do you remember an Inn, Miranda?"

Well, Jack Quist certainly wasn't a Porold, she thought, putting down the melon on the kitchen sink and observing him through the window where he sat laughing with Geoff on a grass bank under the jacaranda tree. He was a goldfish among these tadpoles, he gleamed. If anything he was too intensely right in his dark blue and white striped *matelot* shirt and his white duck trousers and, even righter, he had not committed that heinous offense of wearing socks with his tennis shoes.

Why then this peculiar qualm, this nervousness in the stomach? As though something duennalike in her was saying to her to watch out, watch out now.

"But I won't," she said aloud and cut out the watermelon so savagely the little black seeds spat out.

Approached boldly across the lawn.

"How about some watermelon?"

"No thanks, Tilly. I reckon I'll stick with the gin and T." She sat down on the grass knoll beside him and spooned her watermelon over her qualms, telling herself she was only keeping him company because Geoff had gone off somewhere. He had put away his pipe and was chewing on a stalk of grass. He was just minus being handsome, she thought, as though creation had left off work early. Sidelong he was goodlooking but full-face he was over-symmetrical, planned.

"All those old frips over there, chewing the fat with their dentures. Lady novelists in *turbans*. Jesus. Henry Wolf *Wister* for Christ sake. I didn't think she was still alive. We had *Tasman* in high school and bloody boring it was too. They didn't tell me it was going to be one of *those* Sundays." Now he lifted an arm and described an arc in the air in greeting, and turning her head Tilly saw Loli pass by ignoring it.

"She's off me," Jack said, and laughed. "Well that's *her* hard luck. We had, if you want to know, quite a thing going last year."

"I hadn't," Tilly said.

"What?"

"Wanted to know."

This appeared to please him, the mouth widened to show the straight perfect teeth. Out came the empty pipe for them to clench, he rolled over on his belly and gazed up at her; it was the expected illustration of the scene he was creating. She almost laughed in his symmetrical face where there were now two dimples. Now would come palaver.

"Tilly Beamis. It's like new sheets. Shiny, like clean milk cans standing in the sun."

"Yes, I come from a dairy family."

"No kidding. Geoff just said from out West."

But of course he'd known, the milk cans were too pat. Then why would he dissemble? And looking all innocence. "It must be ESP," he said.

"I'm really Anna Matilde. My Mum had a passion for anything French."

"Matilde's a cross queen, champing around in cold castles like Eleanor of Aquitaine." (It came out Aquityne.)

He made sucking, gurgling noises on the pipe, then tapped it against his shoe.

"So," he said, "you're from a dairy family. My family's in the undertaking business. We've got a nice sedate funeral parlor out in Randwick."

He was to have been a mortician. He would have been, she imagined, splendid at funerals, in cutaway suit and striped trousers with just the right combination of solemnity and polite concern for the grieving.

But what got you down, he said, wasn't the dead but the living, the sometimes bizarre requests to have odd things put in the casket with the body, the family squabbles over what suit or tie or dress he or she was to be cremated in. As if it mattered. That and then the weirdos, necros who came around to the back door with bundles of banknotes and had to be got rid of smartly. Well, it was all in the game, and you got used to it like the smell of embalming fluid.

But somehow he knew it wasn't for him, that way

of death. Then, when the Old Vic came out he'd seen Olivier do Richard Three and it had transformed him; electrified, he came out shaking and knowing that there was nothing for it but that he must be an actor.

"Are you doing anything at the moment?" she asked.

"Talking to you."

"I meant, are you acting in something?"

"I'm the septic tank repair man in 'Dingo and Daise' on GB radio four nights a week. Ever listen to it? Then *don't*, I beg you. But it pays the rent. Lean over a minute, you've got a seed on your chin." He patted her chin gently, his hand smelled faintly of lavender water.

"But I'm up for a play at the Minerva."

"Is that good?"

"It's the stage at least, starvation pay but it's the legitimate theatAH. It's as good as anything gets to be in this Christbitten country where the highest culture is dirty blackout skits in vaudeville at the Tivoli. Unless you count a bunch of old queers and elderly dames mouthing their way through *Love's Labour's Lost* on the ABC in evening dress on the *radio* and calling it drahma. Or you can get to do *Peer Gynt* in burlap drops in a reclaimed men's lavatory basement out in Balmain on weekends and talk about repertree. My arse it is. What it is is crapola. What it is is your cousin Dorothy and her Russian pooftah putting on *Coppelia* at the Conservatorium for two nights to half-empty houses and calling themselves the National Ballet. What they want, the dear people, is the Community Singing, is the Amateur Hour, is Bob

Dyer's Lafferthon. Jesus, this town, this country, you might as well be dead as try to be a serious actor in this blighted land. The boongs have it better on their frigging reservations chewing on their wichetty grubs and going Walkabout."

His face, even his voice had darkened as though a cloud had crossed the sun, as though a bitter wind had sprung up from the West.

From the veranda came the intoning entreaties, the pleadings in iambic pentameter of a woman urging men into fire and blood. Panthia was reading them her unfinished play. Rodomontades of contralto histrionics poured through the wisteria. "Your dastard hearts, of curd and whey," it sounded. Or perhaps turd and hay.

"They're paying for their lunch," Jack said, and smiled cynically. "Poor old farts, taking all the crap she hands out to them, believing they're a part of some literary enclave and her doling out beer so someone will listen to her bloody awful verse. Have *you* heard it?"

"Yes, but I'm not to know if it's good or rotten."

"It's piss, absolute piss. And she's never going to finish that play, somebody might read it who *knows.*"

This had crossed Tilly's mind also.

She set down her watermelon rind and drew her knees up to her chin, her thin arms around her legs.

"Where would you go if you could?"

"Away."

"Yes, but where?"

"Samarkand."

"Yes?"

"London, New York." He was looking darkly down at the bay; fishing and pleasure boats heeled and yawed.

"I don't know. All I know is, I'll shoot through once I get the dough, I'll shoot through so fast on the first BOAC flight out of this shithole. Excuse me, I don't often get so porno in my speech but I guess you've been around farmhands."

In an instant there was a total metamorphosis, he turned on his back, rolling over and laughing.

"Oh my dear, my dear, what's it matter? We're specks in the great firmament and we're all going to go out with the great Boom when it comes, and if you think anyone or anything really gives a hoot in hell about what happens to Jack Quist and Tilly Beamis then you're nuts, my dear. Except——"

Fell silent, fell serious again, it was like the shadows of clouds chasing across sunlit fields.

"——mind my saying do you? You *are* like your name, plain and simple and as a matter of fact you're the realest thing I've come across in a long time."

"I've hardly said a word," she protested.

"You don't have to. I like it, I like seeing you without makeup on."

"Oh Lord, I forgot. I was just going in to get my lipstick and I got sidetracked——"

"Stay yourself, Tilly."

Funny he should say that, as if he knew something about her only she knew. He was giving her a warning look, as though it were the most mandatory thing in the world that she remain "herself," and just for a split second she despised him for it, that tic in her, that frisson when something else took over inside of her, repudiated his assumption that this was the reality, this, the plain Jane scrubfaced soul from down to earth bark and gumtree, new, dazzled by him. Then it ceased and she was herself in every sense of the word.

"I will," she said.

Someone called from the house that Dorothy wanted Tilly in the kitchen toot sweet.

"Will you excuse me, Jack?"

"From what?"

Always, she was to find out, the grinning postscript, as though he were in need of the last word. Just as one day he would say to her (she would never forget) as if it were an imprecation, fiercely, "Oh, you are the pure in heart."

And when she came back he was gone and looking down the hill to the bay, she thought that she could see the blue and white of his striped shirt on the ferry wharf and there was an emptiness where he had lain under the tree.

JQ [she wrote in her journal, conveying by initials the sense of secrecy being required or that by not spelling out the name, she could disguise joy and perturbation] came into the airline office today just before lunchtime. Wearing a double-breasted blue blazer with gold buttons and grown a foot taller I thought till I remembered he'd been lying down all the time. The girls were galvanized. Can I help you, sir? Sheila called out like a shot but he pointed his unlit pipe at me and as I was with a client I smiled and said I'll be with you in a moment, kindly take a chair, which he did by picking one up and pretending to carry it out to the street, which made the girls laugh. When I was finished ticketing my client, he sat down at my desk and indicating the posters said, Commonplace places. Where would you like to go? I asked. Samarkand. I said we only have one flight there a year and that's on Leap Year day. Book me on it, he said, and what are you doing for lunch. Usually, I said, I take a sandwich into the Botanical Gardens if it's fine. Usually's a rut, he said, get yourself out of it and come with me to Wentworth House where they serve lunch in a bosker old family dining room. Can't, I said, that's all the way out in Vaucluse, I wouldn't get back till four. So what, he says, naturally. I say how about Cahills just across the street? Oh I hate Caahills, he said, it's all flowers and butterscotch sauce and North Shore Line ladies in white gloves. They give me the tits, he said, let's go to the Wintergarden and get a drink. I said the waiters there are stuck up as hell and it's about ten bob a drink and he said I got the job, I got the part at the Minerva and I want to celebrate with you, Till. So I got changed and we went out into the hot sun and the mob on Castlereagh Street and I found out I only come up to his shoulder, I also found out women look back at him on the street as if it was Gary Cooper, some kinds of men look too. I have on new shoes, he said like a proud schoolboy. They were the kind of golf brogues with a tongue of leather over the toe, very fancy. He walks in beauty. We were shown to a window table and he ordered gin slings. I'm glad to see you haven't changed, Tilly, he said and I said, Well it's only been ten days. That long? he said. Well, he said, the thing is we go into rehearsal Monday so in a few days I won't be available. It sounded like an ad: 'Last chance sale of mens knitted cardigans.' So we'd better make the most of these few days. Couldn't you get some time off? We could take a day or two at the Lapstone Hotel halfway up the Blue Mountains. Do you play tennis? He was rushing me so, that and the gin, I was afraid I'd show my excitement and I knew instinctively he wouldn't be drawn to young excited girls acting like brumby ponies from the bush and I was trying to act as if there was nothing new in being taken to the Wintergarden for drinks by good-looking men but I must have fallen into a kind of parody of composure because he said sharply, Don't sip your drink in that ladylike way, *drink* it. I can't stand piss elegance and anyway you're not ladylike, thank God. I know you, Tilly, and underneath you're as tough as boards (bawds?). Funny he would sense that in me. I felt disrobed. But not distressed. I liked his perception, it's like being naked in front of a warm fire. At the same time it's rather alarming, his knowing of me, it catches my breath. Well, we had more gin slings and perfect little curried prawns on silver dishes and I was quite relaxed, quite at home with him until I saw that it was twenty past two and that I must have been spellbound, he has the way of capturing your whole attention and spirit so that no time exists. I am twenty minutes late back to work, I said, and he said, Other people are in worse emergencies, and outside in the lobby when I began stuttering my goodbyes he said, Wait, what is another five minutes? He disappeared into the hotel flower shop and to my own surprise I waited until he emerged and handed me a little spray of deep violet pansies. Sweets to the sweet, farewell, he said. I don't know what 'farewell' may mean. Perhaps goodbye.

This evening I pressed them in a book. I hadn't noticed the odd coincidence until I closed the book and saw that it was Marcus Clark's *For the Term of His Natural Life*. Is that how long I expect to love JQ? What a life, what a laugh.

I think that loving him could be marvelously shocking. It may be like being shaken to death.

"Do you believe in God, Tilly?"

They were sitting on the stone wall at the edge of Elizabeth Bay, eating ice cream cones. It was the Sunday afternoon before the beginning of his unavailability.

"Oh yes," she said.

The voice that so often spoke the truth in her said in her ear what a liar. What a liar you are Tilly when you want to present that pure-as-a-lamb side of yourself. He means it in the ecclesiastical sense, you boob. Yes, but I can't explain it in the way *I* mean it, I can't tell about the Oneness with cows and tin cans and ethereal light and silence.

"What's He like?"

"Can anyone say? Like Himself."

"But who do you think He might look like?"

She realized he was not being frivolous. This was a side of him she didn't know.

"Oh, like Abraham Lincoln. But of course the Methodists would not approve of that."

"Good God, are you a Methodist?"

"Well, we were brought up Methodist because it was the nearest church to us, only thirty miles in dry weather, so my brothers and I went to Sunday school at Rotten Creek Methodist. The only thing I liked was in the summer I wore a panama hat with a silk rose on it that came off my mother's wedding dress. What about you?"

"What about me?"

"Do you believe?"

She was half expecting a passionate admission of agnosticism but instead he said as mildly as if she had asked was he comfortable, "Oh yes."

"Do you go to church?"

"Sometimes. Easter Sunday, Christmas Eve. I like to go to Saint Andrews, the stained glass windows are so congenial. But I don't give a shit about the ritual, communion, body of Christ and all that hooey, and I like to think that whatever the hell the Ark of the Covenant is is something I carry around with me wherever I am, on the tram, in the street, even if I'm pissed to the gills or with one of the girls off Kellett Street. That I don't have to be in a pew singing Glory, hallelujah where I can be quote seen of men unquote."

"I like that," she said. "I like the idea that God might be anywhere."

So she told him about her Revelation on the dusty road in Bogong that sunset when all sound stopped and light pervaded her and about everything being the same thing and perfect.

He listened with a seeming intensity that verged on the pious but when she had finished he said, "Pantheistic, I think is the word for that theory."

As though she had been merely theorizing about what had been to her, transcendental. She looked away across the green translucence of water slapping at the encrusted pilings of the jetty nearby to hide her momentary displeasure at him. And at herself for having divulged something immaculately private and precious—she had never before told a living soul about her experience—only to have it contorted into a matter-of-fact definition. Oh, that's pantheism. It was as though he had taken her gift of it and tossed it into the flotsam of cartons, pieces of driftwood, and coke floating under the jetty as he did now with the end of his ice cream cone.

Serve you right, her other self said, you were cockeyed with vainglory telling about yourself as if you were Saint Matilde of the outback.

"Well," he added laconically, "it must have been quite startling." This was too patronizing to answer so she kept staring away at the lucid bay. "But you know I sometimes think there is a touch of the mystic in you."

"Why?"

"The times when you go off into yourself and you do, frequently, you do so in a peculiar way as if you were listening to someone." Sharp as a tack, her other self said at once. Or likes to think he is. Likes to make you think he's privy to your most secret self. Part of his vanity. Vain, vain, not in the gaze-in-the-mirror sense, but vanity of intuition, of which he has none really. He's really very commonplace under all the fancy blazers and Shetlands.

"Like as of this moment," he said and played

with the curls at the back of her neck. His clear hazelnut-colored eyes were pure of the slightest guile, so he could not have been aware that he was trespassing on a clandestine part of her. Any more than he would have been aware that he had short-changed her. Her irritation dissipated, but she felt washed over with the urgency of keeping herself inviolate from the animal magnetism of him, just as someone sick with fever of the blood waits for it to pass.

"I'm stiff," she said, getting down from the embankment wall, "let's walk a bit."

Yet, as they walked off, she did the very thing she had just been counseled by her good sense not to do, she gave him her hand as if they were lovers.

For his opening night she spent nearly a month's salary on a cocktail dress, black and simple as a nun's habit. She considered the effect in the mirror and felt that it successfully reduced the look of ingenue ebullience she so disliked in herself, that she caught distressing flashes of in the shop windows and mirrored signs as she passed trippingly through city arcades in her sunny Young Mademoiselle prints. Now she sought to heighten the effect of sobriety by parting her hair in the center and drawing it back behind her ears to disarm the slight snubness of her nose and accentuate her chin, which she felt was her best feature. She added pearl earrings and then decided against them. She borrowed a black satin evening purse from Loli, who stared at her with the Buddha face and said finally, "Well, wish the silly bugger good luck from me."

He wasn't in the first scene. The play itself seemed to cringe back from the lights like a nocturnal mole affronted by a flashlight.

Something to do with a blind peer and his unfaithful wife who when reading his mail aloud to him discovers a letter anonymously exposing her promiscuity, which she hastily translates into a harmless note from an acquaintance. After a lot of tea and sherry has been served to no useful purpose, the blind man asks his wife why when reading such a trivial note was her voice trembling.

In the second scene, which was set in a lawyer's office with a lot of panelling, brass, and green blotting paper, Jack made his appearance as the wife's younger lover unaccountably dressed in cream pants and brass-buttoned yachting jacket, striding about a lot and saying things like, "Monica, we must get to the bottom of this come hell or high water." But his voice was so different, Tilly could not relate this person on stage with the Jack she knew. Gone was the casual teasing Australian twang with the relaxed lazy vowels and here, horrors, were prunes, were prisms, a "produced" voice, every a e i o u dry-cleaned to within an antiseptic inch of its life. His movements, she thought, were just as prescribed, not awkward but mechanized as though he had been graduated only that morning from a class on sitting down, crossing legs, standing up. And the worst of it was she knew he was convinced he was giving a carefully-thought-out performance, full of subtle nuance and insight, and that she would be expected to discuss aspects of it. By now her dress was sticking to her back.

And what to say?

At the curtain calls he was the one who bowed the deepest as if to an ovation, but in fact to mostly departing backs. Moving up the aisle, Tilly heard someone say, "Well, *she's* always good old tired reliable but the *juvenile*, good-looking but a stick."

"Enough to give you a nosebleed, isn't it?" he said as she climbed the final flight. "It's not true you have to climb in the theater, you *descend* to stardom." He was smoking rapidly and laughing a lot. He was wearing a rich silk paisley dressing-gown. He took hold of Tilly like a possession and drew her into the little poky dressing room where several people, some in evening dress, stood or leaned around, holding drinks. The room was dazzling with light and hazy with smoke.

Judging by their fervent manner, Tilly guessed them to be fellow actors and by their frenzied manner and forced laughter that they, like herself, considered both Jack and the play to be disaster.

"This is Tilly Beamis. Judith Appleton, Rex Goodsall, Robin Day, Janet Dunrich, Gordon Havisham."

Hello, hello, they all said. Hello, Tilly said.

"Well, did you approve?" he asked.

"Oh yes," she said wanly. It was all too disconcerting, the brilliant lights around the mirror, the smiling faces, the fawning, the unmistakable air of failure, and the desperation not to let a pause fall.

She wondered whether he had the perception to know that it was a dead flop, and whether or not he was putting a brave face on it.

But no, "That unmistakable silence for a moment

after the curtain fell and then that *roar*, it does the heart good."

"I know what you mean," someone said.

"It's the ultimate signal of approval, that pause."

"Absolutely, *the* sign."

"Fantastic."

She knew by the pinched expressions on the over-lighted faces and the sparseness of their conventional phrasing, fantastic, marvelous, that they would not be clear of the building before they would be muttering, "ghastly," "an utter bomb," "poor Jack, ghastly." But for now they were slopping down his Johnnie Walker and uttering hot air, claptrap. Was this what he wanted? Was this his place in the sun? Was this what the theater was?

Then he spun round suddenly and said, "Oh there you are, I thought you'd got lost."

An intensely blondined woman of painted-over years leaned around the door in crimson taffeta. Around her neck was coiled a rhinestone snake.

"Jean," Jack said heartily and embraced her.

Jean Magnus, he introduced her in staccato biographic sentences. Former Miss Australia. Now lived in America. Had married Mindy Magnus of Schonfeld Arts Management. Back home to visit her two sisters.

"Of Melbourne and Paramatta," Mrs. Magnus said in her American voice, which was interlaced with a hint now and then of her vestigial Footscray.

"Darling," Jack said and then, dangerously, "What did you think?"

"Well this is a dud, isn't it?" she said gayly, "there isn't anything anyone could do with this play except drop it in the deep blue sea."

This caused nervous laughter but also a riffle of relief like a cool breeze blowing through the hot glaring room.

"Oh yes, absolutely," Tilly burst out as if Jean Magnus had said it for her.

"If this were Broadway," Jean said, snapping a big ugly Zippo lighter, "they'd close it tonight, they'd have closed it in the first intermission. And face it, Pretty, there's nothing you could do with that constipated galoot except play him like a constipated galoot, which you did, honey."

Everyone agreed, yes he'd done all he could with it, all that anyone could do with such a lousy part and *sotto voce* direction and *sotto voce* Muriel who was one-half of the management, had money and cast herself in these leading roles in these fiascos, not Jack's fault. They stirred, they were relieved of pressure now, now they could go with their hands unbloodied because Jack was free of blame, thanks to good old Jean. Goodnight, goodnight.

"Tilly's coming with us," Jack said.

"Oh swell," Jean said

They were to go to Jean's flat for champagne.

"And whitebait, don't you adore it? But Pretty, I'll wait down in the car, these dressing rooms give me the heebies because the lights make me look a hundred and five."

He swung around so fast that Tilly thought he had meant to knock her to the floor, he grabbed her by both elbows in a grip that was Herculean in its intensity and yet she could feel his whole body trembling from top to toe.

"Was I good?"

The painted face with dewdrops of perspiration on the lip and around the eyes was bent toward her like that of an agonized saint in a fresco, the eyes were crucified, beseeching, the mortification of Saint Sebastian, she could almost feel the arrows coming through his flesh into her.

Incredible that this was all about make-believe, that make-believe was power and lust to this young man, a mediocre actor in a mediocre part in a silly play, which even if it lasted a month would be as forgotten as a salt pond that had dried up in the vastness of a desert.

But the beseeching eyes bored into her, begging her crumb of approbation as if it were the crux of life, the dynamics of the universe without which the galaxy would cave in, they would be crushed by blazing stones.

Jack Quist's Adam's apple rose and fell in trepidation of this, the apocalyptic.

How could you say no, smash the atom?

"Oh yes," she lied fervently.

Thank God, he said and swooned into a chair, because it mattered to him above everything what she thought, didn't she know?

"Oh yes, Jack," she said again.

And felt, accused by the other voice in the ringing silence, like a traitor.

Because if she loved him well and truly, why not speak the truth? Risk everything and let him have the sharp blade, said no, you are artificial, an amateur, my poor dear, don't linger on in this fantasy that you will ever make good.

"What have you done to your hair?" he was asking and fluffing out the drawnback hair over her ears. "I like it in the usual style." Why are we all such constant liars to each other? Is it to preserve the status quo and is the status quo worth preserving? Would life be insupportable if someone declared a National Truth Day so that everyone could revel for twenty-four hours in blissful honesty? Of course, it would be worse than anything conceivable, nuclear.

Jean Magnus' sublet flat was on the second floor of a converted house in Billyard Avenue overlooking Elizabeth Bay. It had two conical towers and steep slate roofing that glimmered in the strong moonlight.

"Oh how pretty," Tilly said, "it's like a little French chateau," and they stood a moment looking up at the towers holding hands, "and have you ever seen such moonlight, you can practically feel it."

"It's the night we change into hairy monsters," Jack said.

"And I might change into——" What? the thought was snatched away from her as if something had run up behind her and put a hand over her mouth. "A silver fish," she said and laughed.

The drawing room was solidly Sydney upperclass rosewood and cretonne sofas and armchairs on which eight or ten people were scattered drinking champagne while a small overflow sat on the stone balustrade of the balcony in the moonlight, from time to time pitching their cigarette butts into the dark gardens, which they had been asked particularly not to do.

On a sideboard were set out dishes of cold ham and roast beef and a chafing dish held something over blue flame.

"What a nice place you have," Tilly said to Jean, grateful for a straw of truth.

"Oh honey, you think so? Well, it's not my style. You should see my New York apartment, all white. Carpeting, walls, furniture, even the baby grand, all white. I thrive on white, honey, because I grew up in a little dark suburban house out in Footscray that was all fumed oak and dark-brown linoleum and black velvet sofa cushions with scenes showing lighted windows in luminous paint, and Saturday mornings my mother put me to work painting the front steps with oven black. So now I live in white with lots of lights, lamps everywhere. But you see I'm subrenting this from a pal who's in Chile, her husband's in nitrates, so I can have it furnished until winter when I go home to New York for the spring."

Momentarily deserted by Jack, who had squatted down on an ottoman with an earnest black-haired girl who had come up saying in a plaintive voice, "I'll bet you won't remember me, Roma Linton, I bet you don't, do you?"

"Can I help do anything?"

"You could lay one of these each on these pieces of bread and butter," Jean said, handing Tilly two small round bottles.

"Oh bottled oysters, how I love them."

"Yes. One thing you can't get in the States that I miss. That and passionfruit. I daresay you never lose your childhood tastes. Sometimes when I'm dining out in New York at Twenty One or Pavillon I think suddenly, oh, I'd give my right arm for a Sargents' meat pie with the gravy spilling on my chin."

"Eaten standing up."

"Hot in the hand under a piece of greaseproof paper as you walk down the street."

Jean dabbed a scarlet-nailed finger deep into a large chocolate cake and scooped a dollop into her mouth.

"Tell me what you thought of *him*."

Jean Magnus asked through cake in such a *sotto voce* undertone that Tilly almost missed it. She held her breath a second. Was this invitation to conspire in betrayal? But no, Jean's wide blue eyes were without guilt, trustworthy as a spaniel.

"Not good," Tilly said in almost a whisper, "not real."

"No, false as a toupee, more's the pity. Well say no more. Well here *you* are. When he said, 'Tilly,' I thought red hair, orange lipstick and here *you* are."

Tilly looked down at the floor and pondered the "you," it was so immense and uncircumscribed. Crammed into that mote of a pronoun was every potential for good and evil that existed. You are everything that people rightly or wrongly think of you to them, good or bad, seraph or demon or both in the millions of attitudes clicking away every second like a mammoth computer in the vast outer space of human nature. Yet people attempted to read each other, said how do *you* do? Said I love *you* to each other's enigmas.

Jean said, "Here you are fresh as a spring onion. Well, I've seen him through innumerable Junes and Shirleys and even a Dagmar."

"I know about his reputation," Tilly said a little coolly, laying an oyster on a bread square like a shark's eye.

"Oh now, precious, I wasn't presuming you don't, and anyway I'm sure you can take care of yourself, you seem like a smart chick. How old are you?"

"Twenty-one."

"Yeah? Make the most of it. Well, I'd been married two years when I turned twenty-one. Too early, too soon. And Mindy was twenty years older than me. And I'd been Miss Australia, don't you see, and had notice taken of me and been on the newsreels and kissed by the mayors of all the capital cities, so it wasn't as though I'd had to put myself in mothballs so early on. Not that I didn't have fun, mind you. But it wasn't until Mindy kicked the bucket a year ago last April all in a second in the lobby of the Paramount Building on Times Square that I said to myself, well now girl, it's time for you to be young now, and here I am." Jean struck an attitude, clicked invisible castanets.

"And do you have children in the US?" Tilly asked.

Jean took off her spangled apron and hung it.

"My little girl died when she was six."

"I *am* sorry, Jean."

"No need now, hon."

And she is lonely and cheerful and easily taken. She is ripe for the plucking by almost anyone with an ounce of guile and a gift for the right words, Tilly was being told by the other voice in her and blushing deep at the shame of it, the idea of taking advantage of poor gullible Jean Magnus, now spitting an olive pit into her hand but seeing in her, oddly, some form of rescue, that Jean stood for a kind of salvation in her terrible innocence.

Much later, supper done, Tilly and Jack stood under the dying moon in the half light on Jean's balcony. Nearly everyone had left and it was quiet enough to hear the waves slapping against the small boats moored in the bay. In mid-harbor the last Manly ferry twinkled red and green on its way toward the Heads. A breathing of air stirred eucalyptus silkily, and in the sepulchral light the stone Buddha perched at the curve of the terrace steps seemed to be moving, opening his serene eyes, grinning at her. Tilly put out her hand and touched the stone face and the illusion vanished.

Then Jack put down his glass and said, "Well, are we ready?"

"Yes," she said.

Knowing exactly what he meant. As if they hadn't been ready a long time for the inevitable, and now here it was at last and with the added pleasure of being spontaneous (and how gritty if it had been planned, some overnight place in Dee Why or Narrabeen and with her having to decide what to take, which nightie, what slippers?) on the spot and their both knowing, intuitively, that yes, they were ready. Pure and simple as mathematics, she thought and felt a rapture about it that she knew she probably would never feel again in her life, the heart beginning to beat, the bird emerging from the egg. In her state of grace she impulsively kissed Jean Magnus goodnight.

"Oh, I *have* loved meeting you, Jean."

Outside in the deserted street of parked cars and streetlamp shadows she said, "I ought to have phoned but it's after one."

He said, "They'll know where you are."

Which was true.

He put an arm around her.

"Don't wake that conventional sleeping dog in you."

He had a rented room in a large dirty beige stucco house in Roslyn Gardens. The iron gate screeched loud enough to awaken the neighborhood and as they crunched up the path a figure momentarily parted a curtain at a lighted window. His landlady, Mrs. Pearl, often sat up late, he said. Fortunately his room had an entrance from the back yard so he didn't have to "trek" visitors through the house.

It had a strong masculine smell of bay rum and pipe tobacco and tweed jackets. The three-quarter bed was coverleted with tapa cloth; an enormous old-fashioned wardrobe adorned with whorls and rosettes in mahogany took up almost one wall adjacent to a dressing table and mirror.

It was a nice room, she thought. She felt at home immediately in the soft yellow light from the big chrome art-moderne standard floor lamp, saw herself reflected in the wardrobe mirror as if she actually belonged here, looked tenderly on his things, his comb and brush on the dressing table, his brown bathrobe crumpled on a worn-out tapestry chair, his old leather slippers pointing away from each other like two old people in a huff. He had "use of the kitchen," the bathroom was just outside in the hall, he went to get ice for their nightcaps. Just make yourself at home.

The sepia woman framed on the dressing table she guessed to be his mother, probably taken about thirty years ago judging by the ribbon across the forehead in the style of the early twenties; the wife of the undertaker gazed mooningly from her frame into which, disconcertingly, had been stuck snapshots of her laughing son with a variety of girls. What, she wondered, was the standard length of time for these affairs? How long before he became bored or sated and did they end precipitously without warning or in long drawn-out scenes of bitter accusation or tearful beseeching.

Whatever happens, the other one of her said (for a moment the light winked, the room receded), you must not let him get away with it, you must be the one to call a halt.

But waking in the early hours of the morning to faint birdsong, she wasn't sure of herself any longer, her willpower had been enervated by his stunning triumph over her, for that is what it had seemed to be, ravishment. She had been ravished in the fullest sense and, conversely, she had felt that she had departed from her aroused body into his and they had merged.

"Sweet, sweet," he had kept saying. "Oh God, my sweet."

"No you, no you."

They raved on senselessly in the dark, bit and

sucked juice from each other's mouths, twisting and turning down the whirlpool of rapture, each passionately needing to assure the other of the delight, and then after the explosion that tore them both apart, they fell into an entrancing peace, into dumbness and almost immediately into bottomless sleep.

So now she wasn't sure anymore that she required safety through strength, she felt divorced from the other one of her, as if the other one had been exorcised completely by his strength entering into her and in this blissful state as if she would never heed any warning again. Come rain, come weather, hell or high water, what was to be would be. She would not compromise when it came to giving her whole heart, she would not entertain any doubts, those harpies that spoil the feasts of love. Because the joy of it would be to believe in it fervently, believe in him constantly no matter how inconstant he might be. That would be love.

And I love him.

Totally.

No. Don't confuse love with just good energetic sex.

Yes, *totally*, I want his heart.

As if she had spoken aloud he opened his eyes and stared at her like a child, wonderingly, and then drew her to him.

This time when she once cried out in the moment of truth, he said as if she had apologized for it that, not to worry, this was an old house and the walls were thick as a bank vault. She wondered at the need men seemed to have for propriety.

"Tea or coffee?"

"Coffee, if you have it."

"Instant."

"Fine."

"While I'm fixing it, would you do me a favor Till, so's I don't have to get dressed yet, and as you already are, would you slip up the road and get the papers?"

"The papers?" she was blank, papers?

"The *reviews*."

"Oh, of course."

My God, was it only last night? The dreary play, his stiff performance.

"There's a newspaper magazine shop up on Elizabeth Bay Road just up the hill around the corner. Get the *Herald* and the *Telegraph*."

"First, I'd like to use the bathroom. Can I borrow your toothpaste?"

"Oh yes, sure, just outside on your left. Here's the Ipana and this is a new brush."

There must have been half-a-dozen toothbrushes in cellophane in the drawer.

Spick and span in her dead giveaway black faille, she was not prepared to meet the landlady nor for the surprise of Mrs. Pearl who, instead of being as imagined, landladyish in dowdy cotton, felt slippers, and iron curlers perhaps in iron hair, was sluttish, a poor man's Venus in abbreviated shorts and a loose denim shirt open to her deep cleavage. She was smoking and turning the pages of the *Australian Women's Weekly*. A dirty-faced child in grubby overalls staggered toward Tilly brandishing a plastic oboe and sat down bump at her feet.

"Hello darling, hello cutie pie." Tilly bent over the child to cover her confusion. "What's your name?"

"Come here, Sharon," Mrs. Pearl said, got up and swung the child up into her arms, her face contorted by cigarette smoke. She gave Tilly an appraising look as she may have given many others seeking the communal bathroom. She had the look of a fallen-short Dietrich, the cheap allurement of a girl in a vulgar advertisement for, say, Tintara Wines.

Don't give me any airs, you puss, Mrs. Pearl's lemon-juice green eyes said to Tilly. "Right there," she pointed to the bathroom. Mrs. Pearl, who sat up late to hear the front gate screech and his footsteps up the path.

They had parted demurely, with him carefully knotting the belt of his old brown bathrobe and her making sure she had her gloves, and with sedentary remarks such as, Hope you don't feel too hung over, did you have a coat? It was strange, this metamorphosis from comets in the darkness to commonplace daylight. A bottle of milk had been delivered to his doorstep.

"We'll be in touch," he said, seeing her out.

"You bet," she said too brightly.

But then he had been deflated by the lackluster reviews that didn't portend a run for the play and by the fact that he was mentioned only as "others in the cast."

Nevertheless, something had changed, something was subtly changed in her she knew as she crossed into Darlinghurst Road to get the Erskine Street tram, an enrichment, a pathos had taken root in her, had actually aged her since yesterday, even if she should never see him again (and that couldn't be possible, could it? Not between two people who had experienced such ravishment). She felt a change even in her walk. She was sometimes critical of her walk, felt it too eager, too trippingly anxious to be there, to do whatever was expected of her lightheartedly, such enthusiasm of going up and down stairs, her feet were always echoing pleasantries it seemed to her. It was an ingenue walk, and now this morning, this gray overcast morning but glistening just the same, alive with possibilities, she felt her walk changed, longer steps denied she was in such a hurry to please, she walked now from the hips with unhurried grace.

And, getting onto the tram ahead of everyone else instead of lagging back with after-you smiles, conscious more and more of the sense of unity in herself. That so far the other side of her, the one who criticized and bullied her had not obtruded into her state of bliss with the usual nudges of censure and cynicism. She had awakened in Jack Quist's bed fearful of the morning recriminations and self-accusations she would ordinarily expect of herself, but there had been a miraculous silence and her relief had been so intense that it was as though she had been starving and had been fed a nourishing meal. She felt blameless and happy as the tram hurtled down William Street to the city and, on passing Saint Mary's cathedral, that the two bronze cardinals were lifting their arms to give her their personal benisons. Felt that she was nobody else but Tilly Beamis, felt voluptuously that she was in control of herself and that this could be a continuity. Had love fused the two apposite sides of her? That brown penumbra around the edge of her generous good nature making her look facts in the face, and facts looked in the face were generally ugly. Had it dissipated? Could it be possible that the cold marble girl inside her would no longer pinch and nudge her to remind her life was a bitter unfair joke, that people were treacherous, greedy and fools.

The first time she had become aware of this ambivalence, the fact that she was in a conspiracy with herself, had come about when she was nine. She had victimized the Felumb children. And for no other reason than that they were harmless and stupid and should be made to pay for it.

The Felumb family had a scroungy little property ten or fifteen miles over the ridge in a sunless dell where they barely made ends meet raising pigs and growing turnips and potatoes, and every so often Nell and Sis Felumb rode bareback over to the Beamis' place on their dirty piebald pony, sat silent but sniffling in the kitchen where Mum gave them bread and jam or peanut butter. "Ta," they said, reaching out with their grubby little hands. "Ta" was all they ever said, and "Ta-ta" when they rode off. Sis who was nearly eight actually dribbled like a baby.

"Oh, Mum, here come the Felumbs, must I stay?"

"Of course, Tilly. What harm can it do you to be nice to those poor backward little girls for an hour or so?"

"Oh but *Mum*. And they *smell*."

"Well praps you'd smell if all you had to bathe in was the cow hole."

So she was nice to the Felumb kids, showed them her dolls, Babe Lily and Tanya and the dolls' house made out of a packing crate. "Want to see how the separator works?" she asked, and they nodded although they'd seen it a dozen times. The week-old chicks, the new calf, kittens, when there were any; she quickly ran out of things to show them so sat them on the rail fence or in the barn and told them stories, which they drank in with their large brown eyes fixed on Tilly as if she were some oracle.

Then one afternoon as they lay sprawled on piles of sacks and hay bales in the barn and sucking on sour loquats something snapped in Tilly, and she saw Nell and Sis Felumb as oafish and lumpen, two living toadstools.

"Did I ever tell you this barn is haunted?" she asked.

They shook their heads.

"A girl hanged herself in here. Years and years ago, nearly a hundred years ago. Right up there where that big beam is."

The Felumbs glanced up toward the shadowy roof, Sis edged nearer to Nell.

"Her lover had *abandoned* her so she climbed up the ladder to the top and tied a rope to that beam and around her neck and jumped."

The Felumbs were drinking it in she could see, the little simps.

"When they cut her down her tongue was as swollen as an ox's and her eyes had burst out of her head and her neck was broken so her head fell down on her chest like a rag doll and her long hair fell right down to her knees and that's how people see her now, when she comes, sometimes in the late afternoon like now when it's getting shadowy in the barn. She comes just up there, see where that old saddle's hanging on a hook? That's where you see her come with her broken neck and her bulging eyes as big as glass doorhandles and her great thick tongue hanging out and her long hair hanging down to her waist and she moans this dreadful moan."

Errrrrghh, she gave the awful moan.

Look, she said, I can see her coming now, see the shadow of her moving on the floor planks, look Nell, look Sis.

It was only the shadow made by leaves moving in the failing daylight but the Felumbs saw the hanged woman. They were bright enough for that and screaming, holding onto each other for dear life, they rose and stumbled together out of the barn, ran sobbing with terror to their pony and rode off.

"Now whatever possessed them?" Mum said. But the thing was, of course, whatever had possessed *her?* Making up such a tale to scare the wits out of two backwoods gawks. A good kid like her, a favorite at school, would give anyone her last stick of licorice, known to ride bareback twenty miles in the rain to visit a sick chum, didn't have a mean bone in her body. She couldn't explain it to Mum any more than she could to herself, muttered something about a rat, they had seen a rat run along the rafter.

That night at supper she refused Mum's blackberry tart with cream as penance. She knelt and said her prayers fiercely on her bony knees. "God, don't let it, her—get the better of me."

Now, in this newness of feeling all one, stopping outside a flower shop in King Street, feeling the blessing of morning sunshine on her face, feeling an exaltation of oneness, she said to herself, "It's because I wholly love him that I'm whole, that is it, isn't it?" She was neither agreed nor disagreed with. In a rush of happiness she pushed open the door and went in to buy her one red carnation.

"Let's go to Manly," Jack said. "I haven't been to Manly for years. Let's take the boat over and have lunch on the Corso." It was the morning after his play had closed, they were having tea and raisin toast in his bed-sit. "What do you say?" he chucked her chin. "The sea air will blow away our miseries."

"Do we have the miseries?"

In a sense she had one, she was ruminating on victims.

They had been to a closing night party at Oliver Sly's, which had disintegrated rapidly when Oliver (who had been Jack's dressing-room mate and was in Jack's words, "As odd a sod as you'll ever find outside a normal freak show") and his wife Jan began a scene so violent as to be epileptic; drinks were thrown in faces, a kitten was rescued in the nick of being flung from the eleventh-story window, accusations as corrosive as nitric acid were spat.

"This can go on for hours," Jack said. "I'll get our coats."

"But how terribly unhappy they must be," Tilly

said later as they came in Jack's screeching gate.

"Oh, they need each other," he said, turning the key in his lock. "They've trapped each other. Listen, once you need someone you're their victim."

She was brooding over this. If he needed her would he become her victim? She could not conceive of such a thing. Even as a state of mind. She was not even unconsciously predatory, the opposite. Was she then *his* victim? By loving him? But except in bed he was as undemanding as light and air, never making inroads into her spiritual existence, was not forever asking what was she thinking. Quietly accepting whatever mood she was in as placidly as the weather. It was a kind of small miracle. Well, it was love. It needed only the confirmation of continuity.

They caught the midday ferry to Manly, crowded with Sundaygoers, and when the big boat rolled and dipped passing the Heads he put an arm around her and they steadied themselves against each other, and it seemed to her symptomatic, that this bolstering of each other was their bulwark against being over-needful, was joy. But Manly Beach was no longer joy.

It had become Coney Islandized. Shop windows were crammed with inflatable rubber animals and the plastic dummies showing off bathing suits were offensive parodies of the human figure. Street vendors peddling coconut ice and Fairy Floss were importuning aggressively and the couples maundering along the Corso seemed to have come off some mediocre cruise. It seemed to her that Jack, by contrast, had acquired additional height and grace. Standing in line in the crowded Quarter Deck restaurant he was more than just physically head and shoulders above the tatterdemalion young men in their hopeless rayon reefer jackets.

After lunch they strolled over to the ocean, where a spiteful wind had kept most of the swimmers on land. There was a high surf, white combers curled over the dark blue.

They sat on a bench and he had difficulty lighting a match in his cupped hands against the wind. Lately some distress had set him off smoking heavily. Not because of the cigarettes, but because of not knowing what distressed him, Tilly said, "You smoke too much," and instantly regretted it, it having the overtones of the chiding wife or mistress and then as though to excuse it, expiate herself, said headlong as if in grief, "Only meant because I love you."

He looked grim, sucking at the cigarette trying to get it going, the spark fading, going out, he tossed it away. "I know you do," he said, almost curtly.

"Oh, I hope to God it doesn't make you feel like a victim." He was watching the surfboats tip down from mountainous waves, his strong jaw set in awe or disapprobation. If anything was going to be said, it would be now appropriately against this bitter wind.

"Don't be a goat."

"It's just a matter of not being able not to," she said helplessly, brushing away the tears that the wind had made "pure and simply."

"I know it's pure and simple, Tilly," he said, staring at her in a grave concentrated way as

though he were a physician having to break the news of a fatal malignancy. "You don't have to say it, I know, and furthermore you're okay, you know? You're, if anything, too okay. You see, my trouble is I look for imperfection in the other person, it consoles me. It comforts me to discover that someone is possibly a liar, that somebody is unscrupulous and disenchanting, it makes them human and vulnerable and then I don't feel hooked. I don't mind their faults, it's their pretense at righteousness that makes me sick. I was brought up in an atmosphere of formaldehyde and righteousness. My mother was the living definition of holy respectability sponsored by Christ. She washed her hair every single day, she climbed ladders to scrub the tops of cupboards nobody would ever see. She washed the leaves on the aspidistra fern and the tomato-sauce bottle wore a little crocheted coat. That was her epitome of refinement, that little jacket on the sauce bottle. She lived a spotless, impeccable, barren life and as far as I know still is. We haven't spoken for years, not since I explained to her very gently that she was a castrating monsteress. I daresay she is still pulling the window blinds down to exactly three inches from the sill, it was the kind of thing she took pride in. As far back as I can remember my mother never consciously did a wrong thing in her life nor ever had a pleasant desirous thought, and when she dies the friends will be able truly to say Jessie Quist was a good God-fearing woman. Well, shit."
So he had had to escape from rectitude (she pictured the stifling suburban house, the blinds al-

ways half drawn down, the funeral parlor downstairs) and from the meticulous mother putting lace jackets on phallic bottles. And so now he was bent on pursuing the imperfect. In doing so he had taken on the role of trifler, seducer, and (she saw in a flash of insight as sharp as a pistol shot) he was no better at acting it than he was on the stage; it was amateurish, the little boy putting on mustachios and a cloak to act the villain in the high school play, it was almost endearing that through the cracks in his veneer of disillusionment she saw the gleam of his harmless natural self. He was a natural puritan and in order to prevent this being found out he would resort to any fraud. Without meaning to convey that she was touched to the heart she put a hand on his knee, but he cringed away, stood up abruptly and said crossly, "Let's go, this wind gives me the tits."

Then standing on the wharf, waiting for the boat, she said, "Have you found my imperfection?"

"Oh, you're the pure in heart," he said.

When it got to be Thursday without hearing from him, she telephoned, but there was no answer. She imagined him to be doing the rounds of radio studios because, calamities coming in tandem, along with the closing of his play, his long-run radio series had also come to an end.

Thursday evening however his landlady, Mrs. Pearl, answered the phone; she sounded as though she had a bad cold.

"Mr. Quist."

"Who's calling?" Mrs. Pearl asked huskily.

"It's Miss Beamis."

She thought Mrs. Pearl said, "He's got a new ceiling."

"I didn't hear you."

"He's gone to New Zealand."

No. Couldn't have said that.

"New———"

"He's gone to New Zealand."

There was a tearing convulsive sound as if someone were attempting to throttle Mrs. Pearl, but she was merely blowing her nose.

"Gone on tour there with some show. They wanted him there the next day. He only had a couple of hours notice to get on the plane that evening. I think he tried to get in touch with you, but you were out or something."

"When?"

"Tuesday."

"Tuesday. But I was in my office, I was at my desk the whole day."

"Well, I don't know for sure. He mightn't have had time. I really don't know. That's all I can tell you."

It wasn't possible, she was dreaming. He would never. Without a word. It was a mixup, one of Mrs. Pearl's other boarders had gone to New Zealand.

"Mr. *Quist*," she said loudly to clear up the confusion.

"Yes. I told you. Mr. Quist isn't here anymore."

Silence fell between them, broken only by Mrs. Pearl clearing her throat.

"I see," Tilly said eventually, not seeing, understanding nothing except she was suddenly fearfully hot, the phone booth stifling. On the wall was hand printed SUSY SUX XB 4648.

She was clutching the receiver so hard that it hurt her ear.

"Did—did he leave any forwarding address?"

"Auckland's all I know."

"But to forward letters———"

"He said he wasn't expecting any mail. I have to go now, there's someone just come to look at the room."

And the small click might have been the metaphor for the end of this chapter in her life.

She walked out of the GPO where she'd been telephoning into the evening rush-hour roar and began to walk rather rapidly up Martin Place. By the time she reached Macquarie Street she was running, dodging in and out of traffic and brushing past people, running. She ran past State Parliament House with its uniformed guards standing to attention, ran helter skelter toward the Mitchell Library standing conservative and dignified among its dusty palms. A few people turned their heads casually to observe this hatless girl tearing by them, little pearl necklace flapping, handbag swinging from her arm as she ran, ran as if she were pursued by furies. "Watch out where you're going," a woman called out who had been almost knocked to the footpath. But Tilly heard nothing but her own panting heart, felt nothing, knew nothing but that she must run until she dropped, and only then would she begin to consider her obliteration.

Because at the moment, running, crossing, recrossing Macquarie Street, hurtling back now toward Queens Square and Hyde Park, it could be held back, limited to a little black dot at the very back of her consciousness, a few words spoken on the telephone with a stranger that had no meaning whatever; could do nothing to alter her life.

Because running (past all these neat doorways studded with the brass names of physicians, podiatrists, chiropractors) it was easier to invent the plausibility of a future in which, when she arrived home, there would be a message from Jack explaining everything lucidly and which Panthia or Dorothy had forgotten to give her (or if it were Loli, had held it back out of spite) and reassuring her of his love, telling her that he would only be gone for six weeks, two months.

But even the champion long-distance runner has eventually to stop. She had by now such a stitch in her side that she had to slow down to a hurried walk, then stop, flop down onto a park bench at the edge of the park.

Took a clean handkerchief from her handbag and wiped her forehead.

But

if there were no message at home, no letter come in the afternoon mail.

Then

he'd cleared out, shot through. And she would have to face it and wonder at it perhaps for the rest of her life, and it must seem at this bitter moment like the slap of his hand on her face that would leave its red impression there forever.

Summer.

The worst anyone could remember, this unbroken

streak of heat. Hundred and one, hundred and two. They seethed, boiled through molten January. In the Botanical Gardens they lay on the browned grass like dead fish. The tar melted on the pavements and stuck to shoes, asphalt softened so that it became like walking on plum pudding. The unfortunates working in non-airconditioned offices were permitted to remove jackets and ties, even banks broke precedents and the icy movie houses stayed packed day and night no matter how dreadful the film. On the ferry, the breeze was tepid, lukewarm, even to the lucky ones able to get a seat outside and who averted their eyes and thoughts from the hell below decks where the wretched stokers shoveled furnaces. Still perhaps, Tilly thought, looking down to where great shafts of steel chugged back and forth in the blazing inferno, perhaps they were immune to it. Oh well, she said aloud to the woman standing beside her as they neared Valencia Street, maybe we'll get a nice cool southerly buster. What we need is a cracking bloody good thunderstorm.

These days she held out hopes for herself. These days she opened up conversations with strangers, it helped verify her existence. As if by commenting on the headline in the newspaper, the library book in the lap, she might assure herself of her own presence and assume a posture of survival. She implied a normalcy and the lie helped to perpetuate her outer self. She was prone to laugh a lot, became uproarious over peoples' weak jokes and drab puns. She had begun wearing more makeup than usual to hide the little clouds under the eyes that came from sleeping poorly.

These days she existed only in the literal sense. She got up in the morning and washed her face and put on lipstick and had her tea and cornflakes and took the ferry into town reading the Sydney *Morning Herald* and all day long she cheerfully booked people on flights to Melbourne, to Brisbane, to Cairns and Hobart, and it would have taken a prescience as deep as the ocean to discern that she had been murdered.

Oh, he's gone on tour to New Zealand, she told the Gardenses. She told the lie for him as well as for herself. For his shame. For she had telephoned the offices of J.C. Williamson Limited, the theatrical entrepreneurs and asked in as casual a way as possible for an address for their touring company. But there was no address, she was told, for the simple reason that at this time they had no company in New Zealand, sorry.

She felt clubbed from behind, mugged in the dark lane.

Over and over again she tried to reconstruct that last Sunday, the trip to Manly, she tried to recount their conversations down to the flattest exchange of opinion over anything at all that might yield a clue to what she had said or done wrong, or to uncover a nuance of the scope of such desperation that would have precipitated this necessity to put a distance of sea between them in order to save himself from her. She wondered about the way he had said, "Oh, you're the pure in heart," whether she was correct in thinking that he had said it with a hint of the caustic. It seemed out of the whole day the only thing she had on which to hang her wreath of funeral lilies. And what had been the very last thing he had said on parting? She could not for her life now remember, possibly only something like Cheerio.

Had her imperfection been a pure heart?

"———heat and the continued long dry spell," she read in the paper, "has caused enormous bush-fires to ravage the South West. Hundreds of acres of property and homes have been destroyed in the last week and in the Meridew section the burned corpses of sheep and cattle litter the dry river beds." Well, it *was* over, it was all as dead as the incinerated sheep, she told herself, and she would somehow get over it, somehow, she told herself, and beat her head with her savage palms.

Thought it must be the heat, this astonishing apocalyptic heat when just after lunch she fainted at her desk.

"And you ought to wear a hat, Tilly, this sun's murderous," said Fay who had the next desk to hers, applying eau-de-cologne. Tilly lay on a couch in the ladies room and said, oh but she was used to heat worse than this. Where she came from they had summers that could melt tin at noon.

Never fainted before in her life.

Surely not *that*.

It would be altogether too preposterous, fiction. Tess. Hester Prynne.

Yes.

Early October, the doctor said. His weary tone suggested that lately he had broken this ancient-as-time news to too many unmarried girls who, like herself, had not resorted to fictional names or feigned husbands.

She walked away, carrying it inside of her, aware

now of its presence somewhere below her heart like a smaller heart beating. She waited for a bus in the simmering heat. Across the street pavements, shops, cars shivered, danced in glycerine tide. She put a hand up to her hair and it was as hot as if she had just used an electric dryer. The brazen sky was aching blue.

It is too hot to think what to do, she said to herself. It was as though the heat were cushioning the shock of the doctor's confirmation. Scorched, she was cauterized against perplexity. I can't think now, I won't think yet. I don't have to decide anything yet.

She didn't want to reassess or reevaluate her situation. She wished the heat wave might continue unabated (it was already into the third week and the fanatics in the Domain were invoking Armageddon, UFOs and the A Bomb testing) in order to forestall her having to make any move. She wanted to lie down somewhere dark and cool and drink ice cold grapefruit juice in great quantities and think about nothing.

Most of all she didn't want to think about *him*. When she thought about him it evoked scenes of enjoyment. She pictured him, perhaps unfairly, with some ravishing Auckland girl in bars and restaurants or picnicking under snowcapped mountains. When she let herself think about him it was in a void, neither bitter nor castigating. She felt only a vast separation and an aloneness so totally enveloping it had the finality of widowhood.

Heaving herself up onto the bus was a girl who must have been into her eighth month. The girl appeared to have an inner radiance and for a moment Tilly was shot through with the quicksilver idea that she might go through with it. Dressed him/her in the baby clothes, gave her nipple, smelled the warm baby smell, cradled the downy head, saw the tiny hands curl and uncurl like sea anemones around her finger. For a moment she considered the ecstasy of the possibility.

She automatically crossed her hands over her belly and smiled at the pregnant girl, who smiled back.

"When's it due?"

"Couple of weeks. Boy, will I be glad. Never have one in the summer, I musta been mad."

October, the doctor said. Spring, the budding time. On and off she thought about it during the next few weeks, time slipping by like the tide coming in imperceptibly but inexorable. She began to fancy she was already rounder, but it was ethereal, in the bathroom mirror she was a sapling. She continued to luxuriate in procrastination.

Then one evening without warning at dinner, passing a tureen of peas, she broke the news.

Loli remained silent and deadly still, but Panthia and Dorothy Gardens behaved excessively, out of proportion; old guilt and insecurity seemed to be calmed in them by her announcement, ecstatic at her endorsement of a privileged state they pressed claret and dewy kisses on her, it might well be that she had been visited by the angel of God in a Raphael or da Vinci Annunciation.

"Sure it's him?" Loli asked.

"There's never been anyone else," Tilly said flatly.

"Does he know?"

"Oh no. I only found out two weeks ago."

"I wouldn't have put it past him to have skipped out, he's such a skunk."

"Who gives a fig about him?" Panthia said. "*I* never cared what happened to my fellows afterward. I had all my three children under my own name and never saw the fathers again, and that was back in the days when that kind of thing was unthinkable. Oh have it, sweetheart, have the baby."

"Yes," Dorothy urged, as if it were a validation, this continuity of free love. "You could move into the storeroom next to the laundry. It'd be lovely having the baby."

But Loli said, "She'll have to give up her job. Will they take her back under the circumstances? Who's going to support her?"

"I haven't thought that far yet," Tilly said. She was beginning not to like being pressed this way, like pansies into a book.

"Oh, we'll find some way," Panthia said. "Something or someone will turn up, it always does. Pour me a drop of claret, Dot."

They were crowding in on her, their big faces smiling and coaxing, Panthia's massive face with clotted mascara and chewed-off lipstick, Dorothy's pensive long nose under the plucked eyebrows that looked gnawed off, Loli's Chinese cold disapproval. She felt their heat and coldness and her blood rising in her. Something was happening, that tearing of herself in half, one of those moments she had and could not stop. The floor hit the ceiling and she put her cup down with a sharp crack and said in her other harsh voice with its deep beautiful scorn, "It's mine, not yours. Why do you want it? For another one of your dreams that never come to anything?"

They were staring, struck dumb, Dorothy's cup half lifted to her mouth, Panthia with the cigarette half lit, photographed.

"Plays," Tilly said in this scorched voice, "that will never be finished, ballets that will never see the light of day, perfect lovers that don't exist. Hopeless. Hopeless smooging hangers-on pretending to admire you, toadies, dreams, rubbish, lies." She began to laugh in an ugly sneering way and could not stop, her ugly laugh sounded like wire cutters, gave way to hiccups as she said, "Excuse me but you're pathetic. Nothing will ever happen. None of you will ever come to anything. Never. And you're not free and ingenious, you're as trapped as everyone else. You're as *ordinary* as mustard."

She felt the whirling around, the sparks subsiding into the cool awfulness of reality and put her arms protectively around her belly.

"Well *thanks*," Dorothy said, "but we're the only family you've got, remember."

"I'm going to be sick," Tilly said and rushed for the downstairs lav.

It had passed now. She sat on the toilet with her head against the wall, the nausea subsiding. This was the worst it had ever been, this seizure, and must have been long in the coming, an accumulation of things, shock, the heat, longing, abandonment. Now she had shocked and insulted these harmless people, shaken their only possessions, their dreams in their faces like old strings of broken beads. And she had not done one positive thing to help her own predicament.

"Till, are you all right?" It was Lo knocking.

"Yes. Coming out."

She came out and went shakily toward the stairs. Loli behind her said, "Listen love, I know of someone out Coogee way, he's safe as houses but expensive. Could you scare up fifty quid?"

"Yes, but. But I don't know yet, Lo."

"It isn't safe to leave it too long, you know."

"I know but———"

"If you like, I'll phone him and make an———"

"I don't *know* yet, Lo."

Breathing heavily behind her on the dusky staircase, Loli seemed bent on murder.

So there must have been soft moments in the dark with Jack. Perhaps in the same room Tilly was remembering, the three-quarter bed with the tapa cloth over it, the plaster peaches and rosebuds on the ceiling centerpiece.

Tilly said at her bedroom door, "I'm better now. It was just a sort of spasm. Tell them that, will you? I love them. I love you all, you know that."

Loli said, her lip curling, "That bloody rat."

"Oh no," Tilly said, "why should he take all the blame? I cooperated fully so half the blame's mine."

"Oh, don't try to be fair, that's too bloody much."

Tilly said, perhaps cruelly, "The difference between you and me is that I loved him."

She wrote in the journal (she was herself again). February 12. The dearest thing happened. Last night after dinner there was a knock on the door and it was Geoff Gardens saying could he come in a minute. He was awkward and sat his big frame down in my one wicker chair and fidgeted and finally said, Do you have enough light in here, Tilly, can you read by that lamp? Said, Does the sun bother you early in the morning, this window faces directly east. And I realized that in all the time I've been living here he's never once been in my room and that he and I only meet at meals and on the stairs and greet each other lightly. How's it going? Looks like rain. He usually smiles at me from behind his big tortoiseshell glasses and says, Good on you, Tilly, not much more. Unlike his mother and sisters he's not very outgoing and he's an oddment, scrawny and muscular he has the look of a drover, sunburnt riding behind a herd of cattle and yet he composes weird music based on Aboriginal themes, atonal, ugly but haunting, and sitting at the piano he is transported into some kind of ecstasy, his long thin body is bent over the keyboard as though he's in pain, his eyes are bursting blue behind his spectacles, amazed at some inner power he feels. He plays the ugly chord and then seizing his pencil notes it on the manuscript, plays another chord, notes it. He would not notice if the house were burning. I often sit and listen to him composing, he doesn't mind anyone being in the room, he is transported into his Arcady. Then when he is finished, he closes the piano and spins round on the stool and he is once again the sunburned drover, man of the outdoors, the billabong, coolabah. He winks at me. Good on ya, Tilly.

He was struggling with something he wanted to bring out. He took off his spectacles and blew on them and wiped them on his handkerchief and held them up to the light and blew on them again and wiped them and again held them up to the light, and then he coughed and put them back on and looked at me and said Tilly, if you wanted, we could get married.

Oh Geoff, I said, you are a darling, that's the nicest thing that's ever been said to me. I got up off the bed and went and put my arms around him. He didn't move or try to embrace me, just sat there and I felt his very strong tense back and shoulders in my arms and I just stood there holding him because it was so dear and he knew what I meant, that I intended him to know I loved him for it even though it was, would be, preposterous for us under any circumstances especially in my current situation, impossible for us because we are, will always be total strangers.

A wretchedness began like flu. Persisted. It was only with Herculean effort she could get through the day at the airlines, she took her paper bag lunch into the Botanical Gardens and ate it like crow, the baleful looks she gave people seemed to deter them from sharing the bench with her. Her kind of wretchedness has an aroma and, scenting it, people moved away from her as they might do from lunatics.

Had she been bitter she would have been better off, she could have galvanized herself with it into some kind of action. But wretchedness is soporific, it lulls, seeping into the soul with an anesthesia that deadens. Turning to blue mold, incapable of stopping the rot, the peach browning, spotting, turning to mush, she became the thing she most dreaded, the mourner for herself. She drifted masochistically among places where they had been together, through dull long haunted Saturday afternoons, through empty arcades of coffee houses and record shops, the steps of the National Art Gallery and the nearby Domain where the fanatics, the soapbox demagogues, apostrophizing with clenched fists against America, trade unions, Christianity, vivesection, raised invective to such extremes it made her small predicament seem less incomprehensible.

Then as if she had been nudged, she stepped onto a double decker bus going to Watsons Bay as if a sudden craving for oysters had overwhelmed her, remembering they had been to a small cafe overhanging water that catered exclusively to this delight, and that Jack had eaten two dozen. "All the way," she said to the conductor, holding out her coins and the words seemed as she spoke them, conclusive. It was not oysters she was seeking but a conclusion, an ending. She knew quite calmly that she going to the Gap. Jokingly, she had written in her diary, "Oh well, there's always the Gap," and now that it was no longer just a contemplation she felt suddenly revived, stimulated. She took in the brick houses and gardens flying by as if she were a child out on a Saturday afternoon jaunt that would conclude with ice cream. She got out at the stop and walked briskly up a dusty pathway in a snapping wind to where the lookout was cupped in the rim of a saucer overhanging the ocean and down to where it curled and shrank back over the terrible rocks sixty feet below. It would be temptingly easy. Death and oblivion were two feet away the other side of the fence, the fence easy to climb, the old couple seated on a wooden bench a few yards away would not even have time to cry out before she splintered on the rocks below and was sucked away in the ink blue sea.

And at that moment, the moment of seeing her death in her mind's eye (she saw in a momentary film, herself fling her bag away, step out of her pumps, climb, jump (her wristwatch would be stopped at twenty-three minutes past four), caught and whirled into death by the sea wind like a gull. She felt herself suddenly free and elated, emerging from the apathy and woe that had paralyzed her for the past weeks and then, like the fresh salt wind blowing around her head, felt the presence of her other self stronger than it had ever been, confident, pragmatic, hard as agate and angry, wonderfully angry at the sight of her tiresome melancholy and the mourning for her murdered vanity.

Booby. You were never loved.

"Bastard," she said into the wind. "Fornicating bastard, Judas," she said aloud, rejoicing in it, held onto the wooden fence which had momentarily blocked her insanity. The presence, regarding her fiercely but with a fierce love said Imagine, said imagine you coming to this, you with your brightness. Imagine the waste you have made of yourself.

"You all right, miss?" The elderly man was breathless from running.

Coming out of it, coming back now to herself, realizing she must look rather wild, her hair blown about, hanging onto a fence at the edge of the earth over a boiling sea, over a cliff famous for poignancy.

"I'm all right, thanks."

Righter than I've ever been.

Rid of him, she told herself, told Tanya.

1955

To begin with, America was not the technicolor dream.

New York was not the rose quartz color of myths. New York was the squashed carton of strawberry yogurt on the sidewalk, the steam rising from around the manholes as if hell were just below street level. It was Chock Full O'Nuts' bright, unholy interiors and the Checker cabs that looked like big dented children's toys. It was little pails of dying flowers along Third Avenue and dirty newspapers blowing in the gutter. It was sirens. It was the pinnacles of silver and shining glass against the dazzling blue and the neat woman on the bus who opened her bag to show Tilly the carving knife and said, "I'm going up now and cut off his balls."

It was the gigantic difference after the quiet banality of Sydney, the raw sight and sound symbolized by the monstrous sanitation trucks with their Brobdingnagian brushes sweeping through spotless side streets while a block away the avenue was choked with garbage piled knee high under illegally double-parked Cadillacs.

The nacreous light over the East River in early evening and the liverish neon light of the subway where the faces were like the faces in Daumier. It was the sadness of discovering that in certain grotesque shops near Times Square one could buy a realistic imitation of dog excrement.

It was the moment of discovering you belonged.

It was then, the light turning green and the crowd stepping out, stepping briskly forward to cross Park

Avenue at Fifty-ninth Street, and she crossing with them in the fall evening light striking the golden dome of the Grand Central Building and all at once, glancing south, thinking "I am one of them."

Feeling the elation at this sense of unification, the intensity of community which she would never have felt in her native country (conscious here of how the disparity of background consoled and equalized, whereas in the homogenous congruity of Sydney one would never think of asking where anyone was from when everyone belonged there in the first place) and the beatification of having perhaps stumbled across the secret of coming to terms with this appalling, celestial city. It was this lowest common denominator, that everyone was from somewhere else, that made New York the city it was, unlike any other in the world.

And this is what she had in common with everyone, with the Greek fishmonger and the Irish waitress in Schrafft's, the German Fraulein in the dry cleaners.

So that now this was home, the Grand Central Building at evening was pastoral and real, and the past, the bluegums and the dusty bushlands, was the dream.

First there was Jean.

Toward the end of that same molten stultifying summer.

The first inclination was to pass quickly by Jean Magnus buying soap in Farmers, the connection might be painful or merely redundant. Jean was in a pants suit, hatless, beringed, smoking. The buying of soap was as ceremonial as a Mass.

"Why, *Tilly,*" Jean Magnus said in her half-Australian half-American voice as warmly as if they had known each other a lifetime.

"Aren't you adorable to remember me."

"Smell," she said, waving a cake of pink soap under Tilly's nose. "Nice? Geranium. I didn't know geraniums *had* any smell. Well, how have you been keeping yourself?"

Mrs. Magnus exuded not only a scent of Arum lillies but an aura of exceptional goodwill and the cheerfulness of a nanny. "Oh, I love to buy soap," she confided, "I never can have enough soap. Do you like this French Fern? Is it too persuasive, do you think?"

Boxed with enough soap for forty days and forty nights, Jean took Tilly's arm in an affectionate squeeze as they emerged from Farmers, and Tilly clutched a jumbo jar of bathsalts, which she didn't really want but had been pressed on her.

"Are you on your way anywhere, Till?"

Tilly explained that she was having a day off because she had substituted one Saturday. She was drifting, she said, aware of the truth of it.

The Wellington served Devonshire teas, Jean said, scones with jam and clotted cream. They were put at a table adjacent to the string trio who were playing desultory Chaminade and Rudolf Friml, which could barely be heard above the female chatter of the Sydney suburban matrons; it was the kind of atavistic dining room where one half expected to see the ghost of Dame Nellie Melba appear, buxom and dated, from around a potted palm. But in fact here Tilly was with the one-time Miss Australia.

Who peeled off her gloves and dispensing with caution said, "So Mister Beauty took himself off to New Zealand, I hear."

"Yes."

"Well, I wasn't altogether surprised. I thought he'd eventually succumb."

"Succumb?"

"To Lady Hope."

"Ladddie———?"

"La–dy Hope, widow of Sir Walter. Horses, property. Estate in Otahuna outside of Wellington. I take it he didn't mention her."

"No."

"Naturally. Who do you think paid for all those imported tweed jackets from Richards and David Jones? Not J. Quist, occasional actor in pisspot radio serials, my dear. She's been after him for years, on and off, here and there and he finally succumbed." Jean spooned strawberry jam and whipped cream onto her heavily buttered scone and churned it all into a bloody flux, which she ate with gusto, licking her fingers.

"She was Miss New Zealand the year I was Miss Australia and she landed Sir Walter who was big with cattle *and* around the girth." Yes, it figured. He who would not be victimized had succumbed to the fleshpots, there was a classicism to the irony (and her like an accessory before the fact "I love you," "I know you do"). The fatal admission, the straw she had laid on his back when he must have known already that he was yielding himself up, or about to, would that very evening perhaps make the long-distance call to Wellington, would leave Tuesday and Tilly sitting there meekly with tears from the wind on Manly Beach hoping not to tread on his private perspective of himself.

"Well," she said to Jean, "it's disappointing of him. I'd have preferred a larger sin."

In justice to proportion, what she had been through.

She told Jean about the baby and her decision that day on the cliff. She told about going with her cousin Lo out to the place in Coogee and that oddly enough, the doctor had resembled her father with his thick sandy hair. His breath had smelled of lemon drops. The worst of it had been having to wait so long in a hideous waiting room.

As if she were in the confessional, the weight lifting. As if Jean were her mother and she had come running through rain and storm to kneel at a warm fireside at her mother's knee and pour it all out, the misjudgments and wrong interpretations about love, about the misplacement of the heart.

"I couldn't forget," she said like a hurt child, "some of the things he said in the dark."

"Anything said in the dark, in extremis," Jean said, clicking a big steel Zippo to her Lucky Strike cigarette, "you got to be careful how you interpret it. Better you take to heart what a man says to you in the supermarket than in bed. I've learned. Now honey, you got to cheer up and get your life in gear again, millions of girls have gone through this and later found the right guy and————"

"I don't want to find the right guy, thanks."

"Not now you don't, but you will."

Jean paid the bill and they went out through the potted palms to the tune of "Vilia." Listen, Jean said, she was having some people in for buffet Friday around seven, do come. Do come, Jean said and embraced Tilly fervently like the strayed daughter who has returned to the fold. "Oh you are a duck, you are precious." Unlike Jack Quist, Jean had no preconceptions about herself or others and she was as translucent as a glass of water.

So it happened that Tilly and Jean Magnus entered into one of those mater-familias relationships that happen between women of different ages, without stress of competition, a reciprocity.

Jean lived to give, she seemed to be sustained by the act of giving as if it provided her with some assurance of her own existence. She was restless when not spending, regarded the unbought thing as a kind of waste and having been left substantial means with which to buy anything she liked in any quantity, she basked in amplitude. Growing up poor in the sour streets of Footscray among barefoot children and sunken-faced people humiliated by the dole, she luxuriated in synthesizing her natural Australian generosity with her American prodigality. If she were to order out-of-season hothouse flowers or sugar bananas from Queensland, then it would be three dozen. Why skimp on Strasbourg goose liver? She dissembled prettily, saying as she pressed an expensive evening bag on Tilly that, well she was getting one for herself so why not two, saying that this or that matched Tilly's eyes or that she had happened to notice Tilly didn't have a decent raincoat. She had, within a few weeks, presented Tilly with a radio, kid gloves,

Nova Scotia salmon, three scarves, a raffia parakeet and a gilt-edged leather-bound copy of the poems of Ella Wheeler Wilcox. There was no more stopping her avalanches of bounty than the damming up of the great Murrumbidgee River. Needless to say she fell among thieves, she was exploited, she went unthanked. Her imported Gauloises and Lucky Strikes were surreptitiously pilfered, her Napoleon brandy wantonly diluted in that inexcusable Australian barbarity of mixing it with soda or dry ginger ale.

She appropriated people by the batch with no discrimination: "Everyone back to my place," from out of bars closing, in elevators following dull parties, she sucked them in like a vacuum cleaner. No wonder she was let down, she was ignorant of friendship. Coming into her bedroom, Tilly had encountered a gaggle of young people putting through a long-distance call to Perth. "Oh, *she* won't mind."

"I mind," Tilly said firmly, taking the receiver from them and replacing it on the cradle.

"Who are *you*?"

"Her friend."

Later a little gold and pigskin traveling alarm clock was found to be missing.

Her friend. How could you not be? Without calculating, Tilly had assumed a protective attitude toward Jean because Jean was vulnerable and incautious, and Tilly was doomed to watch over the vulnerable even though the other side intruded, scandalized. She's a fool and so are you, it insinuated. Yes, I know. And maddening. And if only she would eat without spilling.

It was never spoken of but hovering in a gauzy ectoplasm just beyond the contour of their friendship was the ghost of Jean's dead little girl, who could perhaps by now have been of an age with Tilly, and occasionally Tilly caught Jean looking at her in a flash of water quickly winked away.

"Come home with me."

"I can't tonight, I'm cooking the dinner. Pork, and takes time."

Sitting on a rooftop cafe, over a store, after shopping that was more like looting.

Jean said, dropping a blob of hollandaise sauce on her blouse and scooping it off with her paper napkin, "I mean home to New York."

"America,"

Tilly said, and it sounded flat as unimpassioned as if she had said Warnambool or East Maitland.

Without calculating? It was unsettling, exhilarating, victory and defeat. Because the one-half of her, the mostly unseen half, had willed it, coaxed it out of Jean with only half-meant compliments and with which she had insinuated herself by stealthy means, saying did you take your pill? Did you rest? Remember you have to pick up the tickets before six. That color is perfect on you. Encouraged dependency, endured boredom and often repulsion with this mild, brainless generous nitwit and her American vulgarity who was now offering the equivalent of lifting the lamp beside the golden door.

"Jean, I don't think I could accept———"

Now her turn to waltz around Jean with stifling bromides about personal pride, fear of becoming a trespasser, the stigmas of responsibility and of

obligation, those foxes spoiling the vines of virtue.
"I wouldn't want to spoil what we have," Tilly was actually heard to say by her other half, who blushed deeply at her for this atrocious imposture.
"Let me think."
"You think, darling. We'd be going in April. You think."
Funnily, of late she had been resisting the fatality of Australian inertia. She had been shocked by an archetypal exchange overheard on the ferry.
"How's Shirl liking married life?"
"She says she doesn't mind it."
That said it all.
People thought her odd because she felt passionately about things, declared herself entranced by the truth and beauty of things, which was un-Australian and caused skepticism, "Oh, you liked it did you?" "Didn't *you*?" "I didn't *mind* it."
Yet she knew in her blood she was vitally Australian. Perhaps because she was a country girl and her roots were deep in the same harsh soil as the giant gum trees and the scabrous Banksia with its ugly little gargoyle nut faces. That she too was relative to wattle, yellow in the spring, and to cold, fresh winter rain, and that basically she had in her an atavistic resistance to forsaking it. Perhaps it was their inhospitable position on the map of the globe, being the furthest-away continent on earth, that bred in them a fierce loyalty and a mistrust of people and things beyond the horizon, and it may have been this phenomenon, genetically transplanted in them from their great-great-grandfathers who had come in sailing ships, that engendered their fatal chauvinism and the refuge of condescension. And

what was America? The technicolor dream of giant faces on the screen behind symphonic outpourings of emotions generated in tin cans on celluloid. She knew of course it was apocryphal, made up, false as eyelashes. But what *was* America?

Certainly Jean couldn't tell her. Tilly imagined that Jean Magnus saw little or nothing of the sordid and disagreeable in New York, lived high above the sound of sirens in the night, insulated against the pain and inconvenience experienced by people whom she only saw as ants from a great distance above.

And Stanley Kaplan, Jean was saying, her lawyer, *her* Stanley Kaplan could do anything, remove mountains, get Tilly's permanent residence, if Jean sponsored her. Jean had become an American citizen in nineteen forty-five just as the late Mindy Magnus would have wanted. Tilly might merely have to go to Canada for a few days to reenter.

Jean was already tying labels on baggage.

Tilly wandered over to the Botanical Gardens and thought, passing the Shakespeare Memorial statue, that Portia looked down on her disapprovingly. "Leaving?"

There was already a touch of April autumn in the air, it had a dark piney odor. She looked at the lengthening shadows sweeping the grass across to the formal rose gardens presented to the city by Lady somebody, wife of a forgotten state governor, and to the deep blue of the harbor where aptly a liner, last of a line, was on her way to the Heads to sea. All at once she was swept by a tidal wave of emotion and tenderness for it all, for the dusty palm fronds slapping in the breeze, the sounds of traffic in Macquarie Street, the distant tooting of evening ferries, the marble calm of Captain Cook forever looking across his domain, not yet forseeing his brutal end in Hawaii, for all the sounds of Sydney, mellowing around her into gentle evening in its hyacinth light, and she was electrified by the conviction that for all her conniving she could not leave it.

I won't go, she said.

But it was foreordained, it was too late, she had ordained it for herself.

"You *will* go," Tanya said.

Well, there were differences here. Light switches turned UP for on and DOWN for off. Traffic kept to the right. Excuse me, said with upward inflection meant I didn't hear, excuse me said with downward inflection meant sorry. There was the frequent cognizance of welcome; the first words she heard on American soil after thanking the stewardess at San Francisco airport for pointing the way to the baggage carousel, "You're welcome."

NOT responsible for personal property.

You're welcome.

NO checks cashed.

You're welcome.

CURB your dog.

You're welcome.

KEEP off the grass.

You're welcome.

OFF duty.

You're welcome.

There was a certain delight at first in the novel, in softshell crabs, drive-ins, Saran Wrap, carwashes, the Goodyear Blimp, the obesity of the Sunday *New York Times.*

She was quick to tell everyone of her delight in the city. Careful, on constant guard not to admit to drawbacks. That her box of a maid's room (Jean had converted the guest room into television den and bar) was so minute that when she turned over in bed she knocked her arm on the bookshelf. Nor that she was minimized by the blinding opulence of Jean's Central Park West apartment, which was all white, oceans of wall-to-wall whiteness under lamps raining hard grinding light onto great cream furry armchairs that looked like stranded polar bears, onto a white baby grand, milk glass shepherdesses, beaded tulips, and onto paintings that looked in the glare to be concocted of daubs of whipped cream on smoked salmon, which Jean had bought by the dozen (as she did everything) at a bargain from a starving Armenian. As though the room cried out for the relief of color, it got Jean. Jean held court in her strident clothes over this blanched splendor. Many nights a week the huge room filled up with chattering blondined middle-aged divorcees and widows. It was apparent from the start that Jean couldn't be alone for long. Her inner resources were sparse, her attention span short. If Tilly sought the privacy of her little room it would not be long before Jean's plaintive voice would be heard asking was she in there. "You in there?"

Or, "What you doin'?"

And there were the nights when Jean wanted to stay up and play two-handed poker often until way past midnight when Tilly would have to set her alarm in order to be up at seven to get to work. Following her successful immigration, effected by the assiduous Stanley Kaplan, who wore a white carnation and blew cigar smoke in Tilly's face, one of Jean's blondined divorcee friends Lurene De Soto had been instrumental (through a pal on the board) in getting Tilly a job in nail polish at Bonwit Teller. "Oh, wonderful," Tilly had said, "thank you, Lurene." "You're welcome."

It wasn't, she told herself ceaselessly, that Jean was selfish, just thoughtless, never unappreciative. "See how she looks after me," Jean would say to the 'girls,' "see how spoiled I am."

But, Jean pronounced dramatically, Tilly was never on any account to think of herself in the role of companion, paid or otherwise, that was never to be entertained. Tilly was to come and go as freely as a kitten through a little cat door. As if Jean didn't exist. Jean gave Tilly a key to the apartment on a solid gold chain from Tiffany.

Yet when Tilly stayed out for dinner in the Village or a movie with Roddy Staunton, who was in the window dressing department at Bonwit's, was defiantly gay and irresistibly mordant, she was met by pouts. "It's just that there wasn't a thing to watch on TV," or, "It's just that the apartment seems so large and empty, I can't imagine how I lived here all these years alone after Mindy died."

"Why didn't you call Lurene?" Or Lenore, Dinky.

"Why should I call her?" Or them? "She only drinks me out of house and home. What's *she* ever done for me?" Or they? "You're the only one cares about me."

It was things like that. When it came to slow torture, it wasn't the back being broken against the wheel, it wasn't red hot pokers applied to the backside, it was Jean singing "Ol' Man River," Jean forever being a monkey's uncle. Cheesecake. Jean had a passion for cheesecake and especially for the angelic texture and richness of the cheesecake served at Lindy's restaurant on Broadway.

"Oh, I feel like a piece of Lindy's cheesecake," Jean might say, starting up, in the middle of the evening, after a large dinner or almost at bedtime. "Don't *you*?"

It wasn't that Tilly disliked Lindy's, although it was always overcrowded and distressingly noisy. It wasn't that Jean flirted with waiters, became with twinklings and dimplings coquettish, introducing Tilly as her foster child ("Julius, you remember my foster child"), but it was the sexuality of the eating, the turning of Jean into a finicky buzzard that was primeval. First she prinked a morsel of cheesecake onto her fork and then, holding it up before her mouth, let out her tongue to lick it. Then taking tiny bites but not swallowing, she slowly filled her mouth with creamy softness until her cheeks bulged to bursting and all the while at the same time smoking and inhaling into the mass of sponginess, masticating and finally swallowing, gulping and then smiling ecstatically, showing her front teeth caked in yellowish mush. Then starting all over, tiny fragment on fork, held up, admired, then the red tip of the tongue flicking out to lick at it, the maw opening to receive, the cake-clotted teeth. Tilly watched, with a kind of repelled ecstasy, as perverted as the rapture of watching a snake devour a rat. She had once covertly timed Jean and it had taken her twenty-four and one-half minutes to consume a medium-sized slice of cheesecake. At last sated, she would push away the greasy remains, sit back and sigh and say, "Oh, that hit the spot. But what I would give to have a dear old Sargents' meat pie."

Very dearly, Tilly thought of reaching across and pushing Jean's face into the dish.

Or that mightn't she groan aloud when the hat-check girl showed Jean her engagement ring and Jean had to say that well, she'd be a monkey's uncle.

One time something seized Tilly and wouldn't be suppressed, and she in turn, seizing Jean, pushed her rudely through the revolving door onto Broadway, and pinching Jean's baby-white, flabby flesh with her sharp nails (kept long in order to display the nuances of Bonwit's varnishes) she hissed, "You've got lipstick all over your front teeth."

Well, Jean said, you didn't have to almost knock her down to tell her.

Knelt on the floor of her little room as if in penance.

Think now.

Putting clean underwear away in the bottom drawer of her chest (you had to close the bedroom door in order to pull out a drawer) as if she were putting out of sight her grievances.

Think now.

all she's done for you. Not only brought you to

America but arranged for you to get your permanent resident green card, put you up, paid for some expensive dentistry.

What else?

A tap at the door.

"You in there?"

"Yes, Jean."

"What you doin'?"

It could have been a number of things, snow blindness from the white carpeting, the sight of those beaded tulips, the glint of rhinestone heels, lipstick-stained butts in the Delft hand, "Ol' Man River," Tilly broke with the strain of loving Jean Magnus and broke off only minutes before worse things could have occurred to Jean than nail pinching.

On the day Tilly moved to the small apartment on East Eighty-second Street, Jean said, "It just shows no one is grateful in this world. No single person is ever grateful to another person in this bloody world."

"Now be honest, do you like it, Tilly?" Edward asked.

"Oh yes, it's charming."

"But do you like it without any reservation?"

"Oh, absolutely."

"Because I haven't signed the lease yet. I want you to be totally honest with me, Tilly."

"Am I not always?"

"You tend to be accommodating."

"Not about somewhere I'll have to live indefinitely."

They were standing in the empty apartment holding hands like babes in the wood, this quality of fragility made more tangible by the fact of their being virtually the same height. Edward Patterson was a small man, beautifully put together like a miniature with delicate features. At the age of thirty-seven the notion of his marrying had been thought unlikely, undoubtedly by his sister Rose.

Now in his methodical way he had measured all the furniture, sofas, chairs, tables, chests in his own apartment and drawn it on the floors of the proposed new apartment in chalk. Here would be the sofa, here the end tables, there the grandfather clock, the spectral pieces formed themselves in the blank air like ectoplasm. He was a man of order, he didn't allow things to take him by surprise, even furniture. He was of the opinion that ETA should stand for Exact Time of Arrival. Uncharacteristically, this conservative soul, congealed under the faultless suits of Jones Chalk and Dawson of Sackville Street, who had never before done anything in a headlong fashion, had lost control and fallen violently in love.

And to this pert Australian, cocky as a spring lamb and with the remnants of an accent unfamiliar in the environs through which Edward moved, and given to little outbursts of humorous confessions. And in six weeks, engaged. Is it wise? his friends asked each other on the telephone, rattled by this inconsistency.

"I want you to meet Miss Tilly Beamis," Edward said in his Edwardian manner, "who has done me the honor." Straightfaced.

"It's lovely to meet you," Tilly told the friends

warmly and embraced them with their first names, not habitual with this bunch. She was now writing copy for McGrab Hopkins, a small advertising agency catering mainly to FM music stations in and around New York State and Connecticut that provided the half-minute commercials before and after the news breaks.

How this had come about, she liked to say, was typical of New York City in that one thing leads often to another. She had gone against her will on such a hot July night to a wine and cheese party given by one of the girls at Bonwit's down on Jane Street and, worse, had chosen in this heat to wear an orange-colored linen dress that crumpled easily and made her feel by color association, hotter, and plomping herself down on a window sill next to this cool-looking woman in cucumber seersucker she had burst out with, "Oh, I feel as if I'm drowning in boiling marmalade," and the woman had laughed and said, "How apt. Have you ever written copy?" Tilly hadn't even known what copy was. The woman was Patty Hopkins of the McGrab Hopkins agency. "Come in and see us sometime," Patty said.

Things happening like quicksilver in New York (even if that was generally a widespread misconception), a week or two later Tilly had been started off as a junior pro-tem writer, pecking away one-fingered on the old Royal at little pieces of homemade copy for some of the smaller clients, among whom was, if fate had intended, Pease Patterson & Co. Importers of Fine Wines since 1883.

Nonplussed at Pease Patterson and in desperation half jokingly, she had thought up the gimmick of having the announcer say, "And now Pease Patterson, Importers of Fine Wines since eighteen hundred and eighty-three, are pleased to bring you thirty seconds of silence." Incredibly, radio stations reported that their switchboards were being swamped with calls from grateful listeners. A woman had said to thank Mr. Pease for half a minute's peace, people were asking where they could go to procure the excellent wine Mr. Pease and Mr. Patterson, the comforters of souls, imported.

Then Patty said, "Mr. Patterson wants to meet you, Tilly. Can you have lunch with him tomorrow at the Plaza?"

Pretty posh of him, she thought, and put on her best silkprint and a good face. But her cockiness deserted her as she climbed the green carpeted front steps between haughty doormen and then stood uncertainly under the massive waterfall of chandelier, not knowing for whom she was looking, feeling too high-heeled in her patent leather pumps until this neat small man rose from an armchair and came forward wearing a Glen Plaid suit that seemed to have been sewn up by angels to fit him so perfectly, with the speck of white handkerchief and the neat small shoes, and spoke to her as gently as a doctor breaking bad news, and taking her by the arm as though she were something expensively fragile led her into the Edwardian Room where an ambassadorial head waiter placed them at a window overlooking the solemnity of Park and Victorian carriages. But she might as well have just arrived on the milk train from Bogong; she upset her water glass, dropped a bread roll on the carpet. Prodded by these mishaps and a sparking of some wicked inner sprite, she set out frantically on a tale of how her brother had killed a recalcitrant hog in a mudhole while she held its back legs and he slit its throat. Do you know, she asked Mr. Patterson apropos of nothing, how they castrate a sheep? They bite off the testicles, quick as a wink, doesn't hurt, just bite the balls off and spit 'em out. Something in these austere surroundings, the silken cord in the menu, the graceful poise of the people lunching in such security rendered her cathartic. As if, repudiating the Plaza, the stately carriages outside, her expensive print, she was peeling off layer on layer of her outer self for him to understand the freshness of her heart, as if she needed him to know that this was her real self, cowplod girl from the heart of the bush, pure as milk, pliant as barley fields in the wind, relative to eternal things, oats, cowbells, sundown, remoteness.

As if, prodded by her alternative who so often led her astray, she was being gently and positively recommended to him as open and generous and unrefined, and he (she was genuinely attracted to him and some challenge he presented) studying her with steady grey eyes seemed to communicate to her that he was solitary.

As they left and he handed her down the front steps again as if she were faience, said, "I would like to see you again, Tilly, is that possible?"

"Oh yes," she said.

"But only if *you* would."

"Oh yes."

As though she had asked, he turned to face her and looking directly into her eyes said, "I live with my sister and I would like you to meet her."

Rose was tall and impressive with a crown of dark hair and an air of quiet immutability; the kind of inbred authority that could have her mistaken in a crowded room for the wife of the state governor. She imposed a certain awe with her quietness. She poured tea for Tilly and seemed pointedly incurious. "This is the little lass who thought up the ————." "Ah yes," Rose cut Edward short, indicating she was prepared to pass around cake but did not want information passed to her. It had been said of Rose that her accuracy in forecasting the weather was such that never in her life had she carried an umbrella unnecessarily. Whether or not this gift carried over to sensing people, one had the feeling of being quietly appraised and Tilly, sensing a chill as though a window had been opened on her back, suspected that Rose, X-raying her with her jet-black sad eyes, had caught sight of the duality in her. Or perhaps it was that Rose was so perfectly proportioned, without vanity, and that she had so subordinated herself to accommodate Edward that she was now highly sensitive to the slightest deformity, glimpsed the devilish in Tilly's immaturity.

When they shook hands goodbye, Rose's was limp. She had no grasp at all.

Except of the situation.

Six weeks later he proposed. More like an aside than a formality, as though the idea had just occurred to him then and there during the second intermission of *La Traviata* in the red and gold refreshment room at the old Metropolitan.

At the very same moment the warning buzzer sounded so loudly that it drowned out Tilly's reply.

"I didn't hear what you said," Edward said.

"Yes."

Instead of returning to their seats they sat on gazing at each other like two children who had plotted an outrageous act of rebellion against their parents. Tilly, because it had happened and Edward because he couldn't believe it had happened. Sat there like two stunned people, struck by lightning, never saw the flash.

"Have you told Rose?" she asked; Rose appeared to be sitting with them, a solid hulk of resentment and sorrow.

"Naturally I wouldn't mention it to Rose until I had your answer, Tilly."

"I see, darling."

She rarely spoke to him in affectionate terms. He recoiled from even verbal intimacy. It was as disconcerting to Edward as finding a speck of dandruff.

The effort this must have taken, the getting out that aside in the crowded intermission. And it was like him to propose by daylight. It seemed to Tilly that it was exactly right for him not to make a landslide decision nocturnally.

After the matinee, quite rightly, they went their separate ways. There was too much apocalyptic momentum behind the step they had taken for them to be together. He put her in a cab and walked away up Broadway.

Now that it was settled she had a sense of exceptional well-being, not emotional, calm, comforting like a winter sun.

And somehow she would win over Rose or at least they would come to an *entente cordiale*.

Since Edward had come into her life she was beginning to think that everything in the long run was ameliorated, that everything compensated for something lost in the past.

She was just fourteen when her brother Barry was jolted off the mare when she reared up at the sight of some imagined equine terror and he broke his arm, and so Ian Belltrees came over from Manuka Flats to help out. Ian was twenty, the youngest of eight brothers who grew wheat and lucern and were noted for their physiques and their disposition to get into Saturday night brawls. Ian was stocky and rugged, "rough as sacks" Mum said, but a good quick milker, handy with the separator, willing and able. He had tight reddish gold curls that stuck to his forehead when he sweated, and he smelled of a sweetish mixture of new hay and the strong tobacco he rolled in his big stubby fingers, and he had a great smile everyone had to admit, the revelation of such perfect teeth occasioned a weakness at the backs of feminine knees.

Coming at the time of Tilly's recent discovery of the mysteries of blood and menses, the fragility and vulnerability of that cave in her body made suddenly precious, Ian posed the first dilemma in her adult life. What did he mean by those neon smiles he gave her and was he dinky-di on the level or making fun of her? And if he was on the level, what would she do about the swooning feeling of ecstasy it gave her, so much so that she could hardly carry the heavy platter of corned beef back to the kitchen after she had forked his piece onto his plate, saw to it he got the bigger piece of jam tart, refilled his tin mug with the black scalding tea. "Ta," was all he ever said to her but it might have been the sound of harps in Tara's halls. He had been given her little bedroom and she had been moved onto the sofa in the front parlor, which was only used on the rare occasion that visitors stopped by and at Christmas, and when she awoke to this tickling sensation under her nose and saw him sitting on the edge of the sofa twitching this long piece of dry grass she thought at first it was the extension of a dream she had been having. Kitchy, kitchy, he said, smiling his brilliant smile and tickling her again with the grass straw, and in some alarm, confusion and delight she pulled her legs up toward her and half sat up clutching the blanket up to her chin, aware that her flannel nightie with the pink lambs printed on it was scarcely what she would have preferred him to see her in. Look, he said, would you care to go over to the dance Saturday night over at Bogong, and she was so overwhelmed at the invitation and by not being sure she was awake that she could only nod furiously. We'll go then, he said and pinched her leg and went out of the room on tiptoe.

As long as it's only the dance, Mum said, no parking in cars down dark lanes. Mum said, I think you're getting a bit loopy over that boy, I wouldn't if I was you, those Belltrees boys treat their girls like cattle, it's all they know.

All she had was her red and white check crepe de chine, but it had a flared skirt and she polished up her black Sunday pumps with a banana skin and pinned a pink silk rose off one of Mum's old hats in her hair.

"Now eat something," Mum said.

Eat. She wouldn't even sit down for fear of crushing her dress. But standing up she managed to fork some of Mum's Saturday night fried liver into her mouth.

Ian was spruced up in his navy blue double breasted and an imitation silk tie, and his curls had been dampened down with pomade into little greasy curlicues.

"Ready?" he grinned at her.

"Ready," she said, her heart turning over at the sight of him looking so spruced.

"So, we're off then," he said.

"You bet," she said.

"Have a nice time," Mum said.

Tilly hoped to God he wouldn't guess it was the first dance she had ever been to, hoped to God she would somehow be able to follow his lead without stepping all over him, would somehow be able to pass it off without fainting from excitement and the physical fact of his holding her.

She was shivering when she got out of the car down the street from the School of Arts from which came the tinny sounds of Teddy Stropper's band. Under the orange lights and paper streamers they were jiving, there were the show-off boys twisting the girls around them, bending, twisting, side-stepping to the music in frenzied conniptions, and for a moment Tilly felt club-footed.

"I don't go in for this fancy stuff," Ian said, "I hope you don't mind."

"I don't mind," she said.

To her enormous joy and relief they got off on the right foot and stayed that way. He was a natural dancer and she quickly found out that all she need do was to let him lead. In her elation at discovering she was not going to make a hopeless spectacle of herself, the Bogong School of Arts with its naked electric light bulbs and dirty cream walls, the fly-spotted paper streamers and hard wooden chairs was transformed into loveliness and she also, no fourteen-year-old bumpkin in a cheap Bon Marche dress with her hair water-crimped into little waves to make her look older, but a grown-up young lady with a good-looking escort, she was supple, she was composed, she trod on air.

During the first break they had orangeades and smiled at each other. She was too ecstatic to say aloud that she was having the time of her life, and she was overwhelmed at the simple politeness of his staying with her during the interval, sipping orangeade with her and looking at her over the straw with his quiet stare instead of going outside with the boys who automatically deserted their girls and bolted for the back steps where the forbidden beer was guzzled in an alley.

Oh, I'm in heaven, she wanted to say to him.

"Nice and cool," she said, sucking the end of her orangeade.

"Not bad," he said.

If he tried to kiss her in the car going home she would kiss him right back. If he tried to go a bit further she would let him, she might even let him be the first. She longed at this moment to put her hand on the tight blond hair that sprouted over his collar like turf.

"Too many Sheilas," he said, looking around. This being nineteen forty-four.

Most of the local boys who were not exempted farmers being away at the war.

The unescorted girls languished on the hard chairs along the wall, brotherless, dateless, they sat and hoped for the best, they took turns being the "man" and leading, looking pathetic, they held each other at arms length and circled the floor in a parody of a dance couple. Tilly supposed Ian must do his bit and dance with some of them but interestingly he seemed uncommitted to anyone but her, and they danced on, dance after dance as seriously as if they had been partners many times before and thought nothing of it; indeed as if part of the secret of their getting along so well was to think nothing of it. She just hoped the band would not stop too early. Then

"How ya doin', Lil," he said over her shoulder and as they turned a corner she saw Lil Socker jiving away with Ollie Sanders. All kinds of things had been said about Lil Socker and not all of them charitable. Lil Socker's reputation was such that when her name was mentioned the boys took to guffawing and shuffling their feet, and hands automatically went toward private parts as if to connote the incipient erection. It had been said that it was worth the twenty-mile ride out to the Socker place to see Lil on a trotting pony without her bra. You never, it was said, saw such jiggling in all your life. Like two great dishes of jelly being tossed up and down. When it came to tits there was no girl for fifty miles around who could hold a candle to Lil. Not that most of them wouldn't have enjoyed holding a candle to Lil, lit.

Tonight Lil's lettuce-green dress was cut so low across the ramparts of her breasts that you could have placed a good-sized lemon in the cleavage, and she was pressed so close to Ollie Sanders they might have been stuck to each other with glue, and Tilly noticed that now Ian steered her in the same direction that Ollie steered Lil and he then passed little exchanges with her while she threw him scoffing disdainful looks, which was her way of leading any chap on and as Ian now tried to keep pace with Lil and Ollie who were fast expert dancers, he often fumbled with Tilly, lost step and trod on her and made no apologies, only saying "Excuse me," hastily leading her over to where the unescorted girls sat in a row and then beat it over to where Lil was standing by the door, one hand curled on her hip and her posterior stuck out provocatively. As soon as the band started up again Ian grabbed her around the waist and they were off.

Tilly sat on with the unwanted girls until some yokelish boy shambled up and extended a hand the size of a cut of beef toward her. But instead of the physical coordination she'd had with Ian, this was ruin, bobbing, jerking, colliding, they bumped around the outskirts of the floor with her saying miserably, "I'm sorry," "I'm sorry," until in a pause he turned and left her to find her own way back to the lepers.

She sat out the rest of the evening grimly watching the twirling, perspiring figures and wondering at the heights and depths to which the heart can rise and fall in such a short space of time.

It was clear by then that Ian and Lil Socker were no longer among the dancers. But surely, Tilly thought after the band had thumped through God Save with scant patriotism, he'll come to take me home.

But then where was he?

Tilly was jostled out of the dance hall with the departing crowd. Everyone was streaming out into the street, goodnights were being sung out, hooroo Dave, ta ta Else, the cars were starting off, it was amazing how fast they all melted away in the night, backing, starting, roaring off, and she was left alone outside the now darkened School of Arts. She knew of course where he had parked his car, down in Chambers Street across from the old brick warehouse. But should she walk down? Knock on the car window? Interrupt them? For the first time in her life she felt a stab of sexual jealousy at the thought of Ian's mouth being pressed at this moment not on hers but on Lil Socker's and that it was Lil's hand carressing the springy blond hair on the back of his neck. That, instead of to her, whatever hot urgent pleas were being whispered, were being made into Lil's ear. Hurtfully, that he preferred Lil Socker, with her sneering put-down airs and her cow eyelashes all glutted with mascara, to her. Worse, she felt her wretched age, felt fourteen and pastel, lipstick not being allowed her, felt her little inadequate breasts, hardly more voluptuous than a boy's, scarcely nubile, her skinny, coltish legs. Naturally he preferred the orgasmic Lil. But it was a stab in the gizzard because she, Tilly, would have loved him. Whatever that meant, whatever it amounted to, something pure and simple, something you could not put into words or pictures, the great mystery but natural as the air about you, love.

She walked up and down the full length of the deserted street. Under the one street lamp her shadow was attenuated into a long thin membrane. Surely he must know by now the dance was over, surely he'd come now, all apologies, hadn't noticed the time, any old stuff and nonsense but come.

She began edging her way down to Chambers Street, past the old stone post office and the dark windows of Helen's Haberdashery where they had not changed the hats on the plaster models for ten years, and reaching the corner she began to assume an insouciant walk, a careless slouch to advise him, if he were looking, that she didn't give a rap about his bad manners. *Some* people, she would assure him with her raised eyebrows, by not speaking all the way home, just don't know any better.

But the car was gone.

Say ten to fifteen miles in your mind, it's nothing, say ten to fifteen miles while driving it, just words, but walk ten to fifteen miles of dusty stony road in almost pitch dark in high-heeled pumps and you damn well know it is ten to fifteen miles. Now and then she had to stop to shake out the sharp little pebbles that worked into her shoes. There was a faint whitish starlight that barely showed the out-lines of fence posts and the contours of Bandicoot Road, distant haystacks stood humped against the milky sky. About half-an-hour along her trek she became aware of an effulgence of light behind her even before she began hearing the motor and stood by the side of the road waiting to be picked up, nose in the air, ready to show him as cool as cus-tard how that blokes like him were beneath her contempt.

But it was Bluey Walgrove in the pick-up truck he used to cart the big milk cans from their dairy to the train.

"Good Christ, *Tilly*," he stared down at her. "What're *you* doin' out here in the middle of the night? Hop in, kid."

"I spose," he said as they bumped along, "this is the classic case of the girl who walked home, eh? But aren't you a bit young for it?"

Holding her nose in the air she said, "We just happened to get separated."

Too proud to cry herself to sleep, she lay in bed and burned with a fever of indignation and hurt.

Next morning crossing the yard she came face to face with Ian coming around the water tank and was affronted by his casual wave.

"Got home all right, did you?" he said cheer-ily, "I come back for you but you musta just got a lift. Goin' to be a scorcher," he said taking off his sweaty hat and wiping his forehead with the back of his arm. She said nothing, she passed by him like a deaf mute.

In the heat of the afternoon, while Mum was hav-ing her lie-down, she tiptoed down the hall and into her own bedroom, which was for the nonce occupied by Ian, and lay down on her own bed. It smelled strongly of him, of hay and sweat and sweet gingery tobacco, and burying her face into his pillow she let her hurt tears come freely until turning her face she saw that her old baby rag dolls, Babe Lily and Tanya were squashed together on the bottom shelf of her unpainted wooden bookcase. They appeared to be staring right at her. Tanya's black bead eyes and little dot of a painted mouth gave her a look of unmitigated superiority, her little round cloth face contemplative of only herself, not bothered by anything else, she stared unblinkingly at Tilly as if to say, "You're being a bit of a sop, aren't you, for fourteen?"

Tilly got off the bed and took Tanya into a hug. "Listen," she said into the kapok neck, "I'm going to be you for a while and then it won't have happened to me."

So for eleven days she was Tanya and nobody knew it.

Ed Patterson's eyes were hazel and the pupils intense to the point that in certain lights she could see herself reflected in them, which was comforting metaphorically or as the old song went, "I Only Have Eyes for You." Because they were almost the same in height, when they turned to each other, their eyes met on a level and it gave them the illusion of mutual ease. Being at ease with him was the true state of her heart, a kind of bliss like a hum of bees, like winter sun on her hands and as though she had been given a mild opiate, she was sleepy with happiness. Marrying a man who was thirty-seven and beyond, thank God, the white water rapids and into the safe ponds, seemed to her the most sensible decision she had ever made and she went about it as though it were a desirable cabinet post awarded her by the President of the United States. That is, she went about it in a projection, for as yet marriage was still three weeks in the future and she was still composing copy for McGrab Hopkins. In fact, part of the blessedness with which she regarded her future lay in Ed's consideration in allowing that she might want to go on working and if she did by all means to do so, it wouldn't matter to him, just so long as she was happy. "Anything you want," he said. Said about everything. And with such sincerity that she felt dizzy when she contemplated the chasms of his generosity. Not in the sense of gifts and of such perquisites as the Cary Cadillacs and the Quo Vadis and Colony restaurants and the smoked sturgeon she was sent by the pound every week from Old Scandanavia; it was indefinable. She didn't need the definition of it, it was something that worked, like a light switch and it was better not to pry into whatever mechanism made it work. Outwardly, he was easily categorized, Exeter-Yale-Brooks Brothers-Republican. Inwardly he was a knight in search of some mysterious holy grail whose likelihood of being found was moot. If he were to be summed up in a word it could be goodness (no, that was a dull word, it suggested the tediousness of sermons and clean surplices), it could be decency. The kind of oldfashioned decency that cropped up in the Hardy novels; there was something of Jude in Edward.

"I won't change," he said.

They were sitting beside the goldfish pond under a stone faun that leered suggestively at them in Mrs. Gaston Foy's garden in Greenwich after a heavy lunch in Mrs. Gaston Foy's *belle epoque* dining room.

"In what way do you mean?"

"About you, Tilly, I will never change in my feelings about you. Not ever. No matter what you might do to me."

"That's not possible."

"It is with me."

"But we all change, we change all the time, from one minute to the next."

"I don't. I hope you won't find it tedious."

She looked down a moment onto the golden-spotted black movements under the slime and green.

"But how can you be sure?"

"I know. There are certain things you know."

"What if you found me in bed with someone?"

"But I wouldn't."

"Supposing."

"No, no," he rejected it as calmly as waving away a fly, "you would still be you. In the basics, nothing changes. There is a heart to everything that cannot be changed, no matter what the circumstances. I believe there's a core, a shape to everything and everybody which makes it, them what they are, and this can never be changed and that's my religion in a way."

"Do you mean God in everybody?"

"Oh, when you drag in God," he frowned, "it immediately makes everything seem out of proportion and in that sense I'm anti-theologian. I mean the shape of nature, your nature, mine, was decided on by some kind of intelligent mishap and it will always be the shape it is."

She wondered what he would think if she told him that when she was still a kid she'd seen God one sunset out on Bandicoot Road and that He was a rusted tin can. Would he approve of her pantheistic experience or denounce it? When Edward denounced anything it was with the wrath of the Furies. Abortion, for instance (little did he know), was insupportable, murder. But surely, she'd said, not looking him in the face, under certain circumstances———No, absolutely not there were no special circumstances. And don't you bring up that old apocryphal mossback, "What if your child had been Hitler?" And the metaphysical shape of Hitler had been a spiritual mishap of deformity just as Mozart's had been divine. But there was no moving him when it came to abortion or the death penalty even though he considered himself a liberal Unitarian and they were to be married in the Unitarian church on Lexington Avenue where Rose sang contralto in the choir. Benign as he was, gentle as early morning light, you could argue until you were blue in the face against the death penalty, he was rock. You take a life, you give a life, it was only *decent.*

Decency was his structure. Rock-bottom honesty, rock of ages. And in contrast Tilly was water, the river, tides changing, swirling between her banks of reason.

Coming at last, she hoped, to some reasonable agreement with herself, with the other, with that deadly logical girl, her uncompromising twin, that dark opposite she both deplored and embraced (the hurt young girl kneeling on the cold linoleum and crying into the neck of the rag doll, Tanya, thus naming her apposite nature and seeking her true strength to survive had become her for eleven days. What is it? her mother had cried out, distraught. Child, what is it? Why do you look at me in such a cold terrible way, Tilly? Because you only pretend to love me, the child had said, Tanya said cruelly), and the only way she could keep the bold and terrible in her from getting out and wounding was with all the holy strength she could muster from her love and the beatification Edward seemed to inspire in her.

Once at least the struggle almost failed her. Sitting between Edward and Rose at a political rally for the committee to elect some friend of his to city councillor, some satrap position she had never heard of and certainly couldn't care about less. The candidate's speech was long and interwoven with the ravelled phrases so loved by American politicians; free enterprise in a free world in the true American tradition handed down by our forefathers to a new generation for a heritage most precious in this their great land of liberty. Edward had crossed his arms and was listening with what Tilly thought to be honorable fervor. At the end of his peroration the would-be councillor asked the audience to please rise and join with him in singing "America the Beautiful," and as they stood and began to sing Tilly suddenly felt Tanya's extravagant disdain for the situation, the shallow hocus-pocus, the specious appeal to patriotics and in particular to this vestigial hymn full of spacious mountain majesty and sparkling plains when just to get in the hall they had had to step over a reeking wino lying in his own vomit in the doorway. She began to feel her face contorting into a grin of derision and had to look down at her feet so that Ed would not notice, Ed singing out with all his heart about amber waves of grain, while she began gagging on the words about God shedding his light (on fools and mountebanks) and at the notion that He might crown their good with brotherhood when you only had to watch the nightly television news to gain a reasonable assessment of what brotherhood meant in the land of the free and the home of the brave.

Hocus-pocus! Tanya was burning with indignation at this spectacle of pious idiocy and at Edward for wanting to help elect this man who was nothing more than an amiable nitwit. She wanted to cry out, "What balls!" but instead (and to Tilly's deep embarrassment) she let out a low scornful laugh that sounded more like regurgitation, and Edward looked quickly at her and asked, "What is it?"

Stop it. She must sing.

And sing she did.

" 'And crown Thy good,' " she sang, extolling the good, brotherly love, kindness and compassion from sea to shining sea.

"What made you laugh?" Ed asked.

Oh, it was too dumb, not worth repeating. Merely something funny she had remembered. She put her hand in his, feeling safety, feeling that to immerse herself in his decency was like therapy, that in Edward she could find the best of herself magnified into a potential that could be self-sustaining and where she need have no fear of the intrusions of Tanya's scoffing pragmatism.

There was safety in his abiding sincerity. Edward believed, and there the ramparts of his believing safely encompassed everything and everyone he loved (even Rose, poor Rose who was about to be phased out, find herself obsolete like some warcraft the Navy had put into mothballs, canvassed over and anchored up a forlorn cove. And when questioned about her, Edward was heard to say he thought the change would be beneficial for Rose, hoped that her friends could persuade her at last to make use of her excellent French and become a translator at the U.N. Edward believed, like the most blessed of fools, that all things work together for Good); Edward held those he loved in immutable good light.

So could she tell him, Tilly wondered, staring down at the glinting carp in the pond. And if so, how much? Could she explain her duality and retain his confidence in her or would it somehow be shocking to him. In explaining her twinness, how to put it? Say there is a sister? Shadow?

Explain that it was sometimes purgative? That, embalmed in self-pity, she had taken herself to the edge of a cliff intending to do away with herself and at the last moment, Tanya with her sharp common sense had caught hold of her and prevented her from this unreasonable act.

But then she would have to go into the pregnancy, the abortion, and things that would affront him with his sense of right and wrong, perhaps uglifying herself to the point where she would no longer be the sweet bride of his imagination.

"Aunt Bess," he'd said to her, fondling her cheek, "is worried that being from Down Under you perhaps can't speak English," he had laughed at the thought. "It's extraordinary what people misconceive about other people. But then, dear old Aunt Bess has never been exposed to Australians and she is eighty-four."

Tilly and Edward had entered into the sexual end of their relationship, thanks to him, with extreme dignity. He had most neatly folded his Brooks Brothers undershorts on the chair in her apartment before coming into her bed. He had almost said, "May I?" before exploring her small breasts with a sudden increase of sharp breathing. So as they were honest with their lust, hadn't she the right to be honest about her duality? There seemed to be something shameful about lusting with him naked while hiding the most precious part of her, *herself*. It seemed downright deceitful.

Now. While the sun was in her eyes and she could only see his head fuzzily, she took his hand and turning it over gently as if she had been given it as some great reward for her existences, she said,

"I think it's time———"

"There is," a voice said behind them, white sandals appearing on the mossy brick path, "tea going if you're interested."

Averell, Mrs. Gaston Foy's young niece. So it is that destinies are changed not by cracks of doom or fiery eclipses but by the announcements of tea interrupting a confession.

Averell Donner, about a year younger than Tilly

and doomed to be unimportant. Recently out of Bennington majoring in English Literature. Too tall. Spun glass, the doe in the forest quivering with exquisite alarm at the mere sound of the wind in the aspens. At lunch she had talked sensibly about the flat topics Mrs. Foy had passed around the table along with the marshmallow sweet potatoes, but Tilly had not failed to note that when she turned toward Edward her face, like Cassius' took on a lean and hungry look. Now she was saying, apologizing with her grin for butting in on their privacy, that, not her fault, they were expected inside. She half led the way, walking crablike in order to glance back to see if they were following. One felt saddened by Averell's walk, it gave away so much about her that she might have preferred kept secret; it gave away her awkwardness about being too tall. By being nonchalant it betrayed the fact that she was easily breakable, by being jaunty it told that she was sad. She had a slight cast in her left eye and it might have been symptomatic; she was bug-eyed over Ed Patterson. At the door Averell swept them, to their discomfort, a low bow.

"Enter, enter," Averell said.

"Nous sommes arrivés," she said to her aunt. "Asseyez-vous, s'il vous plaît," she said to them. Her color was so high she might have a fever.

"Still and all," Edward said, driving back to New York, "she's a fine girl and she'll make someone a fine wife."

"Oh," Tilly exploded, "I wouldn't want anyone to say that about me. It makes you feel like some sort of *pensioner*."

"Sometime call her up and ask her to lunch,

will you? Make it sound as though she would be doing you a favor, you're good at that and it would mean a lot to her."

Decent of him to care about poor tall Averell Donner. Tilly squeezed his knee and he put his hand over hers and thus they drove on until he asked suddenly, "Are you happy?"

"Today you mean?"

He drove some distance.

"I mean generally. I don't mean all the time, every moment for of course no one is. But generally."

She thought about it the full length of the Triborough Bridge and then said, "I suppose I'm as happy as I ever will be in my whole life."

"Thank you," Edward said, as formally as if she had presented him with a diploma, "I am too."

She thought that she would put down this exchange in her notebook; that it might be interesting to look back on some time.

Nearly dropped the book.

There (when?) at the finish of her last notation about a month previously, in Tanya's poker blunt handwriting was this:

DECENCY CAN BE A FORM OF TYRANNY

She sat down on her bed, the notebook on her lap. This was new, this not remembering when she had had this aberration.

This was new and scary not remembering, like a drunken blackout. And what did it mean? Why would decency be a tyranny? What was there about his decency that subconsciously tyrannized her? Did she feel it stifled her? Was she afraid she could not live up to it? Or was it just a natural subdued hostility to his basic nature, the monotony of his Galahad-ness, like the craving for a sudden black rainstorm to break a spell of boringly beautiful weather.

In any case she was startled to find she was now glad she had been interrupted today in her confession; it occurred to her now that her condition was more serious than she had thought and that Edward was more than likely to have proposed psychoanalysis. Which was anathema. Because Tanya would never allow herself to be exposed in any therapeutic sense to the daylight; practical as she might be, she feared discovery as much as she feared doctors, declared them mountebanks and thieves, said that the moment you let yourself and your confessions into their hands you were done for. Tanya, as bold as she was, would resist treatment because she wished to remain serene in her own conceit of herself, would resist, scream, froth at the mouth, threaten, evade, and as a last resort claim that Tilly was unbalanced.

Therefore, let her sleep on.

A form of tyranny?

She saw a long series of perfect arches, symmetrical, forming a cloister and at the exact center a fountain and at each corner a laurel bush over which was a cloudless blue sky, everlasting noon, and this was unchangeable perfection, and this was how she saw Edward's way of life, and she was at the core of it.

And having to endure it, put up with his goodness, generosity, decency and keep one's mouth shut, smile and keep one's mouth shut, like it, love it, love him. *Was* a kind of tyranny.

So she went out of her way to get him persimmons. There was a little sidewalk fruit shop up near Eighty-ninth Street that usually had them in stock, and she bought him a dozen.

Bertha let her in, it being Bertha's day to clean, nearly time for Bertha to quit. How are you, Miz Beamis, Bertha asked. No, alas, Bertha's husband was no better, if anything worse and the new medicine kills him worsen anything.

They were both on the long white sofa. Rose had a towel over her lap and Edward was stretched out with his naked feet on the towel and Rose was massaging his feet with cold cream. His eyes were closed and Rose was bent over his feet, so for a moment or two they didn't hear or observe Tilly come into the room.

The way they poured themselves into this ecstasy, it was orgiastic. And it was certainly not only Edward's gratification but also Rose's as she bent over the foot in her large hand, spreading the thick cream. Kneading the balls of the foot, the arch, caressing the heel, her eyes half shut, her hands endlessly moving, now searching between the toes, now fondling the instep. All the time Edward's eyelashes merely fluttered, then opening his eyes he saw Tilly standing there and said in a clotted voice, "Tilly, hi," and then closing his eyes again, "She has the divine touch."

Rose merely glanced up and then down again and began on the other foot; slowly she creamed it, making creamy whispering sounds with her hands so that the operation became musical, mystical, a rite. Occasionally he grunted with pleasure and Rose seemed rewarded, breathing in deep satisfaction, her strong hands searching his foot for the known sensitive areas, kneading his sole, her thumbs curving around his ankle bones with exquisite fondness; the hardboned face had the soft effusion of a mother suckling. It was plain that——

(and when Tilly was seventeen, Eunice Rodd and her brother, Ginger, had been found in a hay field just off the Meridgee Road, both with a bullet through the head, and no questions had been asked of their father whose truck had been seen near the spot in the early dawn, no action had ever been taken and everyone knew why).

——they were engaged in a facsimile of incest they had employed many times under this useful guise of podiatry.

And other clues. Rose leaning across the breakfast table to cut off the top of his boiled egg, Rose buttering his toast and giving it into his open mouth like a mother wren, and Edward always holding Rose by the hand going downstairs as though she were infinitely precious and breakable and the way they always waved to one another from a departing taxi, the way——

Oh, what did it matter, what use making inventories. Of course they were in love.

But what was clearest and worst, worse than any touching or placebo love-making, was that Edward didn't know it. Possibly Rose knew, but Edward didn't. That was as clear to Tilly as this vision of them on the sofa. He didn't know. Because Edward's purity prevented him from seeing any badness in himself or in anyone he loved. This was the naivete she had long since perceived and put asunder for his sake and her own. This was the tyranny Tanya had warned about. It was this dense purity that she was going to have to live with, in marriage.

She had sat down and now she stood up as Rose was finishing wiping his feet and Edward said, "Hello, dearest, what do you have there?"

"Persimmons," she said, putting the bag on a side table. He doesn't know about it. But I DO.

"How dear," he said.

"How dear," Rose echoed, and folding the wet face rag and the towel and screwing the top on the cold cream jar, she put away the trappings of their euphemism and went out.

"I can't stay," Tilly said suddenly.

"But I thought we were going to the Armory show—I made a reservation for after at L'Orangerie."

"I can't," Tilly said, childishly near hysteria.

"Why not?"

"I just can't," she said, looking him in the eye and keeping Tanya at bay only with the greatest physical effort.

"All right," he said, "you don't have to give reasons, darling, I just wondered why the change in plans."

"Can't there sometimes just be a change of plan?" she said rather too wildly for the mild occasion it was. "Does absolutely everything in your life have to go according to plan?"

He regarded her steadily, without annoyance, just a little curiosity, in the way Edward had of being as adjustable to the other person's mood, as he could be philosophical about a change in the weather.

"All right, darling. Will you call me later? Or shall I call you? What time will you be going to bed?"

"I don't know. I don't *know* what time I'll be going to bed. I don't know where I may be. I can't always be certain of what, where I'll be. Or who."

"No of course." She must have meant *"with who."*

He was standing in his bare feet in the exact center of a square in the rug, he was frowning slightly but with compassion for her jagged outbreak of premarital jitters, one bar of hair had flopped over his left eyebrow. That was how she saw him before turning and dashing from the apartment. Had she known then, she might have touched him gently, put her hand out to touch his kind face, kind mouth, eyes. Being Tilly. Had she known she would not see him again for twenty-three years.

When she got home she decided the only person she could talk to would be someone who took nothing seriously. She decided to call him long distance in Pennsylvania where he now had his own antiques shop in a little village by the name of Reston Ponds; the name sounded like a haven for swans.

"Roddy? Tilly."

"Tilly Billy?"

Roddy Staunton had been in the window dressing department at Bonwit's and often cooked her suppers and made her little necklaces and bangles out of esoteric things like pine cones and picture wire.

Gay people were immediately drawn to her; she had, they assured her, a sisterly thing about her. They would have been disabused had they been apprised of the cutting remarks Tanya made about faggots and dykes.

After she had run on for ten minutes, explaining nothing except that she was in a state of confusion over her coming marriage, Roddy said, "Oh, you've got the propers." Straight people, Roddy said, got themselves into states over doing the proper things whereas gays weren't expected to be proper, the very nature of their deviation invited impropriety, relaxed standard codes. What she needed, Roddy said, was "a good dose of the funs." Come on down for a few days, he said. "You need to be in a neutral zone."

Indeed it was exactly what she needed, to rest in a neutral zone with boys who were not really men, not altogether women, and so could cast a balance between the two. With Roddy and his friends, she could be brought to laugh at herself and to look at her situation through their witty and pragmatic eyes, she needed both their kindness and their satire.

Roddy said the St. Albans-Pittsburgh bus came through Reston Ponds, it was about a three-hour trip from New York, he would be waiting for her outside Donald's Donuts where the bus stopped. On the phone she described Roddy to Edward as a sick friend, a definition with which he would have probably concurred.

Just took a small overnight valise with jeans and halter tops. Hard pelting rain beat against the bus windows. The driver said gloomily that it had been raining in PA fit to burst a dam, announced that the first stop would be in an hour at Temple, which would be for ten minutes.

In Temple, Tilly got out and bought nougat and was directed to the rest rooms at the back of the small candy and magazine shop. The rain was coming down so hard on the tin roof it reminded her of wet weather in Bogong when they had to shout at each other to pass the butter.

Too late she noticed the envelope stuck on the back of the door to the rest room, which stated HANDLE BROKEN, DO NOT PULL SHUT. The door knob turned around and around uselessly, she pulled on it but the door was stuck fast and needed a shoulder from the outside. She kicked and banged on it, calling as loudly as she could for someone please to let her out. Please, Tilly kept calling, but the facts of the torrential rain on the roof and the rest rooms being so far in the back of the shop made it obvious she would not be heard until someone else wanted the toilet. Once she thought she heard some announcement being made of the bus leaving (then surely the dame at the candy counter would tell the driver someone was in the girls' room, but would she have remembered? She had seemed so apathetic, had not even looked up at Tilly).

Through a small window above the lavatory there was a pocket-handkerchief view of the steep hilly road bearing down on the bridge over the river, which now swollen with the rains gorged up on its banks with dirty brown water flecked with creamy foam. But from this distance the vision was from a doll's house onto a toy scene and by and by she saw a toy bus emerge and wobble down the hill. (Her only real annoyance being that her suitcase was on it.) Then she saw that the engulfing brown ale and foam seemed to be only a foot or so below the roadway of the bridge and as the tiny bus started across the bridge, the brown water became the roadway, then that there was no roadway, no bridge, and the only sign of bus suddenly was the upturned back window, churning, disappearing in beer foam, turning upside down as it went under, and for a moment she thought she heard the sudden gulped-down screams.

And Tilly would have been reading and not noticing until she was upended and flung at the ceiling and then the brown darkness engulfing her, choked with the cold bitter brown water, then sucked down and perhaps out of a broken window into the maelstrom. She would make a superhuman struggle to get up to light and breathing, reaching her arms above her toward salvation, which would be just an oozy star, but then cruelly thrust forward with the current and her body, dying, would be wedged between two jars of rock miles downstream, would be wedged for all time as, imperceptibly, the brown water washes her skin away and eventually the river flows calmly over this dark deep hole and fish dart through her cage of bones.

She heard nothing of the rain outside, she heard nothing of the useless cries of people, pouring down the road out of the little houses in Temple where nothing ever happens and catastrophe so galvanizes them that they run out without hats or raincoats to stand at the edge of where the bridge was and look at nothing but a gap and the amazement of death.

All that was occurring to her, looking at herself in the little spotted mirror over the rust-stained washbasin, was that this was her birth; felt the thrust of birth inside her as if she were changing one skin for another, freeing herself of the all too confining frame she had been born into. Then as calmly as one might feel the earthquake as a mere shudder rattling the cup and saucer on the shelf, she stepped out from herself boldly.

The candy counter woman who pushed open the door to the ladies' room had the stunned look of someone awakened at four in the morning by screams.

"Did you see it?" she squawked.

"See what?" Tanya asked.

"They went under," the woman said. "Oh my God, they've all gone under. Didn't you *see* it?"

Tanya picked up her bag from off the lavatory seat.

"You ought to have something done about this door," she said.

1957

At all times she had the sea. Last thing at night and first thing in the morning was the ocean, tumbling onto the beach only yards from her patio. The tides came in and out of the inlet slapping at her side deck, on windy days spattering her kitchen window. She grew to know the wind directions, the signs of good and bad weather, and she could tell without opening her eyes in the morning, just by the thickness of the sounds, the mewing of gulls and the muffled surf that a fog had come down. Fog often rolled in cutting off the scarps of cliff that hung over her patch of beach, and she enjoyed the feeling of being ostracized. There was a buoy warning of submerged rocks just offshore and its melancholy clanging pleased her, it was like the last sound on earth.

In the mornings she sat, blackened with sun by now, in her patio among the bursting bougainvillea and passion flower which could not be stopped, fertile even in salty air, they took over without any encouragement from her; she didn't know their names, had no interest in them, they were merely beautiful. The only thing that stirred any interest in her about the patio was the long crack in the cement floor like the coastline of Peru made from the earthquake of 1953. Not even an earthquake would have disarrayed her serenity.

Here she was, serene and safe in Santa Helena off the main route, south to Santa Barbara, north to San Luis Obispo and as far west as she could geographically get unless she laid claim to one of the tiny rock islands that her tolling buoy warned of. She had moved west like the sun and she might well have continued west to Japan except for the Pacific Ocean and a shortage of cash. And southern California (it was no accident, she felt, that she was working at the Paradise Hotel in Santa Helena) had turned out to be El Dorado. She must have been directed to it by the same mystic organic sense that directs birds thousands of miles across dark oceans and continents to their winter destinations.

Southern California was seasonless, like herself. She was through with seasons, just as she was through with moods, just as she was through with anticipation and regret. There were no morning awakenings to a sense of responsibility or guilt over something left undone. Awakening in her little rented cottage to the surf, she heard it like her heartbeat, but she didn't have to experience it, exclaim over it, push open the shutters and be ecstatic over it. She wasn't compelled to enjoy the intricacy of the dew-spangled cobweb; she no longer need delay her way through the day stopping to comment unnecessarily over sunsets and accept the banality of other peoples' opinions; she no longer had to be sympathetic to their wants, the everlasting fables with which they cloaked their needs, disguised their failures.

Even now after almost two years she awoke with such a sense of freedom and elation it was as though she had all her life been held down with straps. The morning after the bus accident she had woken up in a motel in a small Pennsylvania town (something beginning with B, Badminton Oaks?

She had hitched a ride from Temple where the bridge had washed away), and the first thing she had noticed was the knob on the drawer of the night table shining dully in the sunlight and it filled her with delight, this knob. It was ambergris and jade and lapis lazuli, stolen from a Maharaja's rose garden by a peacock; it was beautiful because it happened to be the first thing she laid eyes on in her new self.

Remembering that she was free forever now from the stereotype she had been welded to since their childhood and that that suffering, affable, pretty-sweet, nincompoop was gone. Oh, that patient dumbass with the persistence of kindness and devotion, that *mule* of virtue was gone in the convenience of an accident that Tanya had consciously or unconsciously wished on her for most of their twenty-five years.

The body was hers now, her eyes to see the different color of the horse, her nose to smell a rat, her ears to hear the tin note in the oratorio, her taste to add the pinch of salt.

So, Tilly gone, what to say about *her* body? As easy to say she went down into floodwater as to say she died in a plane accident over the Great Divide, that she was bitten by a venomous spider or that she was seen to be snatched up by a great bird on South Hampton beach. If she were now fable, let her be consumed by fable, and being on a doomed bus was like a miss being as good as a mile.

Tilly dissolved into fable, Tanya moved West. Somewhere, buried in the *Chicago Tribune*, she read that baggage being recovered from the sunken bus led police to believe that others missing, believed dead, included E.L. Purvereau of New Orleans, Jerri Mae Humphreys of Huntington, West Virginia, and M. Beamis of New York City. So Edward would by now be receiving the condolences, the choir of the Lexington Avenue Unitarian Church would have been apprised that their services were no longer required. Rose would have taken Edward to convalesce in Nantucket or Martha's Vineyard.

She moved West.

She waitressed her way West, stopping only long enough in each all-night diner or Family Ways Inn to buy her bus ticket on to the next favorable stop; to purchase a nightdress, a vinyl suitcase, or a pair of jeans and a blouse with which to begin the term of her natural life.

By and by she reached Los Angeles, and the scent of it at once convinced her she belonged there, the curious mixture of carbon monoxide and oranges, of burned coffee and eucalyptus brought to her a nostalgia and at the same time a daring sense of potential. She liked the rootless feeling that the rushing freeways gave her, the zip-zooming unceasing traffic, the sense that nowhere was there a center to anything, nothing was arbitrary, all shifting, moving masses of people, forever coming and going and merely pausing like night moths for momentary rest before again casting themselves against lighted windows.

She worked by day at the Hollywood Roosevelt Hotel as chamber maid, she lived at the Ventura Motor Inn out in the Valley, and in her spare time she began gradually to concoct her life, substantiating the insubstantial, signing affidavits to take the place of lost passports and birth certificates, creating Tanya Bond.

She liked the sound of it, the name was balanced in that the over-ripeness of Tanya (which was Tilly's excess) was given its come-uppance by the flat bareness of Bond. In Tilly's old school exercise book, which she had used as a diary and notebook and which Tanya kept with her at all times, she drew a thin line through Anna Matilde Beamis and wrote her name boldly. Then, when a year later she stood up in a Los Angeles court house along with three hundred others including two Taiwanese, four Hungarians, a nun from Crete and a New Zealander and swore to uphold and defend the Constitution of the United States, she became at the same time legally Tanya Bond.

Thus renamed, reborn, she walked out into the peach-colored California morning feeling American, feeling that the last vestiges of Australia had been legally expunged. It would have been too much for Tilly's conscience, Tilly's love of the bush, of the blue gum country, of billabongs and dust, water holes, windmills creaking tinnily over paddocks, vast skies, and the cattle smell and budgerigars and Australian voices singing "On the Road to Gundagai." You couldn't turn your back on that, Tilly would have said, the sight of a Banksia tree, a Bottle Brush flower would break your heart a thousand years from now should you live that long and be a turncoat.

Well, Tanya said, I can and have. Without turning a hair. I have. And when the bailiff of the court had addressed them as to the seriousness of the step they were about to take and had declared that the doors to the courtroom would be left open for five minutes so that anyone who felt not yet ready to undertake the oath could quietly leave, the young man sitting next to her whose tears had run down and hung on the tip of his nose had got up and run out. But she simply had sat on and looked steadily at the American flag without a thought of the Australian Southern Cross nor of there being anything exceptional in what she was doing.

Because it was like the beautiful word, "naturalization," being made natural and as if she were at last being made not only natural but tangible after living a life of being half in darkness, submerged in somebody else, and only coming and going in flashes of commentary on that other person's life, like living in a rented body and putting up with somone else's mind and emotions and now at last being not only rid of that someone but made natural was like being what she imagined God to be, one enormous perfect organ note filling the universe and deafening her with its beatification.

Coming home she was waved to by the Titheridges who inhabited the cabin next to hers and were sitting in their plastic chairs outside, displaying their bare varicose legs. The Titheridges were so English that it was piercing, and yet they had not laid eyes on Clapham (where they had been born three streets apart) for thirty years. Every so often Mayne Titheridge got a call to play an English butler or bobby with a line or so in a movie or television film. More often than not they lived on canned beans, but even broke to the four winds they were never without their gin and bitters to spark up their dreary lives and homesickness for

crumpets and Leicester Square, for toffee, kip-
pers, and people who said righto. Come and have
a spot with us, they called to Tanya, come and have
a spot, ducky. Every Christmas they tied plastic
holly to the dusty branches of scrub oak and cooked
a frozen goose from the Farmers Markets. On the
Queen's birthday they nailed a Union Jack to the
door. Thirty years in California and they were as
unAmerican as Shepherd's Pie. They received
Tanya's news with cautious acclamation.
Mo Titheridge hooded her eyelids and lowered her
voice. "The reason we have never become American citizens is that we still have hopes that one
day our gracious Queen might confer a knight-
hood." Her sunken jaws chewed at the glorious
possibility of Sir Mayne. He cracked a nut between his dentures and said, "Even an O.B.E.
wouldn't be unwelcome, what?" Mo said. "After
all, Cedric was knighted."
Stay and have some "grub" they begged her (it
would be fish sticks or frozen haddock) and "have
another spot, ducky," Mayne begged her, hop-
ping up to refill her glass of gin, which she had
not emptied. They were lonely, they rarely ven-
tured out and then never together so that one of
them was always home lest the phone rang with
the offer of an "engagement"; thus trapped in an
airless cabin in a rundown motor inn in an un-
fashionable section of an alien city in a foreign
country, they rusted like two abandoned Bentleys
on a city dump.
She sipped her gin which tasted more like machine oil and half listened to their chirruping no-
talk. Mo had found a bakery out in Studio City

where you could get biscuits which were not at all unlike English scones. Mayne had heard from a British chum that NBC was planning a series on the life of Nelson; there would be scads of parts for the English. Getting a little squiffy on their gin, the Titheridges grew festive, fetching little glass dishes of cashews and pecans. Triumphant that they had snared her for din-din, Mo burst open a cellophane balloon of Cheese Whiffs. Sodden, they were even less probable, more tenacious in the adoration they professed for their darling "Tarnya"; sodden, they would sometimes tipsily imply she was like the daughter they had never had because every penny had to go toward Mayne's expensive wardrobe of suits for all occasions.

"What do you say," Mayne said, swaying ever so slightly toward Mo sprawled in her green plastic chair, "that we make the trip to Yosemite that we've been discussing for so long and take darling Tarnya with us."

This was one of their ploys. They continually tried to ensnare her in cutrate excursions. The last had been in bottleneck Sunday traffic to Laguna, where to cut costs they had picnicked by a main freeway in thick weeds off what they called "tinned" salmon and warm beer. But it wasn't so much the excursions that were planned to entrap her into their company, it was the subtler interference into her life, the lying in wait for her to come home, the "innocent" runnings into each other getting the mail or picking up the laundry at the White as Wool. She was convinced they spied on her comings and goings through the plastic venetian blinds and lately when she had frankly snubbed them, told them she was busy, a plaintive disappointed tone came into their voices when they tried to assure her they were pleased *she* had a date, like parents being told their child would not be home for Christmas. They presumed, like beggars. Like beggars, they were sickly and greedy to pass their sickliness on to others in the guise of loneliness, assuming that she, like they, must be lonely and therefore they must share their sick loneliness.

Seeing them watching her in a doting way, their pandering smiles, the goatish looks of their old half-nude bodies squeezed into beach wear, the white hair on Mayne's watermelon belly, Mo's bunions prodding through the pink straps of her plastic sandals like mushrooms, she felt suddenly repelled by them and by their familial advances to her, there was a faint dying smell about them like leaking gas. It was time they were got rid of once and for all.

She said, speaking very casually and not looking at them, stirring her viscous drink in the not-very-clean glass, "I don't think I've ever told you, have I? There used to be two of us."

No, she'd never told them. They sat up.

"Twins?"

She nodded. Well, if there had been two bodies, they could not have been told apart.

"One died," she said.

Oh. Their faces dropped into the suitable expressions of condolence.

"In an accident. A bus washed off a bridge."

Oh. My dear, they said. They reached out flabby,

speckled arms. Oh my dear, Tarnya dear, they said.

She threw them back with her laugh. She stood up and said, "I didn't give a damn, if you want to know the truth. I couldn't stand her."

Oh.

It was as if she had farted loudly. They looked away, looked at anything but her, their sweet Tarnya, laughing about her own sister's death. One didn't. One oughtn't to. The more shocked they felt at her callousness, the more they retired behind their British reserve. One simply didn't say such things even if one felt them. "Thanks for the drinks," Tanya said, and left them to their grub.

To be alone is very heaven [she wrote in Tilly's notebook in her own emphatic handwriting as opposed to Tilly's neat Australian high school script with its scrupulously crossed t's] and I'm beginning to find the truth in what I've always heard—that the real riches are in aloneness. What fools people are to be running after diversions and pleasures in other fools. I suppose it is because we are brainwashed from birth to think we need other people or perhaps it is the same herd instinct that animals have, prides of lions, gaggles of geese. I only know that in the last year-and-a-half since T is gone, I find myself searching in my aloneness for the deep treasures it holds, like going down to the bottom of the sea where no diver has ever been. Last night I sat high up in the very top row in Hollywood Bowl to hear Artur Rubinstein. I asked for a seat in the very back row because I wanted to experience the vastness of the place and of being alone with all these thousands of people and holding myself apart from them, alone and apart in the middle of thirty thousand people; it was a majestic feeling, until a girl sitting next to me broke the spell by remarking that something ought to be done to keep so many airplanes from coming over during the concert and holding out to me a paper bag of chocolate almonds. What planes? I hadn't noticed them, I was in a state of grace until she pushed her stupid thoughts and candy on me. I said, "Luckily I am able to ignore nuisances," and she knew I meant her and for the rest of the concert she sat turned away from me as if I had some infectious disease. It isn't that I want to be rude to people, it's that I want to be free, I have been a satellite for so long that I need to express myself freely, uninhibitedly, dangerously. I've learned that there's great happiness in experiencing one thing totally at a time. Like listening. I turn off the radio sometimes and just listen. It's extraordinary what sounds there are in silence, little particles of sound singing in the ears. As if we could actually hear the passage of the earth through space or of tiny things moving, like earthworms, cobwebs being spun. And that if we learned how to be quiet enough we might hear sounds we didn't know existed, like sunlight, and I imagine sunlight sounding like a very low continuous oboe note, and happiness would sound like a rush of glissandi on harps, and the easiest soundless sound to hear would be worry, because there is so much of it, and it would be high B flat on a cornet carried to you on a hot wind passing over stinking quagmires from a country where there was unceasing strife. And if they had been quiet enough the first people could have heard this music in the garden of Eden.

This doesn't mean that I'm flying off in some metaphysical rapture all the time. I'm extremely down-to-earth, controlled, that's part of my strength (unlike poor T, all that rambling through other people's moods) and my endurance. I make beds at the Hotel Roosevelt, I make the very best beds I can because that is all I am doing at that moment, making beds, and all of me, every molecule goes into it, I turn a sheet corner like a sonneteer, my pillows are as consoling as the Ninety-First Psalm.

And I enjoy it. I enjoy getting the best of a room that's been laid waste and leaving it spotless, the bedspreads smooth and pristine as tennis courts, the ashtrays gleaming, the fresh towels hanging two inches apart, the little Lux soaps in their wrappers; I enjoy expunging the signs of people. I can't wait for them to check out so I can start in eradicating them and so I give the evil eye to the loiterers who say, "Come back later, would you?" I repeat, "*Later?*" with a small but deadly emphasis, holding my bundle of clean sheets and towels and swinging my skeleton key and then very quickly turn and go out as if to do murder, and most often they're out of the room in twenty minutes; it's amazing how lily-livered people can be, especially men.

Men can be dealt with, it's women who complicate everything. Conditioned, poor creatures, to be predatory in a world of men, to behave like the trapdoor spider, they tend to become automative

and subtly wily in their battle for superiority; in fact
the only woman whose motives I'd fully trust
would be one who was being considerate to an
eighty-five-year-old person on welfare.

That is why I delight in my new freedom of not
going after a man, of not needing a man compul-
sively or from the point of view of keeping up with
the other girls; that's the threat that harrows and
draws the little worry lines on the face, the constant competition. the fret of will-he-won't-he ask
me? Or will he Take It With Him and go and leave
me in the second-hand goods department. And
what will happen when I get too old and tired and
frightened to be fun anymore?

So I enjoy my new sexuality.

Which is being sexual, undiluted, sexy.

Uninhibited by fondness, regret, anxiety of any
kind. Just having rich rewarding sex for its own
sake, not loving but loving doing it, which makes
it an art and the word fuck itself, generally used
in the pejorative, condemning the truck obstruct-
ing the way or the can opener that has jagged the
finger, can be as beautiful and fine and true as
beautiful fucking.

T always closed her eyes as if she didn't need to
be there. T was the kind of girl who thinks of the
cock as merely a necessary tool for the procedure
(and indeed in her native Australian it was actually called that: his *tool*), as functional as a
wrench, not necessarily to be admired for its contours and virtuosity. I think the only time she ever
enjoyed sex sexually was the first night Jack Quist
took her by surprise and she had no time for mod-
ifications; it was orgiastic that night and very likely

the time he got her pregnant, neither of them prepared with precautions, they dived in. Only later she became wishy-washy, had soapy emotions about faithfulness of the heart and concern for trespassing into his privacy and so he lost his appetite for her. T never saw sex, she saw the shadow of it on the wall. When I was growing up in her I used to egg her on when she'd let me, I even got her curious enough to look through the knot hole in the barn the size of a cow's eye at the older boys swimming nude in the cattle hole and coming up out of the tomato-soup-colored water with their great dangling participles, making her giggle with me until she suppressed me, saying it wasn't "nice" and that Mum wouldn't approve of her watching the boys like a little whore (she pronounced it with a "w" not ever having heard anyone say it aloud); a good clean-minded Methodist Sunday-school girl didn't do such things. Just the same she was a fraud, she thought about cocks and talked about cutting mutton sandwiches for the Sunday-school picnic.

Later on as she grew nubile I used to push her as far as her limited imagination would go wondering about boys, their size and so on, fantasizing about their erections until, poor thing, she was weak with desire and then Christian remorse and would suppress me and revert to her parochial puritanism; she would sit on the overturned washtub in the yard, knitting her thick winter sweaters and as the men came back from the milking, call their attention to the sunset. Other times she would assume her tomboy role, join in the evening cricket game, bowling bravely overarm and with unexpected accuracy, her thin little freckled arms flailing the air, her skimpy hair falling out of its cotton ribbon, her feet in their dirty sandshoes dashing this way and that in the murky dust, crying out, "Got you, sport." The sight of her, red-faced and sweaty with the exertion of comradeship used to aggravate me because it sometimes made me feel ashamed.

She shamed me with her mortifying sincerity. The damned girl meant it, *meant* friendship, *wanted* love. God damn her to hell, her and her precious face, starved heart.

It's strange. I feel funny writing in this book of hers as though
she might be
            watching.

It was Mossy Banks who first introduced Tanya to Santa Helena and its primrose little beaches and confidential coves, the houses almost hidden behind bougainvillea and passion flower, the terracotta-colored Spanish mission cracked from tower to earth from the 1928 earthquake but from whose belfry the iron bell tolled twice a day. And the Paradise Hotel falling into ruins in its once-splendid gardens. Santa Helena no longer fashionable, but welcoming. Tanya was in love with it at first sight, as though it had been thoughtfully made for her, which perhaps it had, even as every sea town or mountain village seems to have been made for the rapture of some person.

Just as the insignificant people in life frequently propel us toward our destiny and then vanish as if that were their only reason for being. They either vanish or are put on a shelf in some dusty purgatory until they are sent out again to propel someone else's destiny and then vanish again; they never die, these people, there is no record of their obituary in any paper on earth, they simply vanish and reappear because no one can ever remember meeting them for the first time or parting from them for the last. Mossy Banks was insignificance incarnate, he was as easily put on or off as a shirt and as difficult to offend. What a ridiculous name, Tanya said, when he offered a card that read, "Mossy Banks, Comic. Rep. Joseph Tinkner, Crossroads of the World." Mossy shrugged. Well, there was Red Buttons, there had been Parkyakarkus. The name had come to him in a dream, he said, where he had seen it on a big billboard outside a "sheek joint"; it looked better than Moses Bogdanov.

Mossy was driving up to Santa Helena to audition for the Yum Yum Tree, a nightclub so off the beaten track it could be excused for engaging failures like Mossy out of desperation. It seemed that all Mossy ever did was audition. In fact the only evidence of his having appeared anywhere were two or three yellowing newspaper advertisements, now whiskery with age, that showed he had performed at the Fireside Inn in Canton, Ohio and at the Millstone in Flemington, New Jersey. What Mossy lived on was a mystery, and it would not have been altogether surprising to have learned that he was a CIA agent; he might have come in and gone out of the Kremlin as unnoticed as he came and went from the Broadway department store on Hollywood and Vine buying rayon socks.

He sported a dated crewcut probably to disguise his age, which could have been anything from thirty-seven to fifty. He pronounced her name with the short "a" as in tan-yer hide. "How's tricks, Tanya?" Mossy would say, turning up at the Ventura Motor Inn on her day off in his 1953 Chevy with a box of crystallized fruit.

"Where'd you like to go today?" She could have said anywhere outlandish, Puget Sound, Mossy would have said OK. Mossy Banks, Comic, was obliging. He was temperamentally as flat as Oxnard, from whose squat environs he had sprung, but in bed he was a revelation. He was, like li'l David in the song, "small, but *oh my.*"

Apart from that, she felt as much for him as she could for anyone now. Without obligations. Fond enough of him to criticize him, which he seemed to enjoy, he would nod appreciatively when she would tell him off about his deafening Hawaiian shirts or his way of gnashing cashews. "Right," Mossy would say, smiling brightly at her and go right on flashing and gnashing. As for his "act," which she had seen at one of the auditions, it was presumptuous of him to describe it as such, he must have watched every lesser stand-up comic on television for twenty years to have accumulated such a variety of worn-out routines. Unable to lie nowadays or even to dissemble a little so as not to wound, she told him it was atrocious, no other word for it. He nodded pleasantly. "Goes better with an audience," he told her cheerfully and went on chasing his wild geese up and down the Pacific coast from La Jolla to Monterey, and often she went with him for the ride. So it came to be that in Santa

Helena on this clammy August day with fog superimposed over the torpid lava-colored sea, over a shrimp lunch in the garden terrace of the Paradise Hotel, thanks to this insignificant man her life came to be changed.

The audition for the Yum Yum Tree had lasted less than seven minutes, a record even for Mossy, and the fact that he came out whistling told everything. The worse the reception, the brighter Mossy grew.

"Let's go have lunch at the Paradise," he said. Set in groves of senile cyprus trees, the Paradise Hotel with its pink towers, its faded striped awnings, the long loggias with their now cracked terrazzo floors, and the great white rattan chairs and terra-cotta urns postulated silent movie stars. They had whisky oldfashioneds on the terrace overlooking the disused tennis courts.

She took slight notice of the man who appeared on the terrace except that even at a distance he seemed inordinately ugly and was dressed all in starched khaki, which gave him the appearance of being a soldier recently repatriated from some minor military fiasco. The moment he appeared the waiter, who had been lolling against the stone parapet with his elbow in the face of a caryatid, unbent and flew across the terrace to a table from which he stripped the spotless pink tablecloth and all the tableware and bundled off with it, returning with a brand new tablecloth which he spread in front of the newcomer with elaborate smoothings out, talking all the time in a low carressing voice, then, whisking out the glittering clean knives, forks and spoons, laid them in front of the man with obeisances. All the time the man stared stolidly in front of him looking neither to the right nor left and only when the pink napkin had been fluttered open and laid across his khaki knees did he make a move. Taking the napkin he lifted the water glass and began carefully to polish it, holding it up to the sunlight and polishing until he seemed satisfied that not a mote or speck remained visible to the naked eye. Only then was the waiter let pour the iced water, which the man then left untouched, sat with his fingertips meeting in the attitude of a praying mantis.

"Spout and dance," she thought Mossy said, his mouth full of poppyseed roll.

"What?"

"Sprout Van Zandt," Mossy said. Mossy knew everybody who was or was not anybody on the Pacific Coast and supplied information about them. "Loaded," Mossy said, "Krofft Industries, Detroit. They make everything from Ping-Pong balls to atomic reactors. His mother was a Hollis from Main Line Philadelphia."

The waiter brought their Crevettes du Paradis.

Mossy went on about him. First name Hollis, had a bungalow on Judas Tree Road along the shore where the "aileet" live. But very few people had ever seen inside it. Was a loner, took no interest in Krofft Industries. Nobody knew what he did with his time, but he had some hobby or other. Mossy had once been "innerduced" to him. On the frail strength of this they stopped by his table on their way out.

"Mossy Banks," Mossy said. "Don't know if you'll remember but we met Thanksgiving Day a year ago when they had the buffet inside in the Hunt Room here. I was with Gordon Kimberley of Domino Films who is an acquaintance of yours. It's always a pleasure to encounter you, Mr. Van Zandt."

Van Zandt, who was spearing an anchovy, held the fork suspended in mid air, achieved a seraphic smile and then said in a voice that was more like a cello than anything, "Go and burst a lung."

But in that moment of eviscerating Mossy, had looked at her, one eye had seemed to catch sight of her, a mud-colored eye, small, the size of a whale's eye, but it seemed to register everything there was to her in a click. She thought about that eye and the general ugliness of Sprout Van Zandt; he seemed to her more interesting than all the beautiful men she had ever laid eyes on.

It was at this time or slightly afterward that a restlessness took hold of her. She sat out the heat of August in the bone dryness of the Valley imagining she could hear the sea beyond the brown dust of Ventura Boulevard, and while scrub fires raced in the Canyons, she thought of the pale-colored beaches of Santa Helena and the little vine-covered gardens.

As if needing an excuse for moving, she set about having herself fired from her job at the Roosevelt; she needed exacerbation, the pink air of Los Angeles subjecting one to lassitude and to procrastination. The easiest way, it occurred to her, of finding the energy to leave it would be to get thrown out. As in everything she did, she put heart and soul into it. Coming on duty an hour earlier in the mornings, she trundled her squeaking laundry trolley up and down corridors and swinging her keys, barged into rooms, ignoring Do Not Disturb signs, crying "Maid" like an avenging Lucifer awakening the dead, disturbing slumber and sometimes love, causing groans and epithets to be aimed at her until Mrs. Tombes, the housekeeper, after twice remonstrating with her paid her off with two weeks salary.

She announced to Mossy she was going to Santa Helena. "I'm in love with it," she said.

"It's only a mouthwash," Mossy said, blinking. She supposed he had meant backwash; when disconcerted, he substituted words, he desired the status to remain quo, disputed change but presented her with a pedicure set in a green plastic case, said he was concerned about her being up on the coast alone. "Gets awful damp in the winter, just you wait and see."

She drove away in her third-hand Plymouth with her own suitcase and a raffia basket of dishes.

A kindly fate, if she wanted to believe it, had killed with a stroke the seventy-eight-year-old widow who had lived in the beach house on Puesta del Sol for thirty years. It was not without the need of paint and some repairs, the agent warned, but because of cracks in the walls and the vines literally taking over (but mostly because of the population decline, the general demise of Santa Helena), she was able to rent it for a song plus forty-odd dollars for the old lady's decrepit furniture which, as she crisply reminded the agent, saved him the bother and expense of having it carted away. Fate continuing to smile, led her to the Paradise Hotel where there was an opening for a night waitress in the bar of the Hunt Room. She was obliged to wear a tangerine uniform with her name emblazoned on a plastic badge but her hours were from five until midnight, which allowed her the days free to wander as she liked up and down the dreamy, often blue-fogged shoreline, often taking a basket lunch and staying out all day, exploring the ins and outs of coves and inlets, tiny lagoons, and the rocky ledges overlooking the sea.

There was always something new to come upon, a cave or a secret path up a cliff face and thus it was that one afternoon, turning into a small unexpected cove, she came upon a low-lying Spanish bungalow she had not seen before almost hidden in cypress and scrub oak. She was so convinced that she had passed this little bay before that the sudden appearance of the house, purple-tiled, startled her as though it had been put up overnight, someone magically transporting it here and then capriciously weaving vines and scattering window boxes of petunias to allay suspicion. But what drew her attention to it was the cat or raccoon stranded on the roof, its back arched in a spasm of terror, and the tide being dead low, she waded ankle deep across the inlet until she stood directly under the deck looking up, realized that the cat was a clever fake among a profusion of animals and birds squatting or perched in trellises— monkeys, wild geese, parakeets, and even a cheetah.

All stared at her with hostile glass eyes. Then a face appeared over the rail of the deck and stared down at her. Snout of a nose, pointy ears, pig eyes, hair like the dull wool on the undersides of rugs,

Neanderthal. She caught a flash of khaki as he waved an arm at her.

"This is private property, go away. Evaporate." The voice in contrast was deep and musical.

"*Evap*orate," he repeated when at first she didn't move, transfixed by the sight of him just as at the sight of a Gila monster. So there must be a plateau of ugliness that can be as astonishing and perhaps mesmerizing as beauty she thought as she slogged back across his bay in the lukewarm water, and all the way back along the shoreline she held that lurid face in her mind's eye, the photograph of the squiggly little eyes, the pathos of scalp showing through the clumps of wool. All the way home she fondled the idea that he might be following to make sure she was clear of his property. She nurtured the fantasy that she might look out a night window and see the face grinning fiendishly at her, but that unlike the bogeyman scaring the child into fits, the sight of him would seduce her.

She hadn't yet come to grips with the truth that all her maneuverings to come to Santa Helena had little or nothing to do with coves and pretty mornings, it had to do with Sprout Van Zandt. That was a fact too unreasonable to face as yet, but dawdling in the shower or drinking her morning coffee she entertained the thought of him and in these entertainments they had ferocious spats. There was nothing remotely saccharine in their ectoplasmic trysts, she knew (without knowing him in the slightest) that he would find sweetness insupportable. (Just to think of how Tilly might have sentimentalized over him! It would have been the princess kissing the Frog Prince.)

Then their cars met head-on in Snookers Lane, a short bypass that was only wide enough for one car to encompass at a time. His big oldfashioned Packard suddenly loomed in front of her like an ocean liner and they both stopped dead a foot from each other.

"Back up," he called.

"Why should I? I was here first."

"Back *up*," he called again, and made a gesture of retreat.

"You back up," she called.

"What?"

"You back up."

"Why should I?"

"Why should *I*?"

He leaned out the driver's window, the small face screwed up with anger was more piglike than ever. Close up the deep organ notes of his voice gave the eerie impression that he was being dubbed by someone else.

"You're supposed to honk before entering the lane," he said

"I did. I didn't hear any honk from you."

At that he climbed out of the car and came quickly toward her on bow legs, pushed his snout into the window at her.

"Back up," he said threateningly, "back up or I'll file a complaint against you for negligent driving. This is a bypass lane and you are supposed to honk and wait before you enter. You women drivers have got to learn discipline."

"I am not women drivers, I am not women, I

am a woman and I will wait here until *you* back up," she said with more calmness than she felt. It was not the nearness of the collision that had disconcerted her, it was the nearness of his face pushing in her car window only inches from her, the hog-face so close that she could now see the little black spiky hairs that grew out of the snout and ears and that the eyes were a mulberry color. But the transcending, terrifying thing was the excitement it engendered in her. This was the Frog Prince in reverse. She had kissed the boring prince into his real loathsomeness. Had she come so far then, out of Tilly, that the need was now for a total opposite, for the quintessence of ugliness to annul the disenchantment with the handsome and charming, the boredom with goodness, charity, the normal requirements of decency and the assessment of worth?

Then she needed dragons.

She looked him fully in the face, provocatively.

She smiled.

Like a torch lit in the face of a bat. He withdrew, hoisting his beautifully-creased khaki shorts. He moved away from her and stood contemplating ferns growing out of the stone wall, then he quickly turned and said, "I hope you die in the Sassafras Gardens."

Got quickly into his big atavistic car and blowing off steam by tremendous accelerations, he reversed, the great black hulk backing down Snooker Lane and out of sight. When she passed it on Whitebait Beach Road, he had pulled to the side and was sulking like a reprimanded child.

She sat on her patio, calmly painting her

toenails and recognizing that she was ready for anything. After all, for what had she gone to all the strain of divesting herself of Tilly if she were not ready for anything?

Even to die in the Sassafras Gardens, whatever they were. She imagined they were out of some violent fairytale that had been read to him as a child and that they had remained as real to him as Persia to the Persians and that whatever happened there was as horrifying as children's dreams.

She was ready for him when he appeared in the Hunt Room Bar at the Paradise Hotel in the middle of one evening's lull when there were only herself, the barman, and two women from Montecito getting drunk on Moscow Mules. When she went over to take his order he looked at her without expression so that she thought for a moment that he had not recognized her in her tangerine uniform and then he said, "I might have expected a last straw this evening." He bent forward to read her plastic name and said, "Tanya. Not a suitable name, it conjures up astrakhan and balalaikas, not a waitress." She looked him right in his pig eyes and said, "I was named by someone overromantic. May I take your order?" Getting up he said, "I believe I'd prefer to be waited on by someone less ornate than Tanya, isn't there a Maisie or Peggy around?" She said, "I'm the only girl on tonight, Tuesdays are traditionally slow here." He sat down again and said, "Kismet." She noticed now that pinned to his khaki jacket was one wilted white rosebud, which suggested there may have been an out-of-the-ordinary date, while the time of evening suggested he had been stood up. There was something poignant about the white rosebud, it projected a sense of required formality like the white flowers worn by professional pallbearers. He said, "Bring me a perfect Rob Roy and make sure it's perfect. And bring me a clean glass with it and a linen napkin. And clear away all this flotsam and jetsam," he added, referring to the ashtray on which stood a fox in a hunting jacket, the fake candle, and the bowl of pretzels.

When she brought the drink, the extra glass, he took the napkin and wiped the extra glass with extreme care and poured the Rob Roy into it, tasted it and frowned. "Too sweet," he said. "It has to be perfect."

Five times he returned the drink to the outraged barman, five times he wiped the extra-clean glass, repoured the drink, tasted, put down the drink. When she brought the sixth glass, the sixth paper coaster, the sixth extra glass she said, "It's your bill. It's nothing to me if you order a hundred drinks, but this has something to do with annoying me and I refuse to be annoyed by you, so that if you don't accept this drink I will throw it in your face and that will cost me my job and I somehow can't imagine that even a pig like you would want to take such a footling revenge."

The little eyes looked at her a long time, he seemed to be weighing possibilities. Then the small hairy paw lifted the glass, and with a daintiness that was somehow repulsive he sipped and sipped until the glass was empty. He set it down with extreme care, wiped his mouth on the paper napkin and got up. Passing in front of her without a glance he made his way to the bar and said to the barman with a mollifying smile, "Put all these on my bill, will you, Marius? Good evening."

When she looked down at the table she saw that he had left a hundred dollar bill.

She stuck it in her uniform pocket as casually as if it had been a one and thought of the patch of damp on her kitchen ceiling she could have plastered but awoke in the night hot with annoyance at herself for meekly accepting insult added to injury. No doubt Mr. Van Zandt handed out hundred dollar bills to anyone whose feelings he had outraged and felt that his responsibility to the human race ended there. This was, perhaps, the prerogative of the rich, given the money, to offend whomever they pleased provided they paid for it. Well not to her they wouldn't, *he* wouldn't, damned ugly little pig. She felt quite Dickensian about the rich at three o'clock in the morning and had she his telephone number she would have called him out of bed to tell him what she thought of him and his insulting largesse.

Judas Tree Road was a cul de sac and there appeared to be only two houses on it. She approached an iron gate on which was a sign that peremptorily hyperbolized that ANY TRESPASSING WHATEVER WILL BE SEVERELY PROSECUTED. Yet, when she touched the elaborate scrolls and storks emblazoned on the grillwork, the gate swung open easily and she went down toward the salmon-colored bungalow by short steps through wild unclipped foliage and rioting tropical flowers quite foreign to her. The imposing sculptured front door was ajar, but this side of the house being in shadow the hall was lost in darkness. She took the hundred dollar bill out of her purse and pressed a bell. Deep in the house she heard it sound and half-expected that dogs would come leaping and snarling, but instead there was only silence and the distant slap of the tide coming in. After a minute or so she rang again and nothing happening she pushed the heavy teak door further open and peered inside the tenebrous hall.

And at a tapestry of unicorns and maidens cavorting with garlands.

And at this shock.

Took a quick step backward in reflex at this embarrassing sight, the private peccadillo she had disturbed.

There lay the parlor maid passed out, dead drunk sprawled on a settee on her back, the glass had dropped from her hand to the carpet and her eyes were closed. But except that her cap was askew and one black-nyloned leg was curved back under the seat, the rest of her appearance seemed pristine, the starched little white apron like a neat square on her flat belly, the cuffs glimmering in the greenish light, her domestic's Oxfords polished to a proper shine. Tanya stood looking down on the childlike face, innocent in unconsciousness, yet nevertheless patently intoxicated. Had she come in answer to the bell and then slithered to the sofa in a sudden blackout or had she been here some time? She had fairish almost-white eyelashes curling against her cheek and what seemed to be the faintest nuance of a smile, as if the boozing had been sweet. But

It was odder than sleep, more like death. She was noticing now that there was no sign of respiration, the black silk breast was as unmoving as the white hand drooping toward the carpet. As she bent closer, it became rapidly clear.

The maid was a doll.

The most incredibly lifelike manikin she had ever seen. The skin, made she supposed from some polyethylene substance, had the exact texture of young human skin, the slight pallor of people whose inside work differentiates them from the accustomed Californian tan. The pale eyelashes were almost certainly human hair.

It was a work of art in its own eccentricity. What was its purpose? If it were to break ice, it must have succeeded brilliantly.

"Hello," she called out, "anyone home?" But the words dissolved in the silent air and the only reply was the sudden distant chirr of a refrigerator turning itself on. She went down the thick-carpeted hall and passing an open door stopped, seeing a woman sitting by a window, or at least the lower-half of a woman in a plaid skirt and low-heeled suede shoes, the upper-half of her concealed by the *Los Angeles Times*.

"Excuse me," Tanya said. Nothing stirred except that the newspaper riffled slightly in the breeze coming in the open window, and crossing the room she looked down on scrupulously coiffeured gray hair and the handsome face of a woman who might be fifty or so judging by the puckers around the eyes and the smiling lines that ridged the well-formed slightly-rouged mouth, which was drawn up in amusement at what was being read. Behind the neck and at the back of the hairline there was almost invisible cross-stitching extending down the spine out of sight. But what really caught the attention was that on the bare shoulder, just above where the bouclé blouse ended over the shoulder blade, a large menacing wasp or Yellow Jacket seemed to be on the point of stinging the lady. On closer examination one saw that the *Los Angeles Times* was three years old. Tanya sat down a moment to enjoy the purity of the hoax; the sensation that any moment the woman would put down the paper and say graciously, "I'm sorry, I didn't hear you come in." And that the moral to the fable was the wasp bringing its venom into the sunlit, placid room with its books and magazines, its dark-green carpet and brass, the secure convention of *Architectural Digest,* the well dressed matron serenely unaware of sudden death.

It was so all persuasive that she almost said "Excuse me" again, going out.

But there were more of them.

Pausing at the end of the corridor where glass doors led out onto a porch screened from the sea by giant flapping palms, she saw through the fretwork of moving light and shadow that a boy in swim trunks and a girl in white tennis shorts were seated on a canvas swing in urgent embrace. The boy's naked tanned back was turned toward the glass doors so that only the girl's flowing flaxen hair and her long white arm encircling him were visible. His left arm was holding her body to his in a passionate arc and she held him as if they were both transfixed by the beauty of the moment, but in his right hand stretched out toward the sun and just behind her neck he held an open razor. The two polyethylene bodies floated on the swing as light as the breeze that gently sent it swaying; light as two empty celluloid ducks in a child's bathtub, they kissed forever. To make absolutely certain that this time she was not being hoodwinked, Tanya rapped on the glass but nothing moved except the speckling light on the tiles and the spittle of sun on the razor blade.

She saw through a half-open door what must be the immense bed of the master bedroom and was mildly surprised that there was no life-size doll mistress lying there, perhaps spread-eagled in a brazen, lusty way, laytex breasts bursting through a see-through nightgown, hair streaming over the pillow, but perhaps the phantasms he strewed throughout his house were for comfort or amusement other than sex. They seemed to be menaced creatures, the wasp, the razor, even the helpless drunken parlormaid with her unconscious limbs spread wide and ripe for abuse.

She was remembering that Mossy Banks had said very few people had ever seen inside the house. Were the manikins, she wondered, put away in closets when visitors came?

And were the dolls in some way related to his life?

Were they people to be burned in effigy only instead of being consumed were left around forever in situations of danger or disgrace to be gloated over by him?

Then why the child?

The child must certainly be his masterpiece, this little boy aged perhaps eleven, twelve, dressed in private-school uniform, in blue blazer with a dull gold crest on the pocket and gray flannel short trousers, knee socks and black utilitarian brogues.

The boy sat on a cot in a tiny broom closet lit by one naked ceiling light that cast a livid brightness on the lonesomeness and sterility of the little room with its cold white walls and bookless shelves peopled only with dusty china figurines of a cheapness that affronted and were perhaps intended to. In his small right hand the child held a fork over a dish of plastic fried eggs while his left hand lay flaccid in his lap, and he stared ahead with an expression of such unyielding mournfulness and despair that the cell seemed to reverberate with the word LONELINESS, its trite furnishings and ugly bright cretonne bedcover and window curtains, garish with their cheerfulness, shouted of misery. Anyone even with a heart of ice, even Tanya, could not be somewhat affected.

But this could not be *him*, the child was beautiful, the heart-shaped face in its deep melancholy and heartbreaking youth was as untouched and vulnerable as a sea anemone, the hand poised over the dish of eggs was like a small hibiscus. No, this could not be the hog, the toad.

Whom she now saw coming up from the swimming pool, exceedingly bandy-legged in khaki shorts, carrying a watering can. And so she stood her ground, cool as the sea air blowing in as he opened the kitchen door and then caught sight of her standing there and squinting in the sunlight, ravaged her with his little squiggly eyes.

"Who let you in?"

"Nobody, the front door was open. I rang first."

"Who are you? What do you want?"

"I came to return this."

He stared at the hundred dollar bill she held out

and then a semblance of a smile occurred across the plains of his face.

"Oh, it's *you*. I didn't recognize you in mufti."

He took the bill and crinkled it up in his hand.

"Is this calculated to arouse my admiration?"

"No."

"Because I think a waitress who refuses a hundred dollar tip is either a fool or a Marxist."

"I'm neither."

"You're the girl who threatened to throw a drink in my face."

"Yes and I would have."

"Tanya, isn't it?"

"Yes."

"Badly named. What accent is that you have?"

"I was brought up among Australians."

"Ah. Then I daresay you've also cottoned on to their sort of pious colonial attitudes about taking money from strangers. Nice girls don't and so forth?"

"No. I just don't care to be insulted."

"It was intended to make amends."

"Exactly."

"Not enough, do you mean?"

"Not nearly enough for the trouble you caused me on purpose."

He tossed the crumpled bill onto the kitchen drainboard.

"Then fuck off in the Admiral Jellicoe Pavilion."

One of his places. The imaginary lands and seas he committed people to. The Sassafras Gardens. Fantasies, like the life-sized dolls.

"The way out is to your left," he said, and

stumped past her on his short hairy legs and went into the study and sat down opposite the woman reading the *Los Angeles Times.*

When her telephone rang in the dead of night, she got up, gathering her robe and her wits about her and snapped on the light in the salt-cold living room.

"Hello."

There was that significance of silence that tells someone is there.

"Hello."

Again.

"I will report this nuisance," she said, hanging up, and went back to bed oddly nourished by the thought that it was he and that he might have taken the trouble to find out her surname and that she was the Bond, T, on Puesta del Sol.

Then some days later she took off on her afternoon walk and very nearly trod on him coming around a sheltering rock. He was huddled up against the gray sodden wind blowing in from the sea, unshaven, his skin a dirty yellow color and wearing a long knitted muffler over a black velour Sloppy Joe.

"Altogether a narsty day, wouldn't you say? Isn't that how the Colonials say it? A narsty day?"

"I'm only part Australian and I'm non-Colonial. They've had their own government for over fifty years. Was that you on the phone the other night?"

"Was someone on your phone? That must be encouraging for you."

"I've heard that people who make phone calls

and then don't speak have some trouble with impotence."

"*Trouble* with impotence? Isn't that redundant? Or do you mean they have trouble trying to
achieve impotence?"

He had stood up and was squishing along beside
her in the wet sand in his bare feet, which she noticed now were flat and splayed like a wooden fork.
They were almost duck feet and very clean.

"Did you see the porpoises?" he asked.

"No. Were there?"

"Oh, there was a school of them. I followed
them down from my house."

"Do they go South in winter?"

"I don't really know what they do, I've never
enquired. What do *you* do, Miss Bond?"

"Mind my own business."

"Which isn't much I imagine."

"Not much, but mine."

"Not good enough."

"What isn't?"

"That snub. Not good enough. Silly little Sydney stenographer snub, 'Never you mind.' Sam-
son: 'What are you doing?', Delilah: 'Never you
mind.' "

"Okay."

"Okay?"

"Okay, I'll do better next time."

"Always supposing there *is* a next time."

He was having difficulty keeping up with her on
his short legs.

He said, "What possessed you to settle in this secluded little place?"

"What possessed *you*?"

"That's another matter. Don't answer a question with another. But the Paradise Hotel bar. It's moribund except for a few skittish old larks from Montecito hoping to run into the ghost of Douglas Fairbanks. Isn't it boring?"

"Talking about it is."

A smile flickered across his face but it was more of a spasm than a smile; muscles moved in the cheeks, teeth appeared, disappeared. Wind was ruffling his hair and he tripped now and then on the long muffler which, dangling from his thin neck, gave him the look of a damaged boy, ruined in some accident, burned or scalded almost beyond recognition and then fossilized into this age, thirty-six or seven but with vestiges of the boy. She thought again of the boy doll sitting over the dish of eggs in a Gethsemane of cretonne loneliness in his house.

He had stopped and was poring over a rock pool. Poking into it with his stubby fingers, he delicately picked out a tiny crab and flung it into the sea.

"Find the Gregorian sea horses," he told the crab and came scampering up to Tanya, his muffler dipping in the wet sand. "Stranded when the tide goes out. Like us all."

She didn't care to be included in his metaphor, it was surprisingly trite for him, a glimpse of him through a crack being himself, vulnerable. He lifted his short arms like wings. "Like us all." So she referred back to the crab. "It would have got away once the tide came in again."

"Ah, but in the meantime it could have been eaten up by a gull."

"I didn't know gulls ate crabs."

"Didn't you?"

Picking up a flat stone, he sent it spinning in the direction of a lordly gull, squatting hugely, landlord of a rock. It took off, mewing.

"Didn't you, Tanya?" he said in a sly mincing tone, skipping sideways along the water's edge in a jerky little fandango. "But then, there may be huge amounts you don't know about the birds, the sea. Why should you when all you're really required to know, I suppose, is that you put a slice of cucumber in a Bloody Mary. Or is that unfair of me?"

"Unfair naturally, but go on. About the sea. What should I know?"

"How can one tell? Have you seen the grunions running? They come up on the beach to spawn and it's a lovely thing, Tan." Strange. No one in her whole new life had ever called her Tan. She turned it over in her mind. Coming from him, it was right somehow, it put her in perspective, and it was as though she had graduated to it quite naturally. Tan, a hard brown stone.

"As though the beach had gone mad with quicksilver," he said, "it's beauty immaculate."

He had stopped jerking along and was standing ankle-deep in the water and glaring down at it as if he saw something loathsome, baby serpents. Or his own reflection perhaps.

He said, "Something *knows*."

"Knows what?"

About beauty? Ugliness?

"Knows. That's all. That's enough," he said irritably. Everything, she supposed. The answer. Like the time when they were a child. She and Tilly (and admittedly *she* would not have seen it, it had needed Tilly's unclouded vision, her gladness), and Tilly had seen in a flash along a country road at sunset that everything was one and was beauty and in her ecstasy had ascribed it all to God. Whereas Hollis "Sprout" Van Zandt, staring into the infinity of the sea, seemed to be transfixed by the pain that whatever the answer might be was horror.

"Something knows," he said again, but this time in a low child-like voice. He appeared to be standing on sharp little stones, he gazed down at the curls of foam around his ankles and even from where Tanya stood further along the beach she could feel reverberations; there was some immense power the man gave off like the hum of electricity, the energy of a ravenous unhappiness that needed to be refueled by little acts of unkindness, and watching him now against the line of waves she knew without any doubt that what he was asking for was for something to be said, harsh as gravel to exacerbate the pain.

"*They* won't tell you anything," she called out to him.

"Who won't?"

"Your stupid *dolls,*" she said and started off along the shoreline again hearing him squidging quickly up to her. He caught her arm and pulled her fiercely around.

"They don't have to," his face was screwed up in pain, "they only remind me of what I already know. What would *you* know about it?"

The wind blowing in now from the north brought fat drops of rain on their faces, and in a minute or two they were struggling through the first downpour of autumn.

"You better come in out of the rain," he shouted and took a key from his trouser pocket. She hadn't realized they had reached his property. He opened a back door and stood aside to let her into a dark basement room and turned on a light over a workbench over which hung tools. There were pots of paint and bottles of brushes.

"Is this your workroom?"

"Sometimes."

He led the way upstairs and stopped suddenly halfway, turned and said flatly as if she had asked, "The *people* are made in Los Angeles by Fred Watts who is a prop man at one of the studios, a fellow of infinite jest and infinite suggestibility. I sketch them out and he creates them."

So they were the people.

"Could I borrow a towel?" she asked upstairs, and he opened the door to a guest bathroom, neat and shiny, normal. No doll was perched on the lavatory or about to be hanged in the shower. His success with his "people" was partly in their having to be come upon unexpectedly. She dried her hair and was dabbing at her wet shirt and shorts when he opened the door and handed in a dark blue terry cloth robe. "Until your things dry," he said.

She found him making hot chocolate in the kitchen. He had changed his wet shorts for what looked like an Indian dhoti in faded colors, grass slippers. On the table was a dish of very sweet-looking pink and green iced cakes. He poured the chocolate meticulously into little gold cups and set them on a lacquer tray together with the cakes and without a word carried it out of the kitchen down the long hall to a large drawing room full of overstuffed chairs and Chinese silk screens. Tanya, being totally ignored, felt like an intruder coming into the twilight of this elongated uninviting room, and as he said nothing nor made the slightest gesture toward the cups she helped herself to one of them and sat down with it into a large cretonne-covered armchair (and now it came to her that it was the same leek-green and cabbage rose pattern of cretonne that was in the make-believe room with the sorrowful boy).

Once he lifted the plate of cakes toward her and she shook her head. Otherwise he paid not the slightest attention to her. He created a sense of solitude, now and then glancing at the long floor-to-ceiling windows outside, against which the palms flagellated themselves in the wet gale. He sipped his chocolate as delicately as a deacon having tea with the bishop. He reached for the little iced cakes and ate one after another without spilling a crumb until the dish was empty. Finally he put down his empty cup and folded his hands, drew up his stocky legs and sat with them crossed under him in the half-dark listening to the rain.

Thus they both sat like strangers in a railroad waiting room while the rain peppered the windows with buckshot and the light faded into evening. Thus, they might both have sat like mum-

mies in a forgotten wing of a museum. Or two
effigies in a glass case in the Smithsonian. Or two
of his dolls. Forever.

Then without warning he said,

        "he————"

It came out in lower case as in midsentence, as
though he had been speaking for quite some time
and her hearing had been cut off and suddenly re-
stored.

        "he————"

Then silence came down again like the thick dusk
that now separated them, almost obliterating him
in dancing specks and motes as the daylight became decrepit, and so when the voice began again,
that being all there was of him and being golden,
it fleshed him in beauty.

   "he only ever saw two people, Katie O'Rourke
and Her. There were other people because he heard
their voices and occasionally caught glimpses of
them at great distances below him on the stairs or
from his dormer window getting in and out of cars
in the driveway. Katie O'Rourke was a big Irish girl
with a mane of shiny black hair and thick ankles
who could turn herself into anything for him, a gi-
raffe, a camel, a monkey, and told him stories about
the extraordinary animals who lived in the Sassafras Gardens, the corkscrew fox and the coffee-pot-
snouted pigmy elephant who were banished there
because they were so gargantuanly ugly that one
look at them could stop a normal heart, but who
were really sweet and harmless and thrived on
Beluga caviar and had bedspreads of silver musk.
And she told about the Gregorian sea horses who
sang madrigals beneath the waves. When they

went for the afternoon walk, he and Katie, they went down the back stairs and through the kitchen and the only people he saw were the stiff and starched maids who only gave him a nod and went on with their work, although once, just as he went out the door, he heard one of them say, 'poor little thing.' Why poor? Why, he had an Erie-Lackawanna train that took up a whole room in the attic and had a dining car that had twenty perfect little green glass lamps on the tables that *lit up* and an exact model of the *Mauretania*, enough building blocks to make the Woolworth Building, a butcher shop with little sides of beef and flitches of bacon made of marzipan, books and books and a papier mâché theater with people sitting in the boxes and a conductor leading the orchestra. Poor? The gifts were unstoppable, every few days there was an elegantly-packaged box the maid brought up with the breakfast tray. And they all came from Her and sometimes She came in Her beads, in Her little knee-high dresses of turquoise and saffron with Her hair cut like a boy's and Her smell of forgetmenot and kissed the top of his head and asked 'How is my precious? Have you had a nice day, precious? Did Katie take you for a nice walk, precious?' But She never looked directly at him, always just to the left or the right of him and she said everything was 'beautiful,' the crayon drawings he did were 'beautiful,' She seemed not to have any other adjective for anything and leaving, She would brush her fingers through his hair and say, 'Have a beautiful sleep, precious.' Once Katie said through her teeth, 'I'd like to give her a "beautiful" smack in the eye,' and once, wonderingly, he asked out of the blue, fitting a piece of erector set to another, 'Is She beautiful?' and knowing there was no one else who came upstairs to see him, Katie answered, 'Yes,' and then he asked, 'Am I?' and Katie was silent for a very long time and her eyelashes blinked furiously and then she said, 'Yes *very*,' and took him in a force of arms.

"Then there came a time when he heard words outside on the stairs between Katie and Her and putting his ear to the door what sounded like this: 'my nurvues and neeces. Slutely no. Footsie other kids? No Katie san invalid. Un Natral? *No.* Some time inna mirror? When s'older, snot now. Slutely not.' Then Her feet going downstairs neatly, clip clop. What was it about? So then one day Katie put her finger on her lips and said not to say a word when next time She comes up. They were going on a visit to the other side of town to visit Katie's sister and meet her nurvues and nieces; he was actually going to meet other children. He was in a thrilling panic over it, but Katie said orra, not to worry, they were only 'kids,' and they took a cab across town and stopped in a street where all the little houses were exactly alike and a big untidy woman rushed out and kissed Katie and then stood back and gave him a look and said, 'Well now, you're not so bad lookin', are ye now?' and Katie said in a warning way, 'Shush, Maureen,' and they went inside to a small stuffy parlor full of bric-a-brac and a picture of Jesus on the cross and he met Colleen, Shannon, Eileen, Kevin and little Shawna, who all shook hands with him, and little Shawna for some reason went into a fit of giggles and couldn't stop until her mother shook her until her curls wiggled and said stop that now, miss, stop it at once and they all took him outside to play hopscotch, which he learned very fast, after which they were served lemon cake and weak tea in the kitchen while Katie and her sister talked in the parlor. he found it was not so strange after all being with other children, only they just weren't as interesting as grownups like Katie and She. Just before it was time to leave, while he was waiting for Katie to get her coat, little Shawna appeared and beckoned him into her room and said she wanted to ask him something but she could only whisper it and standing on tip toe she put her mouth to his ear and whispered, 'Are you a little pig?' and he was at a loss to know what she meant or whether he had heard right so said, 'What?' and she whispered again, 'Are you a little pig?' 'No,' he said, surprised. 'Is your dad a pig?' she asked, and it wasn't a joke, she was dead serious, he could feel her hot breath in his ear. 'No,' he said, because he had seen his father once and there had been nothing piglike about him and going home in the cab he asked Katie about it and why little Shawna would have asked him that, and she covered her face with her hands and said, 'Oh that child, take no notice, darling.' But it was quickly forgotten in what was to come next. *She* was waiting for them in the nursery and there was a quietness about Her which was terrible. She was white and terrible and he was banished immediately to his bedroom. 'You are excused, Hollis,' She said, and to Katie, 'Sit down, please.' They'd been found out. One of the maids had heard Katie on the downstairs phone calling for the cab to take them to Queenstown. So now Her voice went on and on rising and falling interrupted occasionally by Katie's grieving cries, Katie's pleading and finally by Katie's Irish temper, 'Miserable *tyrant*, TY-RANT,' and the attic door closed violently, Her feet went downstairs on angry high heels hardandfast, hardandfast. Terrible. Katie was to go. Terrible. Katie was to go Friday with two weeks salary 'in lyooo.' Unbelievable. He wept, they both wept, held on to each other desperately and wept, no supper, they waved it away, wept. 'I'll go too,' he said, 'you just watch,' and Katie taking him in her arms said in a quieter voice, 'You can't go anywhere. Don't you see, darlin', you live in the Sassafras Gardens.' "

There was a longish pause. The palms continued in turmoil outside in the wind while he grew more indistinct in the murkiness.

"then Katie was gone. So as not to further damage their broken hearts, she had crept away in the early morning before he was awake leaving only a half-empty bottle of Jensen's Skin Tonic, a bus timetable for the greater Detroit area, eleven cents and part of a broken hand mirror. This was very interesting because up until now he had never been able to see himself except in glimpses and at a distance in the glass of store windows and palely in revolving doors, and now he picked up the piece of mirror that perhaps Katie had left behind on purpose and held it up to his face. Except for being so pink, he wouldn't have said pig, he would have said he had the face of a pug dog. But was this why he was shut away in the attic and taken up and down the back staircase? And why She never looked directly at him. And why She talked about beautiful things all the time and had given him a book illustrated with pictures of exquisite children playing in woods and fountains like little nymphs and satyrs and yet had never allowed him to mix with them? Then this must be why the maid said, 'poor little thing,' and why he had never been downtown, had his clothes bought for him, was kept away from everyone so that even his father whom She had divorced had only once come to see him and then it had been awkward, the tall gruff man with the deeply-lined face had only been able to stand in the doorway and look mostly at the ceiling and ask idiotic questions like, 'Did you enjoy the train set? Do you run it much? Get plenty of heat in here in winter? Would you like it if I got you a pony?' Then reached out and touched the child on the head without looking and said in a faraway voice, 'Never mind,' as if absolving it from any guilt in the disgrace, 'maybe when you're older we'll go shooting together and bag us a moose.' But he never heard from his father again except word that he had died flying his monoplane into a silo. 'So now you'll be a little Mister Rich Britches,' Beady said, breaking the news to him over the cold cereal and prunes. Beady (short for Beatrice, though she wouldn't have caused a single head to turn on the Ponte Vecchio) was his nurse-governess, and the moment she had been brought up to the attic he had seen that her smile was all dentures and no meaning and felt something perilous in the way she set down her suitcase and put her feet together and said, 'Well, now, so you're the one I've heard so much about, so *you're* little Hollis Van Zandt, are you? Well you don't scare me a bit. In fact, I'll tell you what we're going to be, young Hollis, you and me are going to be *pals!*' From that moment until he had been rescued from her tarantula clutches by boarding school there had not been a day when he had not been subject to Beady Garside's inventiveness and virtuosity. And there not being a mark on his body, not a bruise to show, there was nothing to prove any accusation about her. And whom to tell except go to the attic dormer window and scream. And who would pay any mind to a disfigured child yelling about abuse any more than one would have heeded mad Mrs. Rochester? In front of Her and the maids, Beady was the picture of the Pieta, her righteousness and propriety were architectural and for the brief periods downstairs or with other people he was sometimes almost persuaded he imagined things. And what went on was quiet, even when she was drunk as a pig, so that had She come softly up the stairs and bent her lovely golden head to listen at the door, nothing would have been heard that would not have been taken for sounds of contentment, of life being normal as pie, pie being a suitable epithet for Beady, bland as pumpkin pie and sunny as June with her all-encompassing smile and her gladness about everything. Impossible to penetrate that gladness, it roused him from bed, singing about the beautiful day it was, reminding him of his good fortune in being alive and well-fed over a breakfast of sickeningly greasy fried eggs which she had usefully discovered made him queasy, then rapping out 'Six times twenty eight, *quick*' when he was hardly yet awake and then 'Too slow,' and imposing gayly the multiplication table recited backward. Biting into her toast neatly, she would propose that for a whole day they not use a word beginning with the letter P and then lay subtle traps for him to ask for something please. Experiments were made to ascertain how long he could stand on one leg without falling over or name all the secretaries of state. Most of it was uneducative and needless but was meted out as discipline, of which he required a 'tubfull,' Beady said. But all her calculated smilingly doled-out punishments were nothing compared to the nights when Beady opened her canvas valise and took out her 'cough medicine,' which was hundred proof bourbon of which she needed little to turn from immaculate counselor into mawkish slattern, drunken Niobe, shaking him awake, her hair hanging in loops of fallen combs, her voice a whining hiccupping singsong of baby talk. 'Does oo wuv Beady just a widdle, piglet? 'En put oose arms wound and give poor Beady a hug,' and nauseated by her breath he would half sit up in bed and clench his arms around her neck only to be pushed away with, 'Call *that* a hug?' Often she got into bed with him, sometimes making little indecent clutchings at his parts and giggling, 'Wassat? Sat your iggie pee-pee? Some day oosel hafta learn what to do with it.' Next morning she would be a stalagmite of virtue, no hair out of place and ready to work out her penance on him with, 'Naturally if a word is ever breathed about last night I shall say you are addicted to sick fantasies, and there will be no going out to the park for a month.' For four and a half years he endured Beady Garside, who became sunnier and more malicious by the year. Who, on his going away to boarding school, knelt and whispered in his ear, 'Don't mind what they say about your face, piglet,' which turned out to be kinder than meant for it prepared him when the boys christened him Snout to pretend they had said Sprout. When the boys went home for summer to families, he went home to Beady, whom his mother had kept on for this purpose while She lingered in Turkey and Cyprus and along the Dalmatian coast, from where She sent cards declaring that everything and everybody was so beautiful, beautiful, beautiful, everything was beautiful to Her eyes, and so he passed Fourth of July and Thanksgiving and Christmas in the big empty house with Beady and the sulking maids and sat alone at the big dining table eating his greasy fried eggs and trying to please Beady or at least not *dis*please her because, after all, she was all he had and indeed he had become fond enough of her to be pleased that on the night she fell from the third-floor attic stair all the way to the second floor landing stone drunk and broke her neck, she appeared to have suffered no pain, sprawled like a broken doll on her back, she was smiling up at him in death with bourbon gladness. About Saint Barnabas School, any further mention would be needless flagellation.

"Poor old Beadie, she was a dilettante compared to the professionals at that school, teachers and boys who combined forces to devise little tortures for him, but he learned how to evade them. He learned not to be there and in this aloneness he became sterilized against their jokes and jeers. To trust no one, absolutely no one is to be totally safe, and he travelled through that school and later through the hideousness of Singleton College surviving with his talent for being invisible, passing through crowds of jesters without being bruised, and he learned to watch lovers dispassionately because knowing there would be none of that in his life he became fulfilled by the pride and the strength of his acceptance of himself so that even his celibacy was gratifying until———"

Now the silence was so long in the dark room against the sea and rain that Tanya wondered if he had fallen asleep in the midst of these other darknesses.

"———Valerie. Who leaned in the door and asked did he have a pencil sharpener? Who was tall and silky, unlike any person he had ever known even as briefly as meeting coming in or going out of the library or in the local tea shop. Who was fully dimensional, wore tartan skirts with a big pin at her hip and tossed her mane of hair like a lion and was the more extraordinary because she stayed, because she looked directly at him without the usual aversion or amusement and talked to him, sitting on his low ottoman with her straight legs drawn up to her chin and her long feathery arms encircling them, and drew him out of his solitude into her brimming light. And they talked of safe banal things, and he was so amazed at her staying that he made sure of not pressing her into any revelation that could be construed by her as making a commitment. But gradually, she leading him out of himself into her light, he began to respond to the (to him) incredible normality of it. Little by little, like someone shut away for years in a dungeon, adjusting to the light, the light beginning not to hurt so that, time passing, the effect of this change in his life became less startling and the wonder and beauty of it less painful for the dread that it would vanish in an instant and leave him back in his empty room. And she seemed impervious to the looks being handed around when they walked around campus or when there was barely stifled laughter in the Merry Onion Cafe and he, born with radar ears designed to catch the softest snidery, distinctly heard someone say, 'Look, the pig has a girl.' But Valerie charged ahead through the smoke and noise like a Gaelic chieftan who has battled with mightier foes and found the snittering, nudging, poking in the ribs, porcine name-calling beneath her contempt. Her gift to him was in her apparent conception of him as perfectly usual. She looked directly at him over the fly-spotted menu and did not recommend the fish sticks. She never smiled at him, only looked steadily into his eyes and he, treated to the flashing brilliantine smiles cast at him to quickly excuse the profound disconcertion he caused, rejoiced in the calm with which she took him and in her continuance (no dates were made between them, no telephoning was done; she appeared, said hello, what are you up to, may I borrow your Ovid, want to go to the Fox and Hound for a hamburger?). In her continuity was the miracle of safety which up to now he had never been granted. One night she said out of the blue, 'kiss me,' and holding down the thudding in his chest he put his mouth down to her uplifted face under a streetlight and felt her open mouth meeting his as if it were a synonym of his opened heart; minutes later heard her triumphant excited voice beneath his window (it was, perhaps, her wish for him to hear) say, 'I won. did you see it? I let him kiss me. So give me the hundred dollars,' and there was laughter. In his dream of her it is always in her daylight, she is in white and they kiss on a porch swing; he cuts her throat."

Said as if the weight of the thought of it was so slight it was almost boring. But then his voice picked up as if it were organically refreshed.

"But the memory that is most vivid is of something that may or may not have happened. His mother is carrying him in her arms along a lonely beach at low tide and he has his little bucket and spade and She sets him down way out on a sandbank and whispers to him to dig, dig down darling to find all the pretty pearls and starfish and maybe if you dig deep enough you may find the secret pavilion of Admiral Jellicoe, where every wish is granted. And he thinks he remembers Her walking away back onto the beach through the wet sand, Her long violet cotton skirt dipping in the little puddles and Her long hair flying like a sail, and he dug and dug and dug and all the time little waves accumulated around his belly and all the time the tide was coming in until it was up to his waist, and it was then that for good or for bad the couple coming from the other end of the long empty beach saw him and waded in to get him and She appeared from around a dune and came running to snatch him, crooning all the lies about his wandering off alone and about Her being frantic, kissing him and crooning all these lies. It is so crystal clear in his mind that he can see Her long blond hair still blowing in his face and blurring his eyesight. But if it was real, if She stranded him on the sandbar for the sea to take him away from Her forever, the worse evil was the fondling and kissing him in front of his rescuers, that was loathsome. If it was not real, the components were there, the potential was there, and the child had only to translate them into terms that he could understand. The very fact of the possibility, the admission of it has sustained him, knowing the capacity of Her scorn for him, the brutality of Her utter distaste for him, even Her alienation from him, Her casting him away, Her rapacious need for beauty to counteract what She believed to be this monstrous thing She had brought forth has strengthened him in the belief in himself, that monstrous or not he is real and more alive because of the anguish he has brought Her."

Outside the rain had stopped and in the long silence that now ensued Tanya heard the slap and wash of the tide coming in.

He said, "The rain seems to have stopped so you can go now."

She was thinking about the little boy doll with the despairing face forever staring out over the dish of squalid fried eggs and that he was as beautiful as a hyacinth. Was that his deliberate distortion of the truth or was it how he really saw himself? Was it his real self disguised under the porcine features, the scraps of wool hair, the pinky-pork skin? If that was so, she was thinking, there was a parallel between them. Because hadn't she, the real person, been captive behind the fake Tilly and wasn't the real Sprout hidden behind the awfulness of Hollis Van Zandt and perhaps beautiful?

She began thinking of him as beautiful. Looking up from painting a kitchen chair Chinese red and seeing him approaching along her beach, perceived in his fastidious walk, a kind of grace. Swinging a green canvas bag of clams.

To be baked, he said, in seaweed among hot stones. "Does that appeal to you? What an ugly house, it's so stricken looking."

"That is beside the point."

"Not necessarily."

Without being aware of it they had dropped into a routine that on the surface seemed so insignificant that they were not aware of any introspection. He came and went, inconspicuous as the tides. If she wished to take a nap she went into the bedroom and closed the door. He might, if he chose, step down off her deck and walk off in the middle of conversation. They walked up and down the shore in silence, haunted by the gulls to whom they threw bread. They defeated each other at checkers and gin rummy. Sometimes he cooked for them in his kitchen, excellently. She had become immured to the "people," passed the drunken maid in the hall without looking. Once, without thinking she said apropos of their driving down to Santa Barbara to dine, "or I could fry us some eggs," and he snapped at her, "I don't like my life being joked about." "I'm sorry," she said, "I'd forgotten." Another time he surprised her by snapping a crayfish in half and asking in a constrained voice,

"You honestly don't have any pity for me, do you?"

"Of course not, why should I?"

"Honestly—not a shred?"

"Not a shred."

As if this were the assurance he needed of her dispassionate self, he proposed. It was like discussing a lease. No animals, no children, no radio or record player after eleven. No sex. She would be free to indulge in any physical peccadillo she chose, provided it was performed in a discreet fashion. The sun room would be made over for her in colors and materials of her choice.

He needed to be married, he explained flatly, in order to defeat the greedy machinations of Her, the mother, whom he believed would go to any lengths, and there were many, to get her rapacious hands on his estate, pay out vast sums to lawyers, postulate with convincing tears in and out of courts, contest the will, break into the sanctity of his tomb, looting and rifling. "Nancy," he said, "is without scruple."

"What makes you think she might outlive you?"

"She has a valvular condition of the heart that she has used effectively for years to get her in and out of situations, and it's my contention that life provides exactly the right irony in such cases. I, who am in perfect physical health, could be struck down in a minute while she lives on with her damaged heart."

Meantime, he added, stay put and think about it.

After he left she stood on her deck and looked over a horizonless calm sea zinc in moonlight.

It seemed to her the culmination of her reconstitution that it should evolve into this bloodless marriage, that after the turmoil, the taking of everything and everybody to heart that she had endured when she was Tilly, it seemed in order that she should attain this seamless unification as if it had been intended for her all along and that here on the other side of the earth she had fully achieved the antithesis of her old self.

Everything, then, is for something.

Not for nothing had the fourteen-year-old child trudged twelve miles home in dancing shoes at two in the morning because her imagination had turned a cloddish dairyhand into a golden swain, curtly reminded that she was a freckled-nosed adolescent. But in the gritty awakening to sensibility she had had the courage to reach deeply into her unfolding psyche to find the nascent alter ego and out of her childish wretchedness to awaken it, speak to it into the cottony neck of the doll she had called by her other name, to grieve aloud and to declare herself to be Tanya and safe from all loving and was for eleven days. For eleven days she practiced the art of being herself, that talent that most people take pains to disguise. She was thought maybe to have a touch of the sun because of her alien swagger.

Not for nothing, huddled in a phone booth stinking of bodies, had the still trickable girl heard from his landlady and ex-mistress that the (to her) immaculate Jack Quist had fled like a rat in shameful haste without having the guts to speak to her.

So everything having a culmination, either punishment or reward, here now was hers, as neat and without conflict as the QED of a theorem in geometry.

"About your proposition," she said, forking sardines out of a can, "all right."

They were married hurriedly in Santa Barbara on a Saturday morning by a justice of the peace.

In keeping with the neutrality of their relationship.

She awoke thinking, "This is my wedding day," but washing her face and looking at her calm eyes in the mirror experienced no emotion, which was, after all, appropriate. She picked some little pinks growing by her kitchen door to make into a corsage and then decided any suggestion of the festive would be contrary to the significance of what they were doing. The witnesses were to be Mrs. Vost, Hollis' cleaning woman-laundress, and Mossy Banks.

Hollis was wearing a navy-blue suit. It was the first time Tanya had ever seen him out of his khaki, regrettably it emphasized his scalded-pink complexion. She climbed into the back of the car with Mrs. Vost, who gave her a tanned glove squeeze of the hand. Nothing was said during the twenty-five-minute drive down to Santa Barbara except that once Hollis turned his head and said, "I'm having trouble getting the curtain fabric in the color you wanted." Mossy Banks was waiting for them in a checkerboard suit and white loafers. His face seemed to be at cross purposes with itself in whether to admonish her for her insanity or congratulate her on bringing off a coup. They went upstairs in silence to an anteroom where three other couples were waiting and eventually were ushered into a dirty walled room smelling of sharp detergent. The ceremony, rattled through at breakneck speed, took under four minutes during which a telephone rang constantly in the background. When advised that he might now kiss the bride, Hollis brushed her cheek with dry lips, but she felt his trembling and going downstairs his knees shook and he held on to the stair rail. Outside they stood in the sunshine like tourists emerging from a cathedral and waiting for a guide until Mossy proposed "a bottle of sparkly" and lunch on him, but Hollis shuffled and said he had to get back home, had things to do, Mrs. Vost had to be somewhere to help at somebody's baby shower, "But you stay if you want," Hollis said to Tanya as if to fulfill the autonomy granted her in the contract. "No, I'd rather get home," she said and Mossy, kissing her goodbye said in a breathy undertone, "Anything you need let me know," as if she were going off to boarding school or summer camp and they drove off with her and Mrs. Vost still sitting in the back seat just as if nothing had taken place. Indeed, being dropped off at her own house because of her room at Judas Tree Road not yet being ready, the only evidence that there had been technically a change in her life was the slim gold band on her finger.

Toward evening the telephone rang and Hollis' clerical voice said, like an operator announcing the correct time, "I want to thank you."

"For what?"

"Showing up today. Many would have lost heart."

She laughed. It was no time for poignancy, considering the odd knot they'd tied.

"Come over and have a drink," she said. "There's no need to be standoffish just because we're married."

But her room at Judas Tree, when she did move in a few weeks later, was the fulfillment of anything she might have wished, might have casually said in passing, mentioned something about afternoon light, wallpaper, comfort. He had even added a small standup kitchen and shower; she could be as alone as she needed.

He seemed short of breath, he bustled, pulled open drawers and doors to closets showing her where light switches were, how curtains closed, temperature and air conditioning could be adjusted.

"And your own door," he said, drawing back sliding glass to show a secluded pathway winding down through clusters of hibiscus to the sea.

"It's all very nice," she said, "thank you."

He was blinking at her through the piggy eyes as though he perhaps expected some show of appreciation, even enthusiasm but she was at a loss what to do; knew that if she waxed enthusiastic he would get that look of faint disgust he always got if anyone offered him approval. He nodded without smiling and set about smoothing the bed cover. "This room gets the afternoon sun," he murmured like a hotel manager.

Familiarity, rather than breeding contempt, bred respect between them. Circling in their separate orbits, they acknowledged a temperate zone between them rather than any division. They met in this zone without ambiguity or pressure and with constant consideration. What they might do, he would suggest, would be to drive up to Monterey for a night *if* she would like that. Or she would hear him rush to still Mrs. Vost's vacuum bellowing up because "Mrs. Van Zandt isn't up yet." But if caution was thrown to the winds it could blow spray back in one's face.

She must never on any account touch or move his "people." Once she had sat for a second to lace her tennis shoes beside the kissing couple on the porch swing and he had come bulleting out from the house waving arms at her. "Don't," he bellowed, *"don't* ever. It intrudes on the picture, it upsets the past."

Then she encountered some hard object in the soup, her spoon had drawn out a necklace of lapis lazuli from beneath the camouflage of lentils. His button mouth was twitching from some kind of schoolboyish enjoyment.

He said offhandedly, "They have a hard dark blueness like blue seen at night. It's your color, I think. You have a dark blue hardness about you. I hope you don't lose it."

"Thank you," she said, but whether it was for the stones or for his appreciation of her hardness she scarcely knew, both were lapidary.

Climbing up the sandy path, the beach grass scratching at her bare legs, she heard singing above her. Into the faint sea wind a true and rather sweet voice was singing "Over the Sea to Skye," and as she climbed up and up the squat head and bulbous outline of him dropped into her eye level silhouetted against a blood-red sunset; his back was to her, he sat with his knees drawn up to his chin looking out at the horizon. She stood very still, watching him, halted as one might be entering a chapel and finding a service in progress, knowing she was witness to a moment of immense privacy, his happiness. Ashamed of it, embarrassed by the nakedness of it, she began to edge backward but some perception of intrusion had occurred to him; he stopped singing abruptly and turned his head to see her standing there, and in the oblique pink light the fat face seemed to contract, to narrow with consternation, his body rearing sideways onto one elbow away from her as though she were threatening him. Then all in one movement he rose, he jumped the twenty feet to the beach and running, dived clothes and all into the sea, emerging only as a head, a black dot in the sunset waves. But nothing was said of it. They ate his beautifully-sautéed bay scallops by the usual candlelight. She had on the lapis lazulis.

"There was a pretty sunset," she said cautiously, "did you see it?" He did not look up from his dish but the muscles around his neck appeared to relax.

Out of the blue, "Don't you ever want friends in? I'd go out. Or stay in my room."

She said, conscious of her ghost, "I used to need people. I've worked very hard to get myself out of that———" She had almost said, "out of her." What she hoped to imply without sentiment was that at the rock bottom of their emotionless union, dry as the moon, there was sanctuary and that she, at any rate, had no need of outsiders and distraction. As if to prove it, she convened a motley group from Carpenteria and Montecito, anyone she could think of, to come for drinks, a last minute thing she told them, casual as you care to be. So casual was her implication that only seven took her at her word and sat around in the forced atmosphere of chitchat and lukewarm canapes. But she had lost the gift of spontaneity and Hollis' silence in handing around the frozen daiquiris appeared to metamorphose into a skeleton at the banquet (the figure of the drunken maid was overemphasized as being delightful and cute) and within an hour or so the preposterousness of the socializing was more than anyone could bear, and the party ground to dust. After everyone had left as one, Hollis and she sat on the back terrace with newly-made drinks and relished the solitude of themselves, said nothing, heard the sea. Then the telephone call came, the one that might have been expected. And she knew by the constriction of his voice, as though a small feather had caught in his throat, knew instantly who was calling; heard him say, "I am married," and repeat it, "I am married," after which in the silence that ensued there was some certainty of laughter coming over the wire, the certainty of someone enjoying throatily a good joke. Heard him say, "Her name is Tanya," and that, having induced some sharp retort he said, "Come and see for yourself," and then stood holding the receiver while faint cluckings went on and he said nothing until the voice spoke up loud enough to be heard. ARE YOU THERE? it said, and at that he hung up. He looked a long time out the window to where the blue eucalyptus tree was chittering its glassy leaves in a stiff wind.

"She," he said.

Tanya said nothing. All he had ever said when she brought up the question was, "She is away, she is abroad somewhere, as usual."

Now he sat down, folding his stubby legs under him as if some weight had metaphysically been put on him.

"She'll come, she's curious. You'll see."

The following week while he was attending to shrubs around the pool garden the telephone rang and after Tanya had said hello, the female voice said, "Mrs. Van Zandt."

"This is Mrs. Van Zandt," Tanya said, and there was a stillness from the other end and then the voice said, perhaps pityingly, "No, *this* is Mrs. Van Zandt."

Curiously, the voice was sweet, it held all the elements of good intention, which put Tanya instantly on her guard.

"Wait," she said, "I'll call him."

No need, the voice said. Only needed to know if it would be convenient if she stopped by in the afternoon a week from Wednesday (as if to give them ample time to anticipate or dread her coming). Tanya said that she supposed it would.

"I'm most anxious to meet you," Nancy Van Zandt said.

Hollis said, "She'll try to win you over. Watch out."

But on the morning of the day he turned to and baked an angel cake light as air.

When the big cream-colored Cadillac turned into the cul de sac he said, "Here comes Nancy, like the Assyrian."

The tall chauffeur was handing someone out, and for the moment they could see only the touch of silk gleaming in the sharp winter sun. Then, as he held open the gate and touched his cap, they saw the slight girl come into the garden and turn and touch the chauffeur on the arm and engage him in some conversation that seemed to involve the house, pointed here and there, turning to and from the chauffeur, who appeared to be laughing at what she said. Even from a distance there was a suggestion of intimacy between the two; it would not have been startling to see the chauffeur make some intimate gesture, perhaps tap her playfully on the rump. Instead, he saluted and got back into the driver's seat as she came forward down the sun-speckled steps between the cactus plants and the birds of paradise with a young girl's step and stance. Nancy Van Zandt appeared to be eighteen until you came face to face with the facts of her spider-webbed face of lines and the gray hair mixed in with the persuaded gold.

"Lovely," she said, bowing slightly at the waist in a mime of obeisance. But whether she meant Tanya or the occasion was not precise.
Mackerel thin under her greenish silks, she was unexpectedly small and vulnerable. Stepping over the doormat into the hall, she put out one thin arm toward her son, not looking directly at him but at the space above his forehead so that her bright smile had a vacuous air to it, slightly lunatic. Hollis said nothing in greeting but merely padded ahead toward the door to the patio while she followed with neat steps in his wake, her walk suggesting compliance indicated a *laissez faire*. "Are we to sit *outside*?" she exclaimed with a congratulatory bridling as though the idea were novel and

delightful. "Lovely," she said as he presented her to the hugely-backed cane chair under the bougainvillea (such a chair was gratifying to the ego and she accepted its prestige, crossed her neat legs, she might have been a movie star receiving the press). "Then I must have my pill at the ready," she said taking an enamel pillbox from her crocodile bag, "and so will you get me a glass of water to have also at the ready." She beamed toward Tanya who was still taking in the unexpectedness of her. "Allergic," she explained, *violently*. To stings. Bees, wasps, hornets. This little pill will guarantee me forty minutes of life in which to be rushed to an emergency room for the antitoxin, otherwise I would be dead in seconds. My weak heart is a collaborator with the insects."

She smiled at the idea.

She herself was a collaborator of sorts, Tanya thought. Had come to terms with enemies to save her skin, which was, in her late fifties, still nacreous. Nancy Van Zandt could be compared to a summer day. She illumined the immediate space about her; she transcended. She blazed with an inner imperturbability.

"How beautiful the sea is from here. In Montecito I'm only half aware of it."

Beauty was the catchword with her. Color and form illustrated her sentences. Her slender hands performed parabolas of delight. This had been lovely, that perfection. She lived for grace and sublimity. She gorged on words like lustrous, polish, gloss, bloom, as if they were fruits. This was luscious, that translucent. Something caught the exact butter color of the wheat stacks she had seen in a field in France. Never in her life had she seen the likes of the handsome Andalusian men with their lovely dark Spanish looks, their silky hair. All the time her lump of a son was bringing thin sandwiches, cake, and muscatel grapes to the table he had set out with the white bone china, saying nothing.

"But now the Taj Mahal," Nancy said, as if someone were pestering her to know, "is too symmetrical, it's unsurprising, like a stunning empty-headed woman."

She ran on as if to fill the awkwardness with some texture of delight. On she raced to Jaipur to the Amber Palace, the Palace of the Winds "the *gentlest* pink," to the gold and scarlet of Knossos on Crete.

Her Mexican silver bracelets rang.

Who was she like?

The likeness of Nancy to someone, no matter how faint, caused a modest disquiet in Tanya. She sat with folded hands while Nancy reconsidered rainbows, butterflies, flamingos. The disquieting thing was the significance underneath the superficial. The fact that under the floss Nancy was scarcely complacent. The fact that under her luster she was naked and hard bone, vulnerable. It was her vulnerability and her struggle to conceal it that caused disquiet.

As they sat down to the white iron table in their wrought iron chairs of wreathed acanthus leaves, Nancy said, "The grapes are the color of storms you see in the Aegean."

Hollis said, pouring, "And have you noticed that China tea is the color of *piss*?"

Accepting the cup Nancy smiled at it and said,

"How you love to cast rocks at people. You always have." She said to Tanya, "He likes to vandalize the impressions I'm trying to make."

"Oh balls."

Nancy addressed herself to a cucumber sandwich. "And yet everything he makes is delicate, like this. How did you meet?"

Before Tanya could answer Hollis said, "It's neither here nor there."

"Nor am I interested," Nancy said. "Except, she surprised me. I half expected some brass chippy from La Brea."

Nancy half looked at Hollis, her eyelid quivered. "Well, you're to be congratulated, under the circumstances."

There was a kind of brutal courtesy in the way she said "circumstances" in order to cover up the venal facts of this marriage of blatant convenience.

Hollis said, "At any rate we have a complete understanding.

"I would think you would have to," Nancy said dryly.

"Assuming?"

"Not assuming. Considering your disadvantages, dearest."

Nancy held out her cup to be refilled. There was bitter vetch in the word "dearest." Hollis refilled the cup and handed it to her saying, "And who is currently in residence at Montecito?"

"Nobody."

"Oh, really? Really? What happened to the Roumanian?"

"Yugoslav."

"*Was* he?"

"Tchenko. He died while we were in Spain last year, over a year ago. In Malaga."

"Oh, that must have been——you didn't mention it in your two cards."

"It was, as *you* say, neither here nor there. Did you make this cake, dear? It's excellent, it is truly angelic. You amaze me."

"Yes," he said, tapping his teaspoon against his cup and watching her, Tanya thought, too fiercely. There was a look of conscious devilment in the way he was watching his mother eat, as if the cake were poisoned.

He said, "Isn't this a new chauffeur since the last time you were here?"

"Yes."

"How long have you *had* him?" The inference was unmistakable. Nancy took the last tiny forkful of cake and put down her plate, wiped the corners of her mouth with the napkin using her little finger, swallowed and said, "Oh about two months. He's a very good mechanic, which saves mightily, and among other advantages he has the most beautiful back of the neck. Which, after all is what you look at most."

She smiled vaguely in Hollis' direction.

Hollis said, "Oh I'm glad. You don't know how glad I am. When I think of you with a chauffeur with no back of the neck I feel I am being suffocated in the Admiral Jellicoe Pavilion."

Again a tic flickered through Nancy's eyelid.

"And is he beautifully Vee-shaped? You once said that a chauffeur in uniform should be broad shouldered and narrow hipped so the back of him formed a perfect Vee."

Nancy stared down at her hands, passed one hand over the other as if she were searching in their smooth whiteness for the beginnings of maculation.

Eventually she spoke. "One time driving back from Baalbek to Beirut I had a French driver, Christian that is, Catholic I suppose, and suddenly on the deserted road a woman dressed all in black ran out from a grove of cedar trees, waving for us to stop, waving frantically——something terrible must have happened, some dreadful thing. And I waited for my driver to slow down but instead he began to accelerate and made straight for her to run her down. He aimed the car *at* her and as she leaped back just in time I saw the white horror in her face and my driver laughed and said, '*Arab.*' "

So *she* was in rags her face said, she knelt in the dust waving beseechingly to the car, the car driven by her son came roaring down on her.

She shook her head, shook it away, she rose and said, "I have to be in San Luis Obispo for cocktails."

Hollis remained seated, so Tanya rose, but Nancy put up an admonishing hand and said, "I don't like being seen off. It merely emphasizes the temporary."

So she would go out on a note of affection. But in the doorway she turned and said like someone with the winning hand in poker, with the victor's smile of triumph, "The chauffeur's name is Flyte."

She cared. That was the astonishment. Nancy Van Zandt cared about her porker son. Nancy's face lingered on in Tanya's mind like the penumbra of some glittering object photographed on the retina;

the flash of the wounded eyes quickly annulled, the wry smile at his expected sarcasm. She saw again Nancy staring down at her hands, then passing one hand over the other while she told the story of the Arab woman. She was hurt or disappointed or both. Perhaps she had been foolishly hoping for a hatchet to be buried. Perhaps she had knowingly prohibited it with all her talk of beauty in front of him, her ravings on about birdswings, skies and dragon flies had been too manufactured to be tactless. Thus they fought and wounded each other, deliberately alienating, accusing, pressing the blame onto each other as in a children's game when an object, a fan, a glove, a silver letter opener is hastily passed on so as not to be in the hand when the music stops. So they pressed the blame onto each other hastily and withdrew behind each other's barricades of withering contempt in a parody of courtesy.

But Nancy cared. She may even in her private tower have wept over him or over the loss of him. Then who was right or wrong? Who was to blame? Was it even possible that his cherished "Scenes from Childhood" stories had no real basis in fact apart from his deeply inbred horror of himself? And had Nancy (with the face as pure as a Fra Angelico madonna) ever run with her fatling runt to her breast along a lonely beach with an eye to abandoning it to the tide?

Layers of prevarication and dissembling covered the portraits Holis and Nancy had of each other like old paint, peeling here and there in minute spots to show potential they had wanted covered up. They were now so practiced at their mutual deceit that any possibility of truth or plausibility had long ago been lost under the varnish. They were pledged to one another's bitter suspicions.

But supposing someone who was neutral could peel away such layers, could they bear to be exposed to each other?

And Nancy had left behind her little enamel pillbox. Tanya turned it over and over in her hand. Forty minutes of life.

Presumably Flyte, the chauffeur with the beautiful back of the neck, would be sent to fetch it.

But what if?

"———as I'm going into Santa Barbara and as she is only a spit away, I'll return it."

He bared his little feline teeth and snorted, "I thought the cunt would win you over."

"Please yourself with what you want to think."

"Oh, *females,*" he said witheringly, "the nether world."

"Think anything you like. Just give me the address."

Montecito was so bathed in calm and security under green palms and vivid flowerings that it could have been almost possible to believe that no hand had ever been raised against another in anger since the birth of the planet, Nancy's garden was so beautifully and meticulously planned that it gave off no surprises, it permeated a sunny joylessness. Behind striped awnings, windows gazed out warily.

Flyte opened the door in shirtsleeves and wearing an apron. In his hand was a chamois cloth.

Nowadays good-looking men disconcerted her as though, married to a gargoyle, she might be thought promiscuous by intent. She averted her head and said that it was Mrs. Van Zandt to see Mrs. Van Zandt. Nancy was sitting in a band of sunlight on a green settee, a scroll of petit-point beside her and she was shuffling yarns, pink, forgetmenot blue, maize.

"How kind."

Tanya put the pillbox on the rosewood sewing table.

"Tea or something?"

Tanya sat and, taking off her sunglasses, stared Nancy in the face, threw the grenade.

"I want to know something and I need to know the truth. Do you have any feeling for him?"

Nancy stroked the yarns, running them through her fingers.

"For *him*, you mean."

"For him."

To her credit she didn't prevaricate, she looked Tanya back fully with her brown eyes.

"You've seen the way we are, the way he acts toward me. Could you blame me if I said no?"

"Understand, I am not taking sides."

"Then why do you want to know?"

"I want to know if he is justified."

Nancy leaned back against her green pillows and gave a small laugh, it had all the tincture of malice.

"You must have had the full brunt of his propaganda hurled at you I expect. I expect you've been exposed to his brutal assessment of me as villainess, ogress, unnatural mother. I guess you've been vaccinated with his fantasies that I hid him away in an attic all of his early childhood, refused him a normal life with other children, abandoned him to drunken nursemaids, all fantasy. You've seen his dolls. Have you noticed the wasp on my shoulder about to sting? What could be possibly made clearer? He would like to murder me. Has he told you I planned to abandon him on a beach to be washed away in the tide? Rescued by kind strangers in the nick of time. Where? On Lake Michigan we suppose there are such underpopulated beaches, only we were never on one. But he prefers the supposition of the sea. My dear, has it occurred to you that the clue to his wild phantasmagoria is in the figure of the schoolboy gazing up over his dinner table with such exquisite pathos and anticipating his next misery, is the quintessence of masochistic enjoyment and that the boy, the child, is *beautiful*? When he first unveiled it to me—naturally I was invited to see it—I had to dig my nails into the palm of my hand not to cry out at the pity I felt for him, for the awful revelation of his agony."

"Why didn't you? Cry out. It might have led to something," Tanya said.

Nancy took a silver thimble and slipped it on her index finger. She said after a pause, "About the ugliness—about *him*, we never refer to it in the slightest, it is the only way we can cope with it. You said you wanted the truth. This is the exact truth about *me*. When they first brought him to me in the hospital—this bristling, scarlet hedgehog *thing* I said, because it burst out of me, 'Are you sure this is the right one?' But they said, babies tend to be ugly in the first few days, wait a few weeks, months, years, there are theories about throw-backs and inheritance and so on. What use are theories? I had a little hog for a child. So we never referred to it any more than we would have if he had been born with six fingers on one hand or no ears. We were both helpless, we *are* both helpless just as I am helpless against his hatred of me." She shrugged her thin shoulders. "I have learned to deal with it as best I can, I have learned not to care anymore."

So she had suffered, naturally. And bravely. She shrugged off her suffering like the good soldier, just as she was shrugging off Hollis now, tapping her thimble on the table as if this were all she intended to say about it forever. I had a hog for a child. She had wrongly been made the villain in a situation determined by chromosomes and genes. A minuscule addition or subtraction to the constitution of a foetus and she may have given birth to Apollo. It was no one's fault. But in her plea for impartiality there was a flaw. Nancy, freed from responsibility, guilt (she put on her glasses and her enlarged solemn eyes gazed at Tanya with the burning intention of an honesty that was disquieting), and while claiming no leniency, desiring only that the bare facts be known, withholding nothing, not even her repugnance, she was too good to be true.

And Tanya *had seen that look before,* the look of self-convinced honesty that was as vain as graffiti. It was exactly the way Tilly had often looked.

Nancy, secure in the myth of golden silence, admitting nothing, excusing her silence by helplessness and abandoning him ("We never referred to it") to years of silence, years of making not the slightest sign to him when she could have let him see her grief as a companion to his loneliness, should have cradled the shapeless body to hers, should have buried the little pig head in her breast. Years when she stood prosaically by him talking in polite metaphors when she could have knelt and kissed. Whether she was, probably, innocent of the accusations he had made scenes out of was immaterial. She had abandoned him just as surely as if she had left him on a deserted beach. She had expunged him, she was the monster, not he.

The word, unbidden rose up in her throat.

"Monster," Tanya said softly.

"Who?"

"You."

As the thimble fell off Nancy's finger and rolled across the floor, Nancy bent, knelt to retrieve it. When she got back to her feet, panting slightly, she had grown suddenly chalky, she staggered back onto her sofa as though the word had penetrated her like a bullet.

"How dare———" she began, she was already affecting a dull routine outrage.

"Monster," Tanya said again, quietly, "you are the ugly one not him. You with your immunity."

"You——even though you're his wife which is the most despicable thing of all."

Nancy began to laugh hoarsely, choking on her laughter as if something had caught in her throat. She coughed, changing from chalk to scarlet, she waved arms across her face, as though waving away the spectral image of herself that had been raised, the mother withholding the love for the child.

When just a gesture, a touch might have averted this thirty-year war.

Too late.

Now she was merely irrelevant.

Nancy said, recovering, "How can *you* allot blame? You are an intruder. How do you know where we stand, Hollis and I? In spite of appearances. I think this is the supreme travesty, being accused like this by such a blatant opportunist as you, milking him for all you can get. What makes you so sacrosanct that you can stand in judgment of me?"

Tanya said, "The difference is that I perform a function for him and you provide nothing, not even pity."

She turned and went swiftly out.

Hollis was making himself lunch, asked would she care for cold curried chicken, asked nothing more. Hunched over his lunch he gobbled his food with the usual furious haste as though it were going to be snatched away, then leaning back lit a cheroot and regarded her with what seemed to be cautionary aloofness as if to discourage her from reporting anything that might have passed between her and his mother.

Just after ten that night the telephone rang. It was Flyte, the chauffeur-houseman, to report, respectfully, that Mrs. Van Zandt had died forty-five minutes earlier of a heart attack while playing bridge; she had dropped her cards to the floor and fallen face downward on the bridge table, it had been instantaneous. Resuscitation had been attempted to no avail.

Hollis kept saying, "I see. I see. I see." "She is dead," he said to Tanya.

Stung.

Not even forty minutes of life, granted her, fell among the cards. There was nothing to be done, sir, Flyte assured him. Doctor Besin had come immediately and was now gone. There was no reason for Hollis to drive down, naturally he would be let known the "arrangements." Were there any special requests? Would he care to———

"No," he said and hung up.

Tanya sat still during all this and said nothing, unable and unwilling to speculate what turn of the tide this sudden immaculate release would have on him; she was mindful of the fact that long-term prisoners were often loath to leave their cells, were filled with unbearable alarm on the day of their release.

He crossed the living room without a glance at her and went out onto the dark patio. She heard the faint creak, creak of the glider as he rocked in the dark.

Roused from sleep (her bedside light snapped on in her face), she turned in bed to see his wild face bent over her.

"What happened over there?" his voice was raspy, harsh.

"What?" She was numb with sleep.

He had gone slightly mad, he ripped the sheet off her.

"Get up," he snapped, "come on, get up."

He was holding out her robe. It was the first time he had ever been in her bedroom, it was as startling as rape. Dazedly, she got into her robe and slippers, glanced at her bedside Westclox, it was twenty minutes of two.

He was sitting on a kitchen stool, there was a bottle of three star brandy on the Formica shelf and a glass in which the ice had turned almost to water. Under the baleful pinkish fluorescent light he looked his ultimate swinish, the snouty nose seemed to have swollen, the eyes like raisins, two little pustules had opened on his upper lip.

"Sit down and tell me what happened."

She climbed on a stool.

"When, where?"

"Yesterday in Montecito. *Something* must have happened."

So he suspected she was the stinging wasp.

She sat with folded hands and calmly recounted what had transpired between her and Nancy. She was ice cool about it. Had she been detailing a guillotining she would have been as unemotional. If this were the supreme test of her strength and imperturbability she had graduated. He listened, apparently without censure. Yes, he said, and then? And what did *she* say? I see.

And then the brandy glass flew across the room to shatter on the tiles.

The wail that came from him was, terribly, the hog tied by the feet, being held to the knife, was ear-splitting and went on relentlessly while his body rocked to and fro on the stool. Through the stubby fingers hiding his face, she was astonished to see little spits of water.

Some words, noises really, accompanied the screaming like a lament in an ancient language.

And here she was, in her calm, in her hard way,

icily watching him in his agony and impotent to put out a hand, to touch him or even to say, "Don't, don't."

Instead, she got up and reaching into a shelf took down another brandy glass and set it beside him. She was as unable to touch him as Nancy had been. Imagine.

"But how could you," he got out at last, "accuse her of being a monster without knowing anything about the relationship we had had?"

He might have been paraphrasing his mother.

"Oh God, oh God," he moaned, "I need her rage. Don't you see, I need her merciless *out*rage, it's been my rescue ever since I was old enough to notice how I look to people. What good would pity have been to me? Sweet words, comforting? She knew that. It was hopeless and it would always be. She taught me never to expect anything, most of all from her and except——except for one lapse I never have. I have never expected or hoped for anything. Yes, yes, yes she behaved like a bitch to me and I resented and despised her for it right down into my bowels. I despised her for it, for all the turning away, the abandonment and for her horrible shame of me and I believed, you see, I really believed she would have been thankful for me to have drowned or dropped dead at her feet. But it sustained me later against any fantasy I might have had about——"

He scratched at his skull and the word when it came was like a bubble of spit, spat

"love."

In the long silence that followed there was nothing to be heard in the kitchen but the white whirr of the electric clock, even the sea was mute.

He said eventually, "We communed in a sense of mutual outrage against each other which, when seen in certain lights, is companionship."

So there had been this dark bridge between their gulfs over which they had crossed to each other and talked in sign language. And he was right, Tanya was admitting, she had wrongfully dealt with a misinterpretation of it.

"I'm sorry," she said.

"Not for me, I hope."

"No. You'll recover."

He wheeled around to glare at her, his eyes were stone black under the fluorescent whiteness.

"Make no bones about it," he said, "make *no bones about it.*" There was intense finality in the way he said it, it might have been an oath sworn on the tablet of something hallowed that it would never be talked of again in his or her life and as if he were performing an elegiac rite over his mother that was both sacred and profane.

When she awoke in the morning, halfway guilty for having slept soundly until after eleven, the house was as appropriately silent as might have been expected of the residence of someone who has lost a close relative.

She dressed and made coffee, cut up an orange. The door to his bedroom was open, the bed had either been made or not slept in. There was no sign of him by the pool or on the beach. Tanya took her coffee into the windy sunshine and passing by the window of the den and glancing in, drew her breath in sharply, put down her cup and went quickly back indoors.

He was stretched on the floor at the feet of the smiling "woman" who endlessly read the *Los Angeles Times* unaware of the wasp that had alighted on her shoulder. Close by were the almost-empty brandy bottle and an empty phial that had contained seconal. He was quite cold. He had become one of his "people," make no bones about it. But so flawless was the manikin of the mother doll, endlessly reading, endlessly smiling that it was impossible, looking at them together, to tell which one had been real.

1978

"But *I* am Tanya," she said aloud to the amethyst mirror (in Sydney late in 1976) taking a comb from her makeup box and running it through her now crisp short-cut blondish-gray hair. As if to assure herself before she took another step in a strange country, in Tilly's country, of her own immaculate self.

Because the feeling of danger was everpresent and something to which she was not accustomed, outrageous, possibly jet lag but nevertheless must be contained, vanquished. This outrageous feeling in the heart ever since she had walked out of the Sydney airport following the old man with the humped back wheeling her baggage (luggage here?) into the extraordinary sharpness of the sunlight and the clarity of Australian morning, the vibrant air tipped with the pepperyness of eucalyptus and the violent, really violent feeling of recognition.

"Your first visit?" the cab driver asked her into his rear mirror.

"Yes," she had said, uncertainly, ridiculous because it was her first visit, for *her*.

If she had ever paused to reflect on her life (which she didn't, she was carried forward in it as if on a train by some diesel force) it would have been in flashes (the lighted train window picking out a white post, an open doorway in the night, a haystack) of disconnected events strung together like the colored slides of a trip she had taken. On. Off.

On. Sometimes with people she scarcely remembers, they have left so little impression on her. Most times alone (then who took the photograph, who is now not recallable?). She stands in white before the Leaning Tower, she stands severely apart from a group of grinning tourists beside a bus in Cadiz. She seems bewildered in Peru. She half leans against a Volkswagen with Matthew Dodd, who is grinning, and although they are posed far enough apart to suggest restraint or reluctance, they were in fact cautiously betrothed for two months. Most often in these flashes she is found to be alone, sitting at tables on alien terraces with her carafe of wine and unread book. She is seldom smiling, she appears to be in a state of becalmed content. Her clothes are scrupulous, her grooming precise, she has gone to pains to be meticulously ready for a situation that will not arise, to greet her rescuer who will not arrive.

However she has never paused long to scrutinize these pictures of her life, she has merely proceeded, moved onward without looking back.

So she has passed on into the regions of forty and on.

She supposed this acquisition of content and reason riled people committed to turmoil, Mossy saying, "Why d'you go on living here with those stuffed dolls? You could have one of the new condominiums with adjustable temperature control."

Indeed Mr. Wilkerson, one of the lawyers who handled the trust for her, said, "Aren't you ever going to *spend* some of this?"

And finally Matthew Dodd, who was six years

younger than she, which could provide them with a convenient excuse for breaking the engagement, baffled at her constant aversion to fraternize, her dark humorless moods which served to ostracize him, said, "The trouble with you is you like to think you're an interesting enigma when you're merely a blank."

This troubled her. Was she a blank? Or was it that people conditioned and educated to expect a degree of fraudulence in everyone could not adjust to her totalitarianism? Hollis had understood it, welcomed it ("you don't have any pity for me, do you? Not a shred."), but then Hollis' need was for neutrality, which she had given to him dispassionately for the whole of their short marriage and never with condescension; she never stooped to betray him with any belittling emotion, she was incapable of it, even at the brief funeral service attended by Mrs. Vost, the housekeeper, Miguel, the sometimes-gardener, and two of the Mendlesohns, brothers from the local garage, she had paid her last respects to him with a passivity he would have approved of; as the ornamental gates closed on the receding casket she turned and walked out of the chapel with a coolness that might have seemed affronting had it not merely served to justify everyone's assumption that she was a compassionless mercenary who had only married the pig for his fortune.

She attended to his specifications. She shook his ashes from the asbestos box delivered to her into the incoming tide one evening, the tiny glistening gravel of his bones was nacreous. She recalled something from her school Shakespeare. "Rest now, perturbed spirit," she told him.

That she became a curiosity, somewhat of a local legend living alone among the thickening weeds and rampant vines of his unkempt garden and with the manikins representing the stages of his various crucifixions, it didn't trouble her. Let people think what they want or need to.

But to be told you are a blank posed certain dark and troubling questions.

Said hastily in a rage over nothing more than her cool neutrality and disinclination to fight back, it had been the parting shot between her and Matthew and somehow it had struck her as being the only pertinent thing he had ever said to her; it was as unsettling as being told an accidental truth by a mountebank gypsy fortune teller.

If it were true then the whole perception of herself, the calm in which she moved, her pride in her content and *con*tent was all a swindle; she wasn't content, she was anesthetized, she wasn't fulfilled, she was emotionally amphetamined.

If so, what had she lost?

In alienating herself from her natural warm loving self into cynical wariness, what had she lost?

Preoccupied with such conundrums she drifted, putting things off, delaying, she procrastinated through the intoxication of a flawless spring. She bought plants for the rock garden and left them to rot in their little sacks. Calling the company that repaired her canvas porch blinds, she was unable to set a date with them. She was bewitched into immovability. She sat for hours at a time without moving as if she were listening to the sound of her own emptiness. When Mrs. Vost made disapproving faces about the unremoved garbage Tanya said, "I know. I have got to get myself together," and went into a fit of laughter at the significance of it, which would have been lost on Mrs. Vost sweeping bread crusts off the carving board.

For that is what had been formulating over the past weeks while she sat in such silence under the bougainvillea. She had been pursuing and at the same time fleeing from furies; she had been contemplating the regaining of what she had lost of herself, the compassionate side of her, the foolish defenseless heart.

Because if such dynamic metaphysical forces could have once been harnessed to release her from it, perhaps they could be reversed and, like a film running backwards, the bus would rise up out of the boiling sandcolored waters, and the bridge would appear from beneath the foaming river, reform itself, the bus rising dripping to raise itself back onto it, edging backward up the steep incline toward the candy and magazine shop in Temple, Pennsylvania, in the curtains of rain, stopping, its folding doors unfolding, and then stepping out of it backward, now stepping backward toward the shop, her back turned to where Tanya was watching, establishing herself, *back* to her would come

Tilly.

Tanya pointed her sandal toward a salamander, which flicked away green and gold. She felt the reconfrontation with Tilly viscerally, as if Tilly had come through the garden gate and was standing looking at her and laughing. In recent years when she thought of Tilly at all it was as remote as looking at an old snapshot of herself. At no time did she think of Tilly has having been part of herself, her body. These were not Tilly's feet, breasts, eyelashes. Compared to the mincing schoolgirl handwriting in the diary, *her* handwriting was dashing and monarchical. So surely the metamorphosis had been immaculate that day in Temple when at last she had been able to yield to the inevitable, out of Tilly's body into her own.

But what had she lost in the process? What genetic chromosome had she excremented that had made her barren? Blank, Matthew Dodd said, cuttingly, as if he could see right through her to where there was no soul. Like the evangelical belief that the body weighed ounces less after the soul had departed it. She felt that something had gone out of her approximately the weight of her soul.

But then what if she could reawaken the part of her she had repudiated? Couldn't the psyche contain many persons (she had done tentative research and read of a man who was at various times and in different places eighteen distinct people) who might remain static and unheard from for years, subdued by the stronger self? Mightn't there be vestiges of Tilly? There were moments when a strange sympathy took hold of her, when an alien sweetness caused her to turn and smile at a child in the supermarket, want to make a caressing motion toward it. The fact remained that as long as her heart still beat and pulsed through her body, the membrane of her former self remained.

"Tilly," Tanya said, aloud, declaratively. "Tilly," she called. But there was only wind and sunshine, hollyhocks nodding. It was as absurd as calling to the dead in a cemetery.

Then one afternoon, slicing onions, it came over her as strongly as the bitter stinging in the eyes. Go.

Go.

Not back, because in essence she had only been there in the guise of someone else's spirit.

But in Sydney there were memories and people and like traces of winter snow caught in the clefts of rocks long after spring, there must be remains of Tilly, forgotten reminiscenses that might begin to reattest to the truth of her, mistakes and stupidities aside, that might reveal what Tanya in exorcising her had lost.

If she had the nerve to exhume.

And she had.

By God, nobody could say she was a flincher; it was as though part of the bargain she made with herself that day in Temple, Pennsylvania, had been that she would never be afraid again, never care, never pity. Made to herself at the moment the bus went over the edge and her gentle defenseless heart went with it.

Go.

Picked up the phone and called Mr. Wilkerson the lawyer, instructing him to put up the house for sale, the furniture, cars, crockery, silver. Not a tea-spoon to be kept.

And all accomplished with Mr. Wilkerson's born efficiency and with such speed that only thirty-two days later she was on the night flight to Sydney.

The sole obstruction had been the disposal of Hollis' "people." Donated finally to a fairground in Long Beach, the dolls were carted away. The last thing she saw was the yearning, grieving face of the young schoolboy. Tossed into the truck, he had fallen against the mother doll, which having been deprived of its *Los Angeles Times* was holding out empty polyethylene arms and smiling, smiling at him at last.

So she flew through a long night, missing a whole day to find the ghost of Tilly Beamis.

But Tilly was not in Lavender Bay, Beauty Point, Parsley Bay, Clifton Gardens, nor Crows Nest. The environs of Sydney, if not all beautiful, attained a comeliness in their names, and in the streets and suburbs the city attested to its cynical beginnings both historic and aboriginal: Bligh, Castlereagh, Macquarie, Parramatta, Turramurra, Banksia. With the elemental and Anglican: Rose Bay, Paddington.

Nor was Tilly half expected to be run into in Loftus Street or turning up in Queens Square, where she would have been surprised to note that the little fat lady holding the orb had been downgraded from the center to the side in order to reroute traffic.

She would have been astounded to find that the conservative Hotel Australia had disappeared into the squat concrete blunderbuss of a skyscraper; nettled to be unable to find Her Majesty's Arcade in a labyrinth of blazing neon squawking rocknroll shops and pizza parlors. She could have been intimidated, looking up at walls of steel and glass, at revolving restaurants in the sky, entranced (her upturned face wide, always young with wonder) at the fluidity of the great silver wings the Opera House spread like an albatross on the waters.

The eerie thing was that Tanya, boarding a Cremorne ferry for no specific reason, recognized all this addition and subtraction subliminally. It was as though never having seen it before in her present incarnation she could yet say with conviction, Ah yes, the old Trocadero stood here, the old Penfold's Wine sign lit up there. It was comforting and disconcerting at the same time to have to ask directions as a stranger and then to turn a corner and know with chilling certainty that it had once sported a fat red postbox with its times of clearance stenciled on it in neat gold. It was creepy to recognize instantly the wet sound of the sodden swollen rope flung down on the ferry deck as the boat pushed away from the wharf, the rattle of the thin little gangplank being upended onto the pier, the gushing and throttling noises of water and engines.

The Australian twang, the long drawn-out assaulted vowels struck a chord in her as reminiscent as the cadence of a language learned in infancy and forgotten. (Asking of the lady changemaker, with her clicketty-click change machine fastened around her waist, in her brass-buttoned uniform and cap, where might she find the Watson's Bay bus, she was given a "wait a sec" gesture while the Bus Lady spat seeds into a hand and said, "Sorry luv, I had a gripe in me mowth.")

Assimilation. Morton Bay Fig trees, lantana bush, cannas, Shasta daisies. The cool sweet wind that blew up from the south at twilight, Kinkara tea,

Airoplane Jelly, KB Lager, the reek of beer from the early morning opening bars filtering into the streets, the houses of Paddington joined together in everlasting terraces of brick and ornamental iron balconies, Australian automobiles shorter and stubbier than American. Sardines on toast and crumpets were on the typewritten menu she was handed in a tea room crowded with suburban matrons knee-to-knee talking in high dainty voices. Crumpets sounded a bell. But they were "off in summer," the waitress said as if one ought to know. Possibly they were some kind of shellfish. Behind her an ultra-refined voice was saying that "Neil and Marge went all over It'ly, they had a gorgeous time *she* said but thank the Lord to be back in Warrabee to see the grandkiddies." It was all dramaturgical, Tanya thought. The tearoom with the dark oak booths and fake brass carriage lanterns and the ladies hired for the scene, extras. Later trucks would haul it all away. She could not make contact with Sydney and she had no real perspective on which to draw conclusions, no tangible way to make comparisons of past and present. She might have felt less disassociated in Istanbul, which might have had a sense of reality with a Blue Mosque that didn't exist in an empty Anthony Horderns store. Because they were mentioned in the diary, she visited the Botanic Gardens and Manly Beach but there were no vestiges of Tilly among the anonymous people eating lunch out of paper bags on benches or the sunburnt children screaming on the Esplanade where twenty-two or -three years ago Tilly had been fool enough to speak to Jack Quist about love.

So what had Tanya expected out of this twelve-thousand mile trek? Reconciliation with phantoms? Tilly wasn't here.

Nor was she to be found with the Gardens family in their decrepit house, they having come to nothing as predicted. Nor was there any semblance of her in Jean Magnus' blindingly white apartment nor with Jack Quist in the stifling manse up in Bullagulla. The past was accounted for and Tanya was resented for confronting them with it like an old unpaid bill, this American stranger with the disconcerting familiarity, the confusing likeness to and yet total dissimilarity to Tilly.

It deepened her feeling of isolation and the conviction that the loving and freewheeling spirit she was hoping to evoke was deliberately avoiding her and that darting in and out of shadows, laughing at her solemn discomfort, the thing itself was saying, perhaps, "Well you wanted me dead, didn't you?"

So the trip had been a failure and she didn't even feel the failure of it.

But on the last afternoon, gusty with April wind, she took the bus to the farthest reaches of Sydney Harbor, to Watson's Bay.

"Up that way," the bus driver said, pointing and giving her perhaps a sharp look for asking for the Gap.

She walked up a path to where a protecting fence had been put around a curving shelf of rock where two hundred feet or so below the ink blue ocean boiled and heaved over the jagged rocks. The Gap Desperation Point

Only a mention of it in the journal. "Oh well,

there's always the Gap," Tilly wrote and appended three exclamation points.

Inconceivable.

But had it been a turning point? Had she in a moment of despairing aberration come here one twilight, come in those days on the old tram, got off and walked up the path and stood at this fence?

Looked down at the sizzling white water curling and uncurling over the fearsome seaweeded boulders, felt the sticky spray in her face, nourished by the graveness of intention? Could she have taken off her shoes, put a note under a stone, climbed the fence to stand on the edge?

Not Tilly, inconceivable.

But could she have come to this brink to dare herself not to deny her strength? Could she have felt then in that moment, in the gray twilight of her moment of truth, that there was something, some reason to continue.

Was it me? Tanya asked the air, the sea.

Yes, it was me.

"Good evening, Mrs. Van Zandt," said the doorman at Beekman Place. Or, Good afternoon, morning, whatever time. Or, "Colder out." Or, "There's a package for you."

Going up or down in the elevator there were usually more women than men. Women dressed in expensive clothes and in the winter, furs, and with chunks of gold on their speckled hands. They stood facing the elevator doors and saying nothing to each other, their eyes fixed on the ascending or descending buttons of light numbering the floors as if to read directions from the north star on a dark night on their troubled seas.

After the Australian fiasco she had turned a page, moved East. But not for any specific reason other than restlessness, no more than the insomniac who turns over and over in bed hoping that the change to right or left side will occasion sleep. And the conviction that her light in California had burned itself out, the scarlet Century plant would not bloom again for ninety-nine years.

Getting the apartment on her second day in New York suggested auguries of concurrence by the fates, or Norns, or whatever was being written on the wind.

The agent said how fortunate, what luck my dear, that this "desirable" apartment with two bedrooms, two baths on Beekman Place had come on the market only that day, a bargain for that situation, it would be snapped up, so could Mrs. Van Zandt look at it that afternoon.

By the evening of the next day the papers were being drawn up to make it hers. She moved in with a box spring mattress and her only possession, Eric Quist's little painting of the Bullagulla railway station framed in unvarnished wood, which she hung on an immensity of white wall.

In the next weeks furniture was being carted in, chairs, sofas, cabinets, sideboards, none of which bore any relationship to each other for she bought at random and haphazardly. A disdainful young man over-adorned in rings and bracelets had been recommended to her for his "conception in design esthetics," but after he had patronized her for twenty minutes with talk of "daycor" and "fabric" she dismissed him frostily. Black and white squares, she said, would make her feel like a pawn on a chess board.

It wasn't a home, home is where the heart is, which in her case was misplaced. It was a place. It was somewhere she was staying or resting in between trains or events.

Good evening, Mrs. Van Zandt.

Sometimes the single women in the elevator addressed her with little pleasantries commenting on the weather or the amount of packages she was carrying and although she replied, her acknowledgement of them was cool and they felt themselves snubbed and brushed past her getting out at their floors saying "good*night*" with a hint of irony.

She supposed they were lonely, cooking for themselves and hoping for the phone to ring.

She cooked for herself a small roast chicken and asparagus, veal patties. She thought nothing of it. Except that in Santa Helena she had had only herself and the sea. But here, glancing out at the night sky hung with the lanterns of lit kitchens, she was aware of the thousands of single women cooking for themselves, and the thought bred a sense of aloneness.

But no lonely. Loneliness implied a need, and what need did she have?

Her mail consisted mostly of appeals, expensively produced on grave stationery, for her assistance in preserving forests, monuments, landmarks. For funds to allay the distress of displaced persons, to support this or that experimental ballet company.

She was encouraged to take this opportunity NOW by placing a tick in a square with the tiny pencil provided. Often her mailbox was so crammed with this flotsam she could barely extract it. Once in a while there would be a postcard from someone from Greece or Antigua to whom she had not spoken in a long time. But then, such is the mail of people who do not correspond.

And the telephone silent for those who never get in touch. But, she told herself, she hadn't the need of people, she was content. Wasn't she? Certainly she had friends, if asked she would have replied that she had scads. But it was difficult for her to keep a civil tongue when they behaved so idiotically, having unhappy love affairs and broken marriages. Come to think of it hers and Hollis' had been nearly perfect with its unpressurized respect for the privacy of each other. If she missed anyone, she missed Hollis with his civilized scorn for the platitudes of living.

She had everything she needed, she was responsible only to herself. Wasn't she?

Then one evening consulting the kitchen calendar (scenes of England, Regency terrace, Bath) she was jolted to realize that today was her forty-eighth birthday. Disconcerted not by the fact itself (she had not kept up even the pretense of celebration for years), but by the proof of her own enervation. She poured a stiff vodka and went out onto her little gritty balcony overlooking the green glass ice floes of the U.N. Plaza and through a fissure between towers to where the East River moved sluggishly. It occurred to her that here she was living in New York City and that she made no use of it whatever, that she might as well be living in Bulla-gulla.

The Aboriginal name slipped into her mind with its lonely sound like a small church bell tolling at dusk.

She sensed the remembered dust, the coffin-like closeness of the little manse, and outside the wind that never stopped blowing, the face of the Reverend John Quist gone into decay, the long beautiful hands protesting in the air, denying with the vehemence of a practiced art the accusations brought against him in the matter of Tilly Beamis who had been only one of his early seducements; protesting perhaps the relative unimportance of Tilly in his overall sexual Odyssey, a small island in the seas he had traversed.

She remembered now the son Eric, the long stag face and blond hair blowing in the wind under the orange light at the door. The only way he would ever get to see New York, he said, would be in the movies. Some extraordinary thought was beginning in Tanya's mind. She went back inside and stood looking at the small painting, the Bullagulla railway station with the milk cans, the falling-down white picket fence running the length of the platform, the faded sign once white on rusted black with letters missing, BUL AG LLA, the now never-used ticket window grown over with wild blackberry, a railway terminal at the end of the world. In the dark blue-gray sky, wild with threatening clouds, he had captured the color of his isolation, his imprisonment in his barren ratshole of a town blown by ceaseless dust winds; his desolate life, the parson's son handing around the plate at Sunday service to the diminishing congregation, now ten, now eight (and the sermon, God and Cucumbers, one could picture his distress at his father's assumption that he knew what God might fancy to eat), and saving the wilting poinsettia to take home after the Christmas service. Perhaps had a dream. "I hope you get out of here one day," she had said.

Perhaps he had faith in a miracle.

Which she could bring about. Keeping in mind that the bringing about of miracles could be dangerous, that the hubris involved in the belief of one's power to affect another person's life could let loose those dogs of war, love, gratitude, suspicion, the eventual need of betrayal in order to regain independence, the almost-certainty of her disappointment because this vast generosity of purse and spirit is for the pleasure of the giver and, more often than not, demeaning to the receiver, so that both giver and receiver are left naked and ashamed.

It would be just the stupid elephantine gesture that Tilly would have made had she the money.

But it was this need of exercising the antithesis of herself, of making the perfect uncharacteristic gesture from the missing part of herself that confronted her with the motion of doing it, that drew her down to her desk to write on her creamy Tiffany notepaper in her bold caustic handwriting, "Dear Eric———"

You may remember me, she wrote. To get to the point. If the idea is not too preposterous. I am also in touch with two people who run a small gallery on Madison Avenue. Adding that he might bring a satchelful of his small paintings.

Anyway, she concluded somewhat lamely, think about it.

He would be, she halfway hoped, too stunned or inhibited by colonial prudence to take her seriously.

But even as she split open the envelope (his letter was neatly typed in a faded brown ribbon) she knew this was not the case. May I, he asked in the second line, call you Tanya?

Eric Quist wrote, or rather typed neatly, that he was flabbergasted. To come to America had been his dream, did she know? Had he mentioned it that one time they met? He was speechless, knocked for a loop by her generosity but hoped he would find *some way* to show his gratitude. (Heavily underlined so that she felt herself unwillingly pulled into his embrace, shuddered and resolved that it must be made abundantly clear from the start that she was not a middle-aged seductress. Even so the obvious conclusions would be drawn, there was no escaping it. What bothered her more was the possibility of her being thought generous.) Well now, he wrote on page four, to be practical for a minute, he wouldn't come over to sponge on her, he was working six days a week and long hours in the local general store and earning a good wage plus room and one meal a day (incidentally his dad had passed away last year), and not only might it inconvenience Mr. and Mrs. Evans, the owners who had been so good to him, to find a replacement in a hurry, but if he continued in the job during the summer he would be able to put aside a nice bit of cash to spend in New York so—could he postpone coming until say September?

There followed a detailed description of the latest paintings he'd done, including *Abandoned Tin Mine, Bullagulla,* and *Old Well at Mulga Ponds*. At the end he wrote in undistinguished grocery-list handwriting, "Would you mind telling me a little more about yourself so that I'm not so ignorant."

He wrote from Sydney on YMCA notepaper that he had passport and ticket on QANTAS (thank you, thank you) and had bought himself a coast-to-coast excursion Greyhound bus seat from Los Angeles to New York arriving October 10. Will that be suitable?

Her few friends said to her, "What fun," and to each other that they shouldn't be surprised at anything, she was the original dark horse.

She looked forward to his coming with the expectancy of the child who has come upon the Christmas packages hidden in the broom closet and attempts to identify objects by their shapes and sizes, as if Eric's coming from such a distance assumed an importance and might present her with a mysterious gift; she could not imagine what it could be, only that it could perhaps define and clarify the something in her life that was missing.

But when she was pressed about him and the reason why she should bring a young man from the backblocks of New South Wales to New York, she grew deliberately vague except to say there had been a connection between his father and someone who had been "close to her."

She took his little painting of the Bullagulla Railway to show Blanche Souter, a cross lesbian who managed the Connaught Gallery. You could not have chosen a worse morning, Blanche said, with all hell breaking loose over a missing Dutch consignment. Blanche examined the picture both close up and at a distance with her eyes narrowed and finally said that, yes, it had vitality. "He must love his country, it shows even in the brutality. That sky has a feeling of Edvard Munch." Well, Blanche said, let her see what else he had and she might "fit him in in the back room for a week in November." The gallery would not pay for the framing, she added.

"That will be no problem," Tanya said coolly. She found the role of *patronne* somewhat abasing in the way Blanche Souter's little raisin eyes suggested the obvious reasons for her interest in Australian art.

Getting off the Greyhound bus in the grimy light of the Port Authority, he was grimfaced until she waved, and signaling back by nodding his head in her direction he jostled his way toward her through the crowd, head and shoulders above them, his lanky six foot four frame in his ardent plaid overcoat, which had an effrontery of being terribly new and no doubt the best they had at the Bon Marché in Main Street, might still have the price tag under one sleeve and which at close quarters gave off the slight odor of wet dog. He put down his suitcase and his tartan plastic carryall and stood to attention and saluted. It wasn't that the gesture was so ill-conceived as much as that it betrayed extreme youth.

Oh, his youth. She was paralyzed at the sight of it, years younger in looks than twenty-one. It must have to do with the simplicity of the bush backwoods. Possibly, taken out of context, out of the remembered orange light over the veranda in the blustery night at Bullagulla or from the snatch of memory he had actually gained youth, freckles, the hard lock of fair hair that fell over the eggshell forehead, the baby pink complexion and she, very much *in* context in her dark wool suit and low-heeled shoes and her hair honestly streaked with the beginnings of gray, must look like one of those youthful grandmothers one saw in swimming pools or riding bicycles in newspaper stories about sensible diets. Appalled by the abyss of years, by what she had done, she could only gather her cool around her like a garment and ask him was he worn out from the long trip. Not bad, he said. In Omaha he had been able to take a shower and use the laundromat.

"This way." She indicated a ramp.

It was then she saw the shoes. Pointed lace-up shoes of jaundice yellow and on his immense feet they were like two yellow canoes.

They were of an awfulness no passing of time would mellow. The pathos of the yellow shoes undid her; the thought of his expecting compliments on them brought her close to laughing or weeping. Very probably he had been told by the locals seeing him off on the dusty train that he looked smart as paint in them. They rode uptown breaking the silence with the stiff remarks of strangers sharing a cab in a foreign country. At Beekman Place, Arthur the doorman relieved Eric of his suitcase and carryall.

"This is Mr. Quist," Tanya said casually. "He will be coming in and out for a while."

"Of course," Arthur said a trifle too unctuously. As though nothing in the lease precluded a little cradle snatching.

And to her "daily," Delia, "This is Mr. Quist who's going to be in the guest room for a while."

Presented him with his room and bath. Left him to tidy up before lunch. To which she sat down without him and to try to persuade herself that she could and would survive this appalling blunder by creating at least the semblance of the normal. She forked crabmeat salad into her mouth as if she had not eaten for a month. When he sat down opposite her in the bright day coming through the tall window, she was able to observe the worst. He had combed and slicked his hair back with water and it gave him the rabbitty innocent look of an adolescent boy who had possibly not yet begun to shave except where the slight prickles of a reddish mustache showed on the waxen upper lip.

"Well," he said, lifting the crystal bowl in his long fingered hairless hands, "you have to not mind my being a bit speechless, Tanya, but it isn't beginning to feel real as yet. I hope you'll bear with me."

It was just to the brink of impertinence, his seeming to be so at ease with her; as if they had been pals reunited after an absence. He effervesced on about his bus trip for her entertainment, gratuitous with information she had not required (and how could he know, poor boy, that allusion to cross country bus travel caused a mysterious uneasiness in her), and she smiled back at him in the confusion of their misunderstanding of each other. "Fancy that," she said, or, "That must have been funny at the time."

Finding herself dead at heart.

"Of course, Tanya," he gurgled, "you have got not to mind me, I'm just the bloke from the bush. I'll settle down in a bit. That was gorgeous," he said about the salad to Delia taking away the dish he had scraped clean. Wiping his mouth he asked, "Prawns, wasn't it?"

He expected response, he drank from his iced water slowly in long slaking gulps making glottal sounds and looked sideways at Tanya as if hoping for the sounds of her breaking ice.

She broke a bread roll into crumbs and smiled.

The terrible invasion of this naive boy made her both responsible and forlorn at responsibility she felt she could not fulfill. She could not yet figure it out. She would have to sit down alone and analyze why this undisguised joy of his made her forlorn. Was it merely the rude Australianness of his elation that so discomforted her, aroused the vestigial sights and sounds of another time, another life?

Like the amputated foot that occasionally itches.

She knew whom it was he reminded her of.

And how they would have gotten along, those two, him in his yellow shoes and her wearing something too young for her. And she would have devised something more fun for his first lunch, not stiff-backed like this with flowers on the table and crabmeat salad, the maid coming in and out silently. With their common bond of outgoing Aussie-ness they would have figuratively romped, he and Tilly, and there would have been no awkward gap of years nor the wet blanket of her, Tanya's cynicism.

For the first time she felt a spasm of jealousy so

strong that when he said the first thing he'd like to see would be Miss Liberty, could they go this afternoon over to see the Statue of Liberty because there was something so symbolic about it being the introduction (he was shiny pink with enthusiasm, he might have been about to quote from Emma Lazarus), she heard herself say in a highfalutin flattening way that she had never been there. "I don't even know," she said crossly, as if he had perpetrated some bother, nuisance, "how to get there. But maybe Delia does." Got up and pushed her chair back roughly, pushed open the swing door to the pantry. "Delia, do you know how to get to the Statue of Liberty?"

Just as she had predicted it was turning out to be a failure. Not that one could put a finger on it, but as surely as in the crescendo one unmistakably hears the sour note from somewhere in the orchestra, it was there, the awareness of failure. In their strained smiles, in their reluctance to look each other in the face, always glancing sideways at each other, obliquely, gauging the other's mood, testing the temperature of the other's temper as a baby's nurse might dip her elbow in the bathwater.

And as she had predicted the fault was hers. Tacitly he implied that his disappointment was somehow connected to her and was deep. As the weeks went by, sluggishly, she believed she saw him adapting to it, making accommodations with an air of surrender. Catching him in one of his brown studies he seemed countenanced in a deep glumness as opaque as dust. Being without imagination she could not (or would not) wheedle it out of him. It would have been her nature to rap at him sharply, say, "What the hell is depressing you and if it's my fault what in God's name have I done *wrong*? Is my entertaining you wrong? Have my friends fallen short of your expectations? Do you not like the places I take you to, the restaurants, the museums, the shows?" All she was able to do was chide him for chewing his fingernails, warn him she would paint them with bitter aloes, but all she got in reply was a faraway smile. All she ever got was that faraway smile that crinkled the corners of his mouth but never the eyes, the eyes remained as quiet and inky blue as a pool deep in a forest where strange animals gathered in constant twilight.

Even when, to her amazement and delight, Blanche Souter offered the small back gallery to show his paintings for a week, he accepted the fact with astonishing calm for someone from the backblocks, not just astonishing, insulting.

"Well?" she asked, putting down the phone.

"Yes, well that'd be all right."

All right.

But if she showed a vestige of impatience he went into his shell like a sandcrab and did not emerge for hours.

A date was set, cards printed. AUSTRALIAN SCENES BY ERIC QUIST. NOV. 17–24 CONNAUGHT GALLERIES. At the framers he became unexpectedly finicky and fretful, frowning at the samples held up against the small canvases and saying this was too "barrock" and that too plain. "What the pictures cry out for is old weathered wood, the kind you see on a paling fence."

In the cab afterward he ran his long fingers through his thick hair and muttered something about having to get a haircut before the opening and she said with elaborately contrived seriousness, "Oh, are you planning to attend?" Saw immediately by the tightening of the skin that her barb had struck home and so, breathing deeply, waiting for her annoyance to abate, she said finally, "I only meant that you don't seem too enthusiastic."

He said huskily, looking away from her, "Oh I am, Tanya, *grateful*. It's only that———" A flat laugh.

"What?"

Head scratching.

"Only what?"

"I only brought the pictures really to show *you*." So she had done wrong, she had not considered his modesty into which she had blustered, forcing him into a limelight he may not have wanted. Neither was she aware of the thin skin around his pride until, blundering again, she suggested the new shoes. In desperation over yellow pointed shoes and imitation silk ties heavily ornamented with heraldry and shields, she led him as stealthily as if she were stalking lyrebirds to the men's department in Bloomingdales where, picking up a slim black loafer she commented on its stylish simplicity and suggested he should take home such a pair? "Won't you let me, *please*."

He had reacted as if to electric shock, the spine ramrod, the eyes gimlets.

"No thanks, Tanya."

"But————"

"I promised myself I'd never let you buy me anything so's not to spoil it."

"Now don't be priggish."

"No."

He strode away and stood apart from her fingering belts hanging like dead snakes and when she came up, took her by the elbow and steered her out of the store.

In the cold street he wiped the wind tears away and said to the sidewalk like an ashamed child, "You see, I happen to know my dad took things from women. Even after he'd become a minister he went on taking presents from women. He had sex with them and they gave him things."

After they had walked a block she asked, "Did you despise him for it?"

"Of course. What do *you* think?"

He was wild with old hurt, he strode along in his yellow shoes, his face in the wind wet with tears, staring into the potholes of Third Avenue, and ashamed of her obtuseness she slipped her arm into his but there was less a response than a slack reluctance to the pressure of her glove and so they proceeded downtown as if he were in her custody.

But it broke some of the ice between them; the revelation of his hurt and shame had activated some emotion in him to which she could react as opposed to the vacuous politeness, the unlit smiles exchanged across the dinner tables, across the vast acres of room between them in the shadows and light from the oversized table lamps. The cold rancor she had held for his father on account of Tilly had accumulated over the years even without it being given much thought and now confronted with his venality and sexual fraud (taking little bits and pieces from parishioners in exchange for his mouth, his groin, it was revolting) she felt a kind of healthy rage coursing through her, remembering the sanctimonious humor, the canonical self-justification, the hairy wrists, the hollow-cheeked remains of good looks. She visualized the metaphor, the black shirtfront and white celluloid collar hanging on the bedpost in the widow's bedroom.

"Prick," she said.

"Who?"

"Your father." She felt a little dizzy, sat down in one of her too big armchairs. "A prick. At any rate he was to her."

"To who?"

"Tilly Beamis."

Tilly Beamis was squashed into the airless phone booth (Tanya had launched into the story to spite her usual caution, shot into it like a launched rocket) and at first she had thought the landlady (and there was more to her than met the eye, believe it) had said that he had got a new ceiling but it was "gone to New Zealand" (and later Tilly found out it was to a rich woman who had been partly supporting him) without a word of warning or as the Australians put it, "shot through." Jack Quist had shot through to Auckland and renounced her, Tilly knew, because of her mistake in loving him and she hung up the phone and ran out of the booth and ran through the Sydney streets like a mad girl or as if she were on fire and trying to put it out whereas the fire only increased and the faster she ran (through Castlereagh Street, Macquarie Street) the faster the flames consumed her until she was burning all over with the knowledge, until she was able in the heat and flames to take it in. He was gone and there was no describing the hurt of this girl (Tanya said, and moved a figurine on the table with a shaking hand). And after a while the fire died down and left her in a deadly cold as if she were encased in ice right up above her heart and no one could help her not even a man who really and truly loved her and no one could touch her. She was shipwrecked.

Listening to her own voice reciting this jeremiad, Tanya could scarcely believe it was her own, it sounded like someone speaking through her, dybbuk-like and authentic. The story of this chapter in Tilly's life, trite enough, familiar as day and night, took on a luster that had a brilliant verisimilitude, and Eric's eyes were fixed on her glassily like someone who is witnessing a person having a fit or an epileptic seizure.

But having begun she was in the capture of wild horses. Nothing could prevent her telling him about the doomed pregnancy during that summer's dreadful heatwave and the final decision. She led the way with Tilly up the slopes to the Watson's Bay Gap, up slopes of rock and brittle stunted bushes and through the faint mist of ocean spray in the bloody brown dying light, seeing the rusted tin cans and bits of newspaper blowing across the gravel pathway, she was with Tilly now at the edge beside the wooden fence and watched while Tilly removed her shoes and climbed the wooden split rail fence painted white——

Tanya paused.

How could *she* have known it was white and that the evening was a burned brown color after the terrible heat of the day now dying. How often had she tossed out expressions like "shot through"? It had all come out exactly as if Tilly had been telling it. And he knew. Eric uncrossed his legs and stood up. He stood in the window outlined by the dark glow of the United Nations Plaza.

He said, "Did you get me over here to get back at my father?"

He went out and crossed the hall into his bedroom.

For a time she didn't move, she was rooted to her chair and to an assumption that there was a cat in the room, let out of a bag. And that she was conscious of relief. That, after all this time it was as big a relief as a confession to murder, which indeed it was. She sat on, cool with the thought of her relief and of the intimacy it had caused between the three of them, herself, Tilly, and Eric until the significance of what he had just said came back to her icily. "——to get back at my father?"

She rose and crossed the hall. His bedroom door was open but he had not turned on a light and in the gloaming from the lamp on the hall table she could see by the soles of his shoes pointing up that he was lying on his back on the bed.

She stood stiffly in the doorway, conscientiously not intruding into his territory.

"What did you mean?"
He didn't move.
"Why would you ask such a thing?"
"I wonder why you got me over here."
"Why? Is it so terrible? Have I hurt you in some way?"
"Not hurt, no."
"Well, what then?"
He was doubly evasive in the dark, she imagined him staring at her, the eyes suspicious, narrow.
"No."
"No? No what? I'm completely at sea."
He turned slightly on the mattress, she heard the rustling. After a time he said in a dusty voice. "No, you've been bonza, Tanya." That meant, she supposed, exemplary.
"Are you unhappy? Homesick?"
"Oh Christ, you'd have to be mad to be homesick for Bullagulla." He went on with infinite slowness as if there were a weight attached to every word.
He appreciated deeply everything she'd done. Arranging the show, the posh cafes, the museums, "That Rousseau with the lions, I won't forget that now."
But you see, he didn't know how to put it.
"Well, try," she snapped, it was unfair this talking to the dark.
"Well, it's like you're not there or only half there and it's like I'm always just a visitor and you're watching to see if I'm having a good time."
"And you aren't?"
"Yes, I have had but————"
"But, but. Say it. Tell me!"

"Having a good time isn't what I came over for. I don't know how to say it. When your letter came I could hardly believe it and I showed it to a chum of mine, Occa Stevens, just to see what he thought and he said, 'I reckon she means it all right,' and then he said what was in my mind, 'Maybe she took a bit of a shine to you.' I couldn't think of any other reason you'd want to spend all that dough bringing over a stranger you'd only met once. But you see I knew whatever the reason was it wasn't in the sense Occa meant it, he's got that kind of mind, he thinks everything's sexual. What I thought was, 'maybe she's lonely and she's guessed I'm lonely too and that———" The rest was indistinct.

"That what?" she asked.

"———that perhaps we could matter to each other. But I've been here seven weeks and nothing happens except *posh restaurants*."

It burst out like fireworks in the dark.

For all her distress over his disappointment she could not move a finger, she could no more reach out and touch his pointed shoe than fly. She imagined that in his green-as-apples way he had appropriated her as older sister (how obvious and impudent of him) or even mother. His mother had died, he had told her without emotion, when he was ten and she had seen his mother as a wan little woman fading away in a sepia light, languishing in the stultifying parlor while the philandering vicar lay under cotton quilts with the ladies of the congregation.

This poor boy, child. She felt his accusation to be fair, she had fed him lavishly and yet here he was famished and she saw right through to the poignant immaturity of his suspicion that she, in her aloofness, was getting back at his father in the name of Tilly. She found herself now despairing, unable to contradict this convincingly, unable to gain credence, impotent. Because on the spur of the moment she had seized her pen, because troubled by a sense of unreality she had needed to provide herself with an illustration of the magnanimous, an illusion of affection, an appeal to her *better self*. It was the better self of earlier times that had flickered momentarily, the leg kicking in bed tripping over the stone of sleep. Poor boy, he was the recipient of her empty intentions and the victim of her lost heart. On top of it all she felt suddenly staggeringly tired, never so tired in her life.

She leaned against the door jamb and she said, almost in tears with the fatigue of a defeated child, "Well, I'm sorry but you see I don't know of any cheap restaurants."

On the evening of the opening of his showing there was a four-and-a-half-inch snowfall. A handful of people showed up, piling galoshes and wet coats on the floor, and wandered silently around the small gallery eyeing the pictures while he stood attentively to one side with his face set in a constrained diffidence. At least they were in tacit agreement at this moment not to act brightly.

He and Tanya for once tacitly in agreement, no smiles.

When Blanche Souter, in black pants and sharp paisley, from time to time inveigled him into the proceedings, introducing him to this or that potential buyer, he merely bent his head and made some laconic comment no more interested in the reaction to *Sunset on Dugwell Road* or *Old Wool Shed* than a guard, fretting over the slowness of time passing in the Uffizi, gives a fig about the *Birth of Venus*. Neither did he seem in the least stimulated when Blanche Souter came bearing red paper dots to stick on the frames of two paintings sold. ("Sold," Blanche said. The fact that her percentage was steep especially with unknowns may have accounted for her jollity.)

"Well, are you pleased?" Tanya had to ask, confronted with his blankness.

"Oh yes. Except one of those she sold I was planning to give to you." As if it were somehow partly her fault, if she had not arranged the showing the painting would have wound up where it was meant to be. No matter what she did she was pleading the wrong case in the wrong court, she was peripherally involved in his annoyance. It left her speechless.

Let it go.

Let him go, she meant. And as if he had caught her thought, he said over the noise of the French restaurant where Blanche Souter had taken them in the Village (for once not posh, grubby aprons, candle grease, she hoped that he would appreciate it), said peremptorily, "I've got to go home soon."

She merely nodded, admitting the fact that they were slipping apart, had been slipping apart from the day he arrived, and in accepting the fact of his going they entered into the kind of somber acceptance that comes in the aftermath of failed peace talks.

Then in the last days of his stay, leaving the Quadrille on Fifty-eighth Street, as unexpected as a meteorite crashing through the ceiling, she had come face-to-face with this staring woman. Who was it? Who was this woman in her fifties, thunderstruck? It was someone from Tilly's past.

Tanya hesitated by the woman's table only a moment, eyes met eyes, hers inquiring, the woman's electrified into glass. Then Tanya walked quickly on and out of the restaurant, Eric behind her.

It had been Rose Patterson, and Rose had lifted her hand to her face as if she had been warding off a blow or seeing the drowned come to life.

So that when the doorbell rang, the inevitability of this confrontation having been accepted from the moment she got his note asking to see her on a "matter of grave urgency to myself," she said calmly to Eric, "You get it, will you. And don't go off, stay." For the moment, blocked by his back she saw only a leg in glen plaid under a camel's hair overcoat and an umbrella and heard Edward's voice ask, "Mrs. Van Zandt?"

"Yes, come in."

Then seeing her seated calmly in the big red leather chair, Edward seemed for a moment to be blinded by strong light, put up a hand to screen his eyes and fumbling with his coat buttons, dropped his umbrella to the floor and then fumbling for it, looking up, holding the umbrella by the wrong end he said in a gulp, "Tilly."

He had to reach out to steady himself, touching a side table he upset a glass egg.

She stood up unsmiling to greet him with an appraisal of formality, but to her utter disconcertion he dropped to his knees at her feet and embracing her around the buttocks buried his face in her crotch, weeping and saying, "Tilly, Tilly, Tilly," the name obscured by her dress.

She unclasped his arms from around her and said, "Please get up, don't do that."

As if to emphasize the melodramatics, thunder rolled outside, there was sudden bullet-like rain and Eric went over to close the window.

"Excuse me," Edward said, rising, taking out a handkerchief, "you must excuse. But it's the emotion of————"

He sat down and blew his nose fiercely, wiped his eyes. "You have to give me a minute to————"

She sat down and crossed her legs.

"This is Eric Quist," she said.

"How do you do?"

Typically, she observed, Edward rose and stretched out a hand. Ridiculously, he and Eric met halfway across the room and shook hands and retired backward to their seats like duelists.

Edward sat again and regarded her through wet eyelashes.

"Tilly," he said again, pronouncing the name lovingly as if it were a benison.

"No," she said flatly, "I'm sorry to disappoint you."

Probably it was like denying the Sphinx was the Sphinx, outwardly ridiculous. But now face-to-face with her metamorphosis under the strong light of his reasoning her denial became imperative. Whether he believed her or not was not important, it was the plausibility of it to herself that constituted her life and in no way could she allow this man to cast any doubt in her mind as to who she was and had been for the last twenty-two years.

She said with great composure, "Mr. Patterson, Tilly Beamis died in nineteen fifty-six in Temple, Pennsylvania, when a bus went over a bridge during a flood."

"She was never found. Only a suitcase was found."

"That is beside the point."

"What are you trying to give me?" He gave a short laugh.

"The truth."

"What truth? Why are you trying to pull this stunt? I'm sitting looking at you."

Already he had the air of the April Fool trying to laugh off being caught calling the zoo for a Mr. Lion. But behind it flickered a genuine bafflement.

"Not to say you haven't changed, we've all changed. But you can deny it a hundred thousand times, I am looking at Tilly. My dear, I know every pore of you, so please. It takes a great deal more than changing names."

Which God knows she knew. She had papers enough, naturalization, marriage certificate, passport, that all showed her to be, without shadow of doubt, Tanya Bond Van Zandt. But they would be insufficient to convince this small man, leaning back in the chair opposite her, eyeing her with a narrowed gaze, who waited, frowning, for some explanation. And how to explain to Edward Patterson about twin souls when he could not see beyond his aristocratic nose? She noticed now that he wore a flesh-colored hearing aid partly concealed by his longish silver hair and it seemed symptomatic of the difficulties she would have appealing to deaf ears. Here was a man untouched by inspiration, while she had dared to change her own soul. His existence went no further than his physical frame and she had travelled incalculable distances of the spirit. He was motivated and limited by conventional decency. Decency was a thing she had had to throttle out of herself before it throttled her.

He was waiting for her explanation. But how could she give it when she couldn't even explain to herself how crack boom, standing in the pink painted ladies' room in the magazine coffee shop in Temple in the roar of the rain that crack boom she split in two and one side of her, the side he knew and apparently loved, was annihilated in a breath, ceased to be and that the explanation she had given for Tilly in order to accommodate the people who couldn't see beyond their noses like Edward Patterson was that she had gone over into the river on the bus. Because being nonexistent it mattered very little what tale was made up about her. People only needed and wanted explanations.

"Explanations," she said aloud and opened her palms on her lap, "could be unnecessary. Had you known her?"

"Known you," he was suddenly galvanized, "you were my girl, Tilly. What is all this? You were my sweet girl. We were engaged, we were lovers." He glanced around at Eric Quist and back.

"Could we discuss these matters in a more private manner?"

She said, "There's nothing that I mind Eric hearing and I prefer not to be alone with you."

Edward Patterson was turning pale pink around the gills but his lips were pressed together and gray with his disapproval of this menage. No doubt he would say to his wife, that pale creature Tilly had once met in someone's Connecticut house, "I found her living with this *boy*."

For a while she let him roll around like a whale threshing his water. She was waiting for him to get the required expected protestations out of the way. Just as he was the kind of man who could not sit through the simplest meal without offering a toast to someone or something, so was it natural that having been forsaken whether intentionally or accidentally it stood to reason that he had rehearsed an inventory of grievances into self-exculpation so that should the matter ever come up he could indulge himself in a fat lather of self-pity. Now he rolled in a froth of it. I wonder, he said grimly, if you ever gave a moment's thought to the anguish of the people you left behind. Had you ever a qualm about their quandary of whether you were dead or alive? Could you picture what it was like for them every time the telephone rang? Do you know what the final black hopelessness felt like when her suitcase was found? He never paused for her reply, it was as unbroken as a litany; he had been readying it for years.

She was contemplating the fact that she knew (through Tilly) his body, head to toe, that he was hairless as a schoolgirl except in the black moss of his crotch and that he always took off his socks last, two red straps of garters clasped his calves and meticulously held up his black silk socks, black and red in contrast to the extreme whiteness of him. Kneeling over Tilly he kissed her eyelids, first the right, then the left, closing her eyes as if what was to come should not be seen by a nice girl because his lust was rambunctious in contrast to his mild good manners and he was ashamed of his lasciviousness.

She could still feel the warm dry lips on Tilly's eyelids and how she had cringed at the fatuity of the gesture and wanted to cry out, "Don't do that, I hate it." But instead, nestling against him, Tilly would murmur dearest sweet, and open her generous mouth to his and thus squirming together they clasped and groaned in delight while *she* felt the ugliness of it and the mediocrity of him, and later the putting on of the socks again and fastening the red garters and him stroking his silken calves and sitting naked in her cretonne-covered chair, he would smile at her and ask had it been good for her too, and Tilly always lied if it had not been successful for her, got out of bed and perched on his naked knee like his good little girl.

It was too much, Tanya was perspiring with the whimsy of it. She had heard nothing he had said for the last few minutes. She groaned and said, "I hated the way you kissed."

He had trodden barefoot on a nail. That was his expression, mouth open.

"You———" Pulled up in the midst of his litany.

"On the eyelids, it seemed so patronizing."

"You never said anything."

"I wanted to, it made me squirm."

"Surely————"

"Your lips were always so dry."

"Well, my dear, if you'd only so much as hinted————"

"Oh, she wouldn't have, she revered you in her infantile way."

"I don't————who revered————?"

"Tilly."

He looked appalled now. As if he had come upon her mumbling and eating hay. Alarmed by the implication of insanity. So much so that she felt a momentary tic of remorse for the trick that had been played on him, this decent dense man.

She said quietly, "There were two of us. Twin souls. All the time. But I was scarcely in evidence then because I was not yet the stronger. It was like me watching me. Sometimes me watching me make a fool of myself."

"Two," he said, flat with incredulity.

"Yes."

"All the time?"

"We were conscious of each other. We were always conscious of one another. Just as black is aware of white and day of night. We were our direct opposite. She saw the dream. I saw the reality. It was constant warfare to see who won and for a long time she won and I had to abide by her regrettable choices. Living on a farm with only older brothers and a mother who was bound down to work from dawn to late at night, it was lonely and she had little or no communication with them, longed to give her heart away. Gave her heart and half her lunch away to a worthless simpering girl at the country school, gave in passion to Nell Felumb and her sister. Blobs. They thought she was what they called 'a ratbag' sharing her raisins and jam turnovers with them and wanting to slip an arm around them, which she needed passionately to do, to hug Nell Felumb, perhaps even be allowed to kiss her even though she smelled of lard (I smelled her). Nell and Sis Felumb, they were stupid little ninnies with flat, freckled faces incapable of recognizing her need. I detested them. One time I got the upper hand and frightened the liver out of them. *She* didn't understand. She was deplorably innocent of herself. It was both heartbreaking and exasperating. Fell in love at fourteen when she was nubile, full of the wonder of her new body, fell in love with a farm hand, a clod, conceited and coarse as hemp. But she saw only the dream of him whereas I saw right through the dream to the slicked-up Vaselined tinpot bumpkin he was, abandoning the child for the first spit curl slut to come along, which he did, leaving her to walk the miles home, broke her silly heart. But she wept to me and called me Tanya, evoked me to resuscitate her, and I took over and I was fully her for eleven days."

As if she had explained more than enough and still nothing, Edward Patterson, overburdened with the weight of incredulity burst out with, "But *me.*"

Tanya said, "Oh with you, she hadn't changed, she was still building houses with soap bubbles. She hadn't grown an inch emotionally since she was fourteen and abandoned on Bandicoot Road in the dark by the goatish farmhand. And you gave her encouragement not to be anything more than herself. You were decent and blind as a bat and I wasn't sure that I could survive your lovingkindness, that it wouldn't choke me with its incongruity. As it grew nearer and nearer to the wedding date I became more and more detached, more and more alienated from the pair of you, it was like a blinding process and as if in the glare of her infatuation for you I was being drowned. I had to struggle for my life not to be totally absorbed into her bland sweetness and light and the only thing that saved my independent spirit was her conscience and guilt over not telling you about *us*. I prodded and prodded and finally one day she was about to tell you—it was in a garden at somebody's house in the country where you were spending a weekend—when she was interrupted by, of all people, the girl you were later to marry. Averice? Averell? Coming in like a stage maid to announce tea. And such are the minuscule workings of forces that chart our lives, that Tilly should be interrupted by an announcement of tea, little cakes and then never speak of us because before she had another opportunity something had happened that changed the whole perspective and shocked her into giving way to me entirely. I had walked into a room and seen two people who were in love. Although the probability was that they had never discussed it and never would. You and your sister Rose." Again as if in a movie, thunder rumbled outside the now dark window. If it had struck him, it had struck him a leaden blow from behind and stunned him, he didn't stir a finger. But after a second he moved his tongue across his lips.

"So she fled. With lame excuses of wanting to be alone for a bit. Bridal tremors you would think and with your infinite patience, permit her. Fled with me, now the stronger and her knowing that she must never go back as herself to you. Knowing that it would be wiser to submit to me entirely. And so the bus, the river provided her in some ways with the exit she'd been really looking for all our life. That's all."

"All?" Edward spoke in a low voice as one might say in a movie house, "Isn't this where we came in?"

He rose, a small man suddenly tall with dignity.

He said, "I find the way you talk about yourself despicable. As if blaming someone else for your loathsome suspicions and deception. And defiling Tilly."

He walked toward the hall, then turned back a moment and said, "Whatever is true or not true in this wild preposterous explanation you offer so disgustingly, I know one thing for sure. You are not the woman I was to marry."

He picked up his coat and umbrella. He had some difficulty with the locks on her front door but as if they were in a conspiracy to avoid any further recognition of even his presence neither she nor Eric moved until he had finally managed to get the door open and disappeared into the outer hallway and later the elevator doors were heard to open and close.

After what seemed as long as the lifetime she had

been reexperiencing, Eric said from where he was still sitting by the rain-drenched window, "I need a drink, do you?"

When she awoke, feeling the pressure in the dark on her bed, felt sheets pulled momentarily back and his weight settling in beside her, felt surprise more than anything else, he never having shown a flicker of emotion, even interest in her, always staring away, beyond into some territory where only he and his alien values existed, now his hand pushing up her nightgown; it seemed ambiguous, insulting almost, as if having noticed his preparations for leaving she had tacitly importuned some token of his gratitude.

"No," she said and tried to thrust his hands away, but he merely caught her hands and pinned them to her sides, moving onto her with unexpected strength and began to kiss her on and around the ears as she turned her head from side to side avoiding him, they were little feathery kisses, like the kisses of some affectionate godson.

"No, Eric."

"Please."

Now on the mouth, forcing in his tongue and moving on her, in on her until there was no going back, nothing to do but submit with the odd feeling that she was still half asleep and in a dream where she was being ravished in a shadowy grove by a young woodsman and also that extraordinarily, it was the first time for her just as it was for him, and they were two ageless children joined in radiant unity in this brilliant dark and giving in to this was swept away with him and by the thought that this was Jack Quist's boy. This might have been the little boy she could have had by Jack Quist (she saw the blue glass light over the porch of the doctor's house on the bleak Coogée Street, the waiting-room couch in desolate mauve), and suddenly the thought was not iniquitous, incestuous, it was sweet, sweet, she gave it all her strength in her arms around him as together they neared the wave that would carry them over their crest, and as it hit them, lifted them, she felt she was being pulled up, up by dormant forces out of the sea like Aphrodite. Or up out of a river like——— No sign manifested itself, no star burst out in flames, no bell sounded to indicate an intrusion, no click of a door softly opening, no creak of footboard announced her. She said in a clear light voice trembling with sincerity, "Oh you darling, you sweet love. Sweet."

Tilly said.

Toward morning, pale light, she thought she heard soft bumpings as though someone were moving heavy bags with care so as not to waken anyone. A little later she was sure she heard the front door close softly. She moved her arm around and found she was alone in bed.

After a little gathering of herself together she got up and slipped on her robe. The door to his room was open, the bed had been carefully made. On the kitchen table was this note:

"I thought I wouldn't tell you when I was going, it would save an unnecessary scene. I'm on the bus this morning to LA and fly Thursday. I probably won't write for a while after I get back,